CONSCIOUS UNIVERSE

Duncan Alexander Maclean

Publishing Details

COPYRIGHT © DUNCAN ALEXANDER MACLEAN 2013

Published by *Australian eBook Publisher*, 1st Edition 2013, ePub and Mobi

No images have been taken from websites. All photos have been altered considerably from any possible copyright material that to my knowledge was in the public domain.

Where necessary pen and ink and drawings have been used to give an accurate image of historical images out of tombs and archaeological sites.

Cover art and drawings by Duncan Maclean

Edited by Sally and Amanda *Australian eBook Publisher*, and Trudy Graham, Creative Writing Services

ISBN-13: 9780987591029
ISBN-10: 0987591029
Ebook formats created and distributed by Australian eBook Publisher
www.AustralianEbookPublisher.com.au

FOREWORD

Within a fictitious love story that covers many thousands of years is the secret of Stonehenge. The connection that joins the 30,000-plus-year-old cave paintings of Lascaux with Stonehenge connects the pyramids of Giza, (Egypt) and the largest in China and Mexico, all the way to Christ and Christmas day. All this explains a belief in your immortality and the effect you have upon your own reality.

YOU THE CENTRE OF YOUR UNIVERSE.
YOUR ETERNAL SOUL.
YOU THE CREATOR OF YOUR OWN REALITY.

An ordinary man tells a different history of humanity.

This is a work of fiction that uses biblical and historical records to create a sense of reality.
It refers to strange coincidence and unanswered improbabilities to create questions and wonder. It connects the work of many scholars to give perhaps, the hoped for readers a chance to

form their own understanding, within the comfort of their own beliefs.

At no time do I think of myself as more than a simple layman who attempts to give you entertainment, romance and a little humour

After THE END, I refer to the beliefs behind consciousness and inform those of religious doctrine of content that may be outside of their comfort zone.

The web site. www.dmaclean.com is available for comment or other titals.

The web sites. www.consciousuniverse.com.au and www. duncanmaclean.com.au are registered to the author at the time of publishing, but are still at the development stage. I hope by the time the readers arrive they will be ready for you.

CONTENTS

DAWN OF PLANET EARTH   ix

ONE. Death and Rebirth   1

TWO. Early Hominid Awareness   5

THREE. Departure for New Land Indonesia to
Australia, 150,000 years before the present   11

FOUR. Settling into My New Home   37

FIVE. On Leaving   85

SIX. Arrival at New Land—Australia 150,000
years before present   93

SEVEN. Reunion and Spacer Communion   117

EIGHT. White Cloud becomes Shaman and Arise
begins to emerge   129

NINE. Child born of spacer world   137

TEN. Ancient Man meets Hobbits of Flores
(2004 discovery of 12000-year-old new species,
Homo-Floresiensis, less than one metre tall).   141

ELEVEN. Arise and Estra. New journey to
old connections   161

TWELVE. Return to Indonesia. The old country.
After Death of White Cloud and Nioma.   169

THIRTEEN. White Cloud (Human Journey)
is born again   173
FOURTEEN. Finish of White Cloud - Nioma   175
FIFTEEN. Location caves of Lascaux—Wildflower   179
SIXTEEN. Return of the Spacers (ALPHA)   207
DRAWING OF TUYA AND YUYA IN
FRONT OF MANY COLOURED SHANTI
BOXES IN TOMB.   212
SEVENTEEN. Time of Joseph—Coat of Many Colours
(Yuya and Tuya)   213
FUNERAL MASK OF TUYA   238
EIGHTEEN. Akhenaten, Sephron and General Aye
to the Exodus   253
SCULPTED HEAD OF QUEEN NEFERTITI:::   266
NINETEEN. 1378 BC Amenhotep1V (Akhenaten)
3390 years before The Time of the
Writing, 2012.AD   267
AKHENATEN   272
ACURATE DRAWING OF SCULPTED
HEAD::: DAUGHTER OF AKHENATEN AND
NEFERTITI::: From Tutankhamen's
exhibition while in Melbourne.   277
TWENTY. The Time of the Exodus   279
CHINA   MEXICO   EGYPT   GIZA
BELT OF ORION   TEOTIHUACAN   286
PICTURE OF THE NEBRA DISC,
GERMANY 4000 YEAR OLD DEPICTION
OF THE SEVEN SISTERS, THE PLEIADES.   289

SKULL OF TUTANKHAMUN AND PERHAPS
OTHER FAMILY MEMBER SHOWING
ELONGATED HEAD::: ABOVE
SCULPTED NEFERTITI..   290
TWENTY-ONE. Malcolm Redome from, The Time
of the Writing, 2012   291
TWENTY-TWO. Three Births, Three Great Religions!   295
TWENTY-THREE. The Present Time.
Many Lives Pass.   303
STAR OF DAVID   DIVISION OF STAR.
64 TETRAHEDRON GRID?   315
EPILOGUE   323

Dawn Of Planet Earth

The surface is cool now and oceans cover vast areas. The mantle buckles and slowly forms the plates, giving rise to the birth of land. Clouds cover much of the sky and rain falls.

Day follows night, and all that is required for the coming of awareness is blown by the wind.

As night settles and a full moon shines down on the planet, a new light flashes towards a calm ocean.

The new world absorbs the impact and time moves forward.

Now a new presence exists.

A living cell; complete, with no evolution, is equipped with all the information for the beginning of life on this already beautiful blue circle.

Intelligent design is present on planet Earth, pre-evolution, pre-natural selection!

Within the nucleus of the cell, a protean machine unwinds a strand of DNA and another machine reads information from more than three billion combinations to form the strand of RNA. This RNA is transported through the gatekeeper out of the nucleus and to the factory Ribosome, to issue instructions to more machines carrying amino acids to form the first protein shapes of life on Earth.

Three billion or so years before the Time of the Writing, one tiny outboard motor machine with forty protein parts assembled in correct order, running at one hundred thousand revolutions per minute, and capable of stopping in one quarter of a turn, was needed for natural selection to exist. We call this Flagellum.

This is one of thousands of complex machines there by intelligent design at the beginning, within the first cell, in order for life to develop on Earth.

This is not to mention the already complete instructions in DNA for all life on Earth.

Over vast time the oceans fill with life; plants to feed animals. New life appears on land; new life appears in the air. A living world exists; a new home for a complete conscious awareness; Mother Nature, Mother Earth.

(In 1993, scientists came together in California and termed the phrase, *intelligent design*)

ONE

DEATH AND REBIRTH

I am old now and my eyes have long grown dim.
My life as Malcolm Redome fades fast. I wonder, after all the
stories I told and sold in connection with the book called *From
the Time of the Writing*, what answers lie before me. Regardless of
the money that came late in life, it was a lonely journey.

As the light fades, the pain recedes. I feel the body becoming
light as if it is less of a part of me. A new clarity of mind is upon
me that I have not known for years - if ever.

I wonder if, after all I told, I am to take my karma to an
eternity of darkness? Or like most people, do I hope there will
be life after death?

The voices grow dimmer and the long ago journey of my
astral youth is re-emerging. I see my body and the activity that
surrounds it. Then the walls and ceilings grow larger and in a
flash, a journey begins.

I am moving now across distances well understood for longer
than the rise and fall of billions of universes. The consciousness

of our kind has penetrated to beyond the boundaries of human imagination. The lights of great clusters pass at infinite distance until finally I am above the plane of the universe. Now there is an unbroken endless series of lights in a profoundly beautiful night sky. It is changing now; the dark of much of the empty space grows brighter. Light sweeps towards me, or I towards light; and I can tell from empty space I am to arrive at what feels like home and total fulfilment.

My mind is now, as I have never known it to be.

All time and space seem to communicate and the feeling of body is no longer relevant. I feel profound warmth of the mind with an intensity I have not felt with my heart or my earthly loins. It seems to encompass all the senses.

Somehow, over all this, there is a sense of harmony, humility and wonder.

In this world that somehow brings body and mass to empty space, the galaxies are spreading their spiral wings and the once beautiful arms are now central to great glowing arenas.

All space seems to be slowly filling with a vast panorama of a consciousness.

Now I seem to become a part of, as well as aware of, a cosmic intelligence. This I cannot explain with the voice of an individual, but with the knowledge of all, coming to me in a way that even with heightened awareness is simple enough for me to understand.

The question comes to me. What is it? Where is it? Where am I? I know I have not been this close to all I see in any spiritual life before. I sense clearly these lives as an endless line stretching back; all with total comfort.

I feel the thought say to me, *you are the spirit of Malcolm Redome, the spirit we call the Human Journey. You are no different to the spirit of any other living creature. In the living flesh, you suffer endless hungers and joys. You still have your share of sin and goodness.*

In short, you are an ordinary traveller and an infinitely small part of the life that makes up the living universe which again in turn is a part of endless other universes that once again are total cosmic intelligence. All life of the spirit is infinitely small and infinitely large; a part of a whole; so Karma can exist as your deeds, whatever their merit, contribute to life.

I see I am to journey to look upon something beyond what I have seen. The light clears and into the far distance, I see endless flat circular plains with what at first glance appear to be galaxies. Then I realize they are universes stretching endlessly beyond vision. Plain upon plain appears so all is full of universes, and even this somehow is all part of a total cosmic intelligence.

I hear myself think, *how is this so?* The answer comes, *on your beloved Earth you wrote that awareness is perhaps reached after about four billion years and that those you dwell amongst have only emerged into awareness.*

Countless millions of species have reached this stage, and some have gone on to survive for billions of years.

What level of wonderment they achieved is beyond the difference of your first life in the Time of the Writing and your last three and a half million years later. These stretch back in time for all conscious knowledge for such as you.

Why am I here?

It is now that you will return to write again the rest of the story for simple people such as you to find a part of their knowledge.

Who sent you? Are you the Holy Spirit?

I am just like you but far older. Still an infinitely small part of all you view.

Who and where will I be to write this?

The spirit is not restricted to a time and space; you will be returned to your body not long after you wrote From the Time of the Writing. *You will live and die again. Malcolm Redome will not be even vaguely aware of this death and return to life.*

This spirit, your life, will be as him and as his guide. It will remember and through Malcolm tell the story.

You will remain the same man, with ordinary human qualities, often with too much desire and sometimes too greedy for strong drink and the gift of the Mother Earth.

Your spirit, the spirit of the Human Journey, is not of high order. Simply the susceptibility or perhaps lack of strength makes Malcolm easy to direct. As both human and spirit, Malcolm will write with the help of computers - primitive machines that are the beginning of human reawakening. The minute storage of information is in the direction of total capacity.

The further they go this way, to eventually biological computers, and quantum mechanics, will take them towards the ancient direction of all you see before you.

Two

Early Hominid Awareness

I am Malcolm Redome and I am fifty-five years old and living in North Australia working on any old job.

I have just written the story called, *From the Time of the Writing*. Much of that work is total fantasy, but with an underlying story of belief that I suspect is a major part of the early development of humankind, removed from humankind's consciences over many centuries.

I am not sure how these stories come to me. I simply write and the words flow. When I need to research, it seems to be almost in front of me. Still the job of writing, even with a computer, is hard. I have to learn to use the keyboard and my English grammar is restricted.

Regardless of all this, these thoughts come to me and I feel compelled to write. I am aware that both this work and the last must include my heart, my lust and perhaps my honour, and if I am lucky, humour.

I hope my work will be entertaining, and if I listen to the quiet voice that seems to reside in me (and in all other people) there will be a purpose and perhaps a rewarding journey to any who read this.

HUMAN JOURNEY

Malcolm is sleeping now and once again, I am free to move from the restriction of his body.

I am the Human Journey, the spirit of Redome. It will be through my mind that much of the Living Universe will be told.

The clarity of the spirit memory will span the ages. We shall return to the beginnings of From the Time of the Writing- those journeys towards which I influenced Redome. Once again I will use his conscious brain to open some of those lives long gone. In reality, it will be through the eyes of Human Journey with many aspects of Redome's future.

I am moving now across distances greater than human imagination. I am to be born on what will be the first of many lives that span millions of years.

The ocean is wild outside the cave. The waves that crash into the shoreline are higher than the tallest of my clan. My kind mostly moves on four legs but may occasionally stand to gain advantage over another. The body of the one who is my living flesh is restless. It has been days since he has eaten properly. Several new births have been left in the cold to die as the milk of the mothers dried up. I see my body's eyes open and I am looking with him through his eyes.

We are trying not to be noticed by *Strong One*, so look without looking, through the sides of our eyes.

Our dangerous world has many predators so to see all without looking helps keep us alive. In the violent weather with the snow on the ground, the large group will not go out.

Strong One protects his preferred and sends those he feels he can spare and who may be successful in finding food.

The one born before the body I inhabit has gone out. Now he is looking at our body.

It has happened and we are trying to see where the ones who have gone before are. We hear the noise and it strikes quickly. The pain soon stops, and as I feel this earthly connection fade, I have a last glimpse of my body serving a purpose for those that are still a part of a living planet.

The light opens up, as the world of the ancient eternal laws of the cosmic intelligence once again becomes my home. The tensions and fears of my physical connection depart and I feel the comfort of harmony and joy. As the memories of my early human and otherworldly journeys clarify, I realize what beauty there is in the design of awareness for all types of life. I see clearly also the need to return to the physical as all conscious thought needs the rebirth to develop, learn and break eternity into constantly reoccurring beginnings and journeys of excitement and opportunity, including the low sides to physical existence.

The people I am born amongst spread out over the land that will someday be known as Africa. Over vast time, they evolve into many forms of hominid. With the availability of room and food in abundance, they sometimes live in harmony side by side. Rarely their blood mixes.

As space becomes an issue in each area the strong move the weaker away from what it is they need to exist. Some perish and their type no longer exists.

The Earth is cold so the ones who have the greatest gifts of observation follow the food, which exists in abundance near the oceans of the world. They move up out of Africa onto the southern coast of Europe. Some reach the coast of the Mediterranean. The cold does not encourage the majority to travel beyond to the great ice sheets.

There are continual waves of people moving eastwards along the temperate coastline, where they eventually reach the lands of South East Asia. Some may have developed separately in these lands. If so my spirit was not, I think, born to these early humans.

Through much of this vast time span, land from the Mediterranean to the Bandar Sea are the lands of greatest opportunity for the spread and development of the home of the Human Journey, my spirit. We learn to travel on the ocean and to use its resources long before humans at the Time of the Writing will suspect.

My spirit is born on and of this planet Earth over eons until at last, those I have been a part of walk tall; still 150000 years before the Time of the Writing.

At the Time of the Writing, the ancient remains of my people will be called *early man*. I will be born in the lands that were called the south part of Indonesia, at a location that will be far below the ocean due to the increased size of ice caps 150,000 years ago.

Where I stand now will be half way from the south-west point of Sulawesi and the Surabaya on Eastern Java in the Java Sea. For most of Earth's history this has been one of the most suitable habitats for our kind of life on this living planet, and probably the warmest. It is the equivalent of the future Mediterranean during the brief times the planet has not been a part of continual ice ages.

This group will pass south of Sulawesi and sweep east with the currents for about 1,100 km and strike the Island of Kep Tanimbar, half way between Papua New Guinea and Timor, eventually to travel the rest of the journey as occurs in this spiritual fantasy.

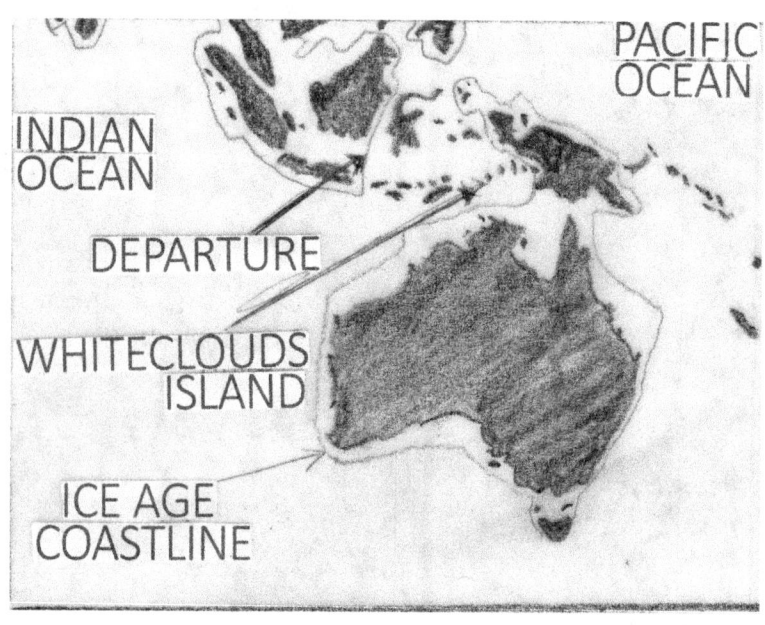

INDIAN
OCEAN

PACIFIC
OCEAN

DEPARTURE

WHITECLOUDS
ISLAND

ICE AGE
COASTLINE

THREE

DEPARTURE FOR NEW LAND

INDONESIA TO AUSTRALIA, 150,000 YEARS BEFORE THE PRESENT

IN THE BODY: (WHITE CLOUD)

I see her coming up the beach. Even though the bags she carries are full, her shoulders are back and her breasts jut out with the rich projections that set my body on fire.

The seven long boats with sleek outriggers line the shore. We are in the final stage of food preparation and storage and other supply gathering before we push off on the next leg of exploration. As we have wandered this land through many generations, we have become avid explorers. Now the ocean has become our great challenge and I love it. Still, as I look at the woman I hope to bond with and think of the risks to her, my body becomes nervous.

We hope the time of the storms has passed and we are on the monkey moon, the fourth finger of the hand that throws the spear from the time of the longest sun.

Nioma is with me now. I feel the touch of her hand on my cheek then the warmth spreads through my body, leaving a gentle ache in my chest. She senses my reaction and smiles quietly with the inner knowledge that is part of the mystery of woman.

We see smoke come over the horizon from south of the setting sun. There can be no smoke without food for fuel. There must be land for a large fire unless we are facing a volcano, so we will travel south when the sea is right. If the Mother is with us we will survive to find new lands.

Tomorrow we will raise stones to pay our respects to the *Earth Mother Goddess*. All we see around us is evidence of her living presence. If one listens carefully, one can almost hear her voice in the wind of the trees, the singing of the birds and the sound of waves breaking on the seashore. Even without all the sounds she makes throughout our lands, her life is everywhere. The kindness she shows in the ever-changing seasons that bring the cycle of life, that gives my Nioma life, makes me happy. The sun sinks low onto the horizon now. A beautiful red glow with a red sun signifies a fine day to come.

The central fire is lit and the smell of cooking meat brings new desire to my body that has lived for as long as the fingers of both my hands plus one more hand. Our group has more people than all the fingers of hands by the number of toes on my feet. We need much water as all will drink for perhaps days before we turn back or find land.

The hides are over the timber frame and our sleeping places are dry and warm with fire to keep animals at bay. Nioma still sleeps with the young girls but her celebration with the Mother will come soon and she will find company with men and, I hope, decide to form a hearth with me. We have favoured each other's company from our youngest days.

Late that night I am woken to take my turn as guard. It is hard to come out of sleep but good to know my place in the tribe.

My name is strong totem as it is a part of the giver of life. I am called *White Cloud*.

As the dawn slowly emerges and the soft golden glow gives life to her new day, followed by violet, then her beautiful blues, it gives me joy to see the givers of my new name following this emerging day. As always, my chest is full of awe as I wonder how the coloured clouds will slowly become white, with sometimes a touch of grey, always changing, as if my name has a life of its own. Then I realize that, as a part of the Goddess, they do have a life of their own. I am full of pride that my people see fit to call me White Cloud. I wonder what name Nioma will take after her celebration.

My thoughts bring desire to my body and I wish the days would go faster. My mind returns to our immediate tasks and the need for food. People begin to attend the fires and bring water and food to give us strength for the journey ahead.

The boats are a great joy to our people. There are still many made of hides stretched over a frame of bamboo, bound together with rawhide. The length is the number of tall men of one hand plus one more body length, at the widest point almost a short man's length. The outrigger is half as big and carries both people and supplies. The weather is good and the heavenly lights show the way. We can survive at sea for a large part of one moon, perhaps more, though I have never known people to be at sea for such time.

Our only fear is that we must leave in the season of the winds that blow in the direction of the smoke over the seas. It can blow for up to one hand of moons before swinging the other way. We cannot travel over the vast distances if the ocean goes against us. This we well know is also the season of the great winds that can tear trees from the earth. No boat will survive such a storm if caught in its path. Even some distance from the storm, the ocean can be dangerous with waves many times normal height.

The day passes with gathering and drying of food. The holy people, elders of our tribe, guide several men in the gathering of stones in order to ask guidance from the Mother on the morning of departure.

I feel the excitement amongst our people, and perhaps quiet fear in some. We may not all leave when the time arrives. I will be tested if Nioma falters. Could I leave her? I know I could not. Although we have not reached the time of a hearth, she has been my companion as often as boys of my age, often to the scorn of my friends. The bond is unusually powerful, especially since her shape became prominent in femininity, from just before her age reached the time of both hands.

Three days pass and those who decide say we must go while the supplies are fresh. As the sun rises, we gather by the shore at the junction of a small stream. Beautiful conifers rise amongst a great variety of plant life. The wonder of the living kingdom brings all the noises and the movement to give the mood for the ceremony.

The simple circle of stones, with the taller as a central symbol, are as they should be to give us a chance of safe journey. I feel the energy of all emotion now in my body and glance sidelong to see a pair of dark eyes upon me. I would ask the Mother to give me strength but am deeply aware that this is an immensely important time for all the tribe. We place all love and concentration for the good of all in the hands of this great Goddess. We are to travel into the unknown upon her back, we hope without her anger, so all will survive.

Regardless of this, I feel Nioma's eyes still upon me and, at the important time of the ritual, desire reaches my maleness and it is lust that is in my body, not my joy of the Goddess. Fear enters my mind for I can bring bad omens to the journey if I am not at one with all the tribe as we seek harmony.

I try to ignore Nioma's presence but a glance shows me her private smile seems to know I am unable to ignore the power she has over me.

The group is disbanding and more than one disapproving glance goes my way as many realize I was not giving my all to the good of the journey.

My desire is gone and I feel unworthy of the great honour bestowed upon us who will journey into where we think no people have ever gone before us.

We are forming up with the boats now. Each boat has a headman and I see they are gathering their favoured people for each vessel. I look hopefully at *Swift of Foot*, the father of Nioma and long a friend. To my horror, he bypasses me and swiftly I am amongst the handful of people holding back. I sense they will not travel. I step forward to separate from those who fear.

Swift of Foot looks away.

I move from boat to boat trying to catch the eye of each head boatman. They look away. My inattention at the ceremony was noted and I am considered bad luck. My heart sinks.

Three boats have already left. I cannot even look upon my departing love. Then as her boat enters the first of the breaking waves, I see a small figure leap into the surf washing swiftly ashore. Nioma stands and walks to stand beside me, still coughing seawater.

My heart bursts, but all emotions are distressing me. I fear for not only myself but also the one I love. The ocean is danger but the family group is strength. I have already left my group to go to the unknown. Great shame will accompany me if I return in the company of a woman not blessed by the ceremony of the Goddess.

Her father's boat turns beyond the breakers and coasts back to shore. The brothers are swift and she is aboard. With a flick of his head, he summons me. I thank all. My body finds an oar and a seat in the rear of the boat. I have a future again. I can redeem myself and find approval from all. I am not game to look at Nioma and could not explain my emotions. I am numb! None of this should have occurred. I am at one with the ocean. I have watched closely the night sky and all the moods of the living world around me. I will give all to this journey.

The sun is up now and with wind behind us, the land recedes. There is much quiet and contemplation for we all have much to dwell on. The headman stands high and, with an occasional command, keeps all within close contact. We will keep together. Our numbers are our survival and comfort on this great plain of water, with land receding swiftly, taking all security and much of our lives.

The men work on the oars, then take cover for shade and rest in the cycle of work that will go on from sunrise to sunrise. I close my mind and work the oar. I hope Swift of Foot will look gently upon me and not be angered. I have friends but most of the men are older and already of hearth, with some children at foot. Most hearth mates with small children looked away at talk of this journey, so young children number fewer than the fingers of both hands.

The three boys of my age are in the other vessel. I try not to look to the eye of my heart, for my worthiness in the eye of all must be restored.

As the day passes and land becomes a thin line, isolated islands on the horizon in turn fade from view. My mind turns to what may lie ahead. A glance behind shows me the trailing rope, which lies behind all vessels. If any fall overboard, the rope is their rescue.

On the morning of the second day, we see large flocks of birds circling and diving. Large school fish are driving small fish to the surface to feed. Our boats enter the boiling water and trailing lines with hooks of strong bone bring many fish to the surface. It is not just food and life, but a sign we are blessed on this journey. I am replaced after pulling several fish as the older hunters take privilege and claim the usually unwanted rear of each vessel.

We clean and eat fresh fish. We cut the remaining fish into strips and hang them out to dry. With all this excitement, I have felt the reassuring touch of Nioma's hand, and I am happy again. Still I keep my eyes to the ocean. I thank the giver as my body travels to what we trust will be our brave new world. Any world with her is complete for me.

The dark clouds come each day bringing warm rain and stronger winds. The seas rise and we surge forward on the running crests. The men of the boats are well used to this, so apart from some quiet amongst women we are grateful for the wind in our favour. I look to the woman amongst us who is the favourite of the Mother, and see her expression of quiet assurance. My confidence lifts. I answer the call and return to oar, and listen to the call of he who guides the stroke rate. Dark falls and my replacement sends me to take my turn in the middle of the vessel and sleep.

HUMAN JOURNEY

White Cloud is sleeping now and although my detachment to the physical life remains, I feel my eyes quietly depart from my body and their living consciousness. Even before I depart, I sense the presence of Nioma's inner self, also free of body as her physical self is deep in slumber.

Although I am in the spirit, the essence of the physical body that is my present life gives shape to me. It is the same for Nioma. In addition to her outline, I see her in a blue cloud with a silvery shimmer surrounding her wonderful form. However, it is not her arms that I wish to enfold me, not even the warmth of her flesh for they, I am aware, are not of this world. The warmth that approaches with her form is reaching out to me.

We reach high and see the long boats as dots on the ocean. Then we are away and for the time of our slumber, forget that life.

WHITE CLOUD, NIOMA

I awoke to movement. The sound of wind, voice and wave bring an awareness of danger. Dreams of strange journeys depart. The battle for survival is again my reality. Today's storm is fierce, but not the terrifying wind that kills and destroys all.

It is not time for me to take oar, so I move to the edge and bail water from the boat bottom. Nioma moves to help me. We work together until I am called to my position in the stern of the vessel and once again dark falls.

Eventually the wind eases and rain comes. Our world, so small now, is full of discomfort. I see the woman favoured of the Goddess cut a notch in her measuring stick. She will keep track of our time. If no land in so many days, she may talk of changing our destiny, or press us onwards, perhaps to find no more land. I put these thoughts behind me.

The days pass; with fruit and fish we remain healthy. It is quieter now, with only bouts of singing. All the boats have managed to stay together. Our people are our future in the hope for new lands.

Clouds form on the horizon and birds lead us to small islands. We find no water to drink but eggs to collect and young birds for fresh meat. Many wish to sleep but we move on, for time is life. The people are losing all sense of optimism.

Each day starts with a call to the Earth Mother to guide us to a new destiny. The ocean calms with only the deep swell found so far from land. Fewer fish are caught and the fruit is all gone. Swift of Foot and the Mother amongst us talk quietly from time to time, but little else happens. I wish I could sit with my Nioma.

I have no desire to attract attention. The start of this journey is still close to my mind. Human nature can turn my way again if all hope is lost. The following morning after our call to the Divine giver, the people ask for direction. They are told again it is in the hands of the Mother. This time the answer is not sufficient.

Then they are told what I already knew. We have come too far. To turn now for homelands would mean death by starvation and thirst. By the amount of fresh water left, I fear it will be thirst, for fish are still to be found, although in decreasing amounts. The stillness of the ocean and the lack of bird life are depressing. There is still great comfort in the deep wonder of eyes of the Mother's woman when they give swift answer to a glance cast her way.

With the knowledge that there is no turning back comes a greater determination to cover distance. The men put all remaining energy into the oar. I am moved to the outrigger where one out of every hand of people takes a shift. Within two days, we are down to half the number of oarsmen. Weakness and illness now afflict all the boats.

The first deaths come. Bodies are removed with little ceremony, with only a tiny part of the outward grief that all must be feeling. Cloud appears on the horizon and birds gather. Hope raises its weary head, and I put my remaining strength into the oar. The Mother takes up the timing and we row together. Land grows as darkness comes and I know we all fear the land will pass in the night. The Mother tells all we have the stars to hold our direction so we work on into the darkness of the living world.

The sound of waves on land reaches us, then the cliffs show against a dark sky. The boats are close together now and move cautiously along the coastline seeking safe landing. As time passes we become a little excited. This is not a rock in an empty ocean. We may find food and renewed hope or perhaps our new world. There is no moon. Starlight reflects off the white water as it breaks on rocks to show us a safe landing. I see only the boat in front and those close to me. Light reflects off the oar as it breaks the surface. Then I see the boat in front move landward and hear the order for those on the other side to hold.

We move towards the land. Waves catch and rush us towards what I feel must be an opening through an outer reef. I see nothing but dark and the fast approach of white water.

My body crashes into the man in front of me. I feel the outrigger lift high, then only space below me for a blink. I crash into the raging surf and rocks that tear into my body. The pain is intense but my struggle is for air. The water calms between waves and I glimpse rocks clearing the water and struggle to reach them. The water crashes and pain strikes again. Then I am in the lee of the rocks protected from the power of the ocean. I grasp hold, and heave myself into a gap between rocks. The ocean crashes again. This time my lungs take water and with a last conscious thought my head impacts stone and the world stops.

HUMAN JOURNEY

They are struggling ashore. All vessels but mine are intact. The outrigger, although damaged, is still attached. The other four oarsmen are on the shore. There are weeping women and most look exhausted. Nioma is with her mother and one brother. If anyone noticed the departure of my physical body, there are more urgent concerns. I see that some of those amongst the recovering are about to depart into the world I am part of.

A form leaves an unconscious figure and moves without hesitation past me and into an existence beyond where I am. I am aware my body is not yet dead. From my position in this silvery blue twilight world, I see the boats pulled high above the water line. Then I am back in my body and White Cloud is struggling in and out of awareness as he resists pain and death.

I drift in and out of his body until well after daybreak. He finally collapses into a state of sleep, close to death as far as I can tell.

They are back in the vessels and moving out with the change of the high tide. This place is not suitable for their needs so greater access to this land, where they are not enclosed by high cliffs on all sides as with this cove, must be found.

White Cloud will not be seen from the gap in the reef they must pass through.

One lone girl stands and searches for his missing form. They are swiftly around the headland and lost to any rescue of my physical form. I reach high and see this land is a large island. I also see that the place the boat people will probably land will see the sun high in the sky for their arrival.

My body is lost to them, but more especially to his beloved Nioma.

His eyes open and once again we face what is to be a desperate, lonely, and perhaps brief journey.

WHITE CLOUD

Slowly clarity returns to my suffering. Where are those who will rescue me? How long have I been lying amongst the debris of washed up vegetation amongst these rocks? Long enough for me to know I must move my painful body or die here. No one is coming for me, not even my beloved. They believe me dead.

My body lies over the forked remains of a tree that, like me, is just clinging to these rocks. Slight movement shows me I would have to swim many steps to reach the beach. As I move, the branch slips and takes me quickly into the sea. I cling to it in order to gain strength but to my horror see that we are already moving through the gap in the reef and into the open ocean. Already I am too far to swim, if that was possible before. The log keeps me afloat so I am at its mercy. I pray the blood of my wounds does not attract hungry mouths from the deep. My mind is somehow numb. Perhaps beyond hope, but the spirit is strong and death is not to be given easy access to my physical being.

Time passes and the ocean remains flat. Fear stops me from looking to the land. I do not know the answer. Do not wish to think.

I do not hear the approach and I am only vaguely aware of my head lifted from the water. It must be a dream that a tiny toothless face of an old woman is staring at me over the edge of a large vessel. Then my world goes dark and I presume with a last thought that death has arrived.

HUMAN JOURNEY

Even I, a spirit who has seen more than the body can know, am intensely interested in this strange spectacle. Tiny people, in most cases of lovely form, are filling two boats that are about half as large as those of our own people. These bodies stand less than half the height of ordinary man and are petite but strong in form. Although I had heard of the little people, many considered them legend.

They are towing him, log and all, towards the land. Perhaps he is too heavy to lift into the boats. I think the reason is that this man is unknown to them and may even in his weak form be a threat to vessel and people. They avoid the cove, moving eastward towards what appears to be sheer cliff face. A quick lift above cliffs shows me an entrance almost hidden from ocean that opens up onto small sandy beach with access to the island above. I see some kind of shelter against the stone, and other signs of human achievement. They are skilful with many oarsmen, so my unconscious form is soon roped and dragged well above the high tide. I sense fear, excitement and wonder at this giant that has come from the sea.

Then the old woman, who peered into my face, speaks and gestures to some of the young at the same time pointing different directions up and down the coast. A group quickly departs to seek any companions of this giant.

White Cloud's people have landed on a beach to the rising sun direction. There is a stream giving fresh water, with fish of the shell and fin. The trees are full of the milk nut so all but three are gathering food in preparation for a feast and restocking of stores. Three are making their way through thick forest towards the high part of this island. They do not know if they have reached the land of dreams, but first sign says this place could support people.

I can see from high in the sky that smoke from fires in at least five hearths is disappearing. The little people do not intend to show themselves. I cannot tell their intention, but they now know they have probably unwanted guests. They are observed as they move through forest and their life is in great danger. I feel

White Cloud emerging and I become, once again, his subconscious mind.

WHITE CLOUD

My arms and legs are bound, but someone is bathing my wounds with something that seems to cool and perhaps dull the pain. My face is blindfolded, and a gag stops me from making noise.

There is no point in struggling until they finish. The gentle hands continue to remove pain and I seem to be placed in a position of comfort. I hear speech as those unseen go about their business. I wonder if the rest of my people are in danger. These people do not see any need for a new people to invade their small land. How do I know this is a small land? My mind focuses on the one who dominates my very small world. The hands feel like that of a child. I had only a glimpse of a tiny wizened face, before my journey into what was to be death. This is not death.

Shock or exhaustion takes over and I slip into strange dreams.

With new awareness comes quiet, with only the sounds of the nearby ocean. By the feel of cool air on my body, it seems night is well advanced. I struggle to sit up, and sense movement nearby. No one touches me, or attempts to communicate. Time goes by slowly and eventually sounds tell me the community is going about the activities of a new day. The lack of smoke or cooking smells tells me something is different; most probably connected to my kind and me.

The day passes and my wounds are tended. I attempt to show them I mean no harm. The tethers stay on my hands and feet.

The covering remains on my face. I am very thirsty. It will not be long before hunger starts to weaken me.

I know night arrives again, but I sink into the sleep of a degenerating body. My dreams are of strange events, as my body seems to rise from the ground and fly high in the air to a silvery blue twilight world. I see my people sleeping on the beach, unaware those eyes are watching their every move.

I move close to my beloved friend Nioma and see the sign of tears on her cheeks. She is sleeping now. Then I am awake and even more alone.

I don't think Swift of Foot is aware this land is not for the taking. Our people will not know it is an island alone in an endless ocean. I think they will rest, replenish supplies and move along the coast in search of what they have been told by those who serve the Mother is a great Southern land, not an island with limitations for their future as it has been foretold to the elders for more than a generation.

My face is free at last and to my relief cool milk of the coconut nourishes my body. The cover goes back on, but the ropes are loosened and some feeling returns to hands and feet. They do not place me in a position where I could see people or settlement. They have obviously decided for the time being that I am worth my place amongst the living. I am not sure if Swift of Foot and Nioma's brothers felt as strongly about my place amongst the living. When all appears to be lost, people are quick to look for reasons as to why the Mother is not present to guide the destiny of her children.

My glimpse of the world showed the light of new day. I hear people moving away and silence follows. Eventually the cool air tells me night has come again. I drink from the coconut and eat a kind of flat bread. My wounds are treated. Then silence again. I think there are fewer people present now, perhaps as many as the fingers of one hand.

I drift into sleep with dreams of new lands and Nioma. The morning comes with food again. This time the mask stays off and when daylight arrives, I turn in all directions and see I am alone, some twenty feet from the water. Steep cliffs rise in all directions but a track leads into a gap between two faces of rock. The boat or boats are gone, as is all sign of people. By sliding across the sand, I reach a ledge of rock with sharp edge, and am soon free.

There is only one direction to go so I am soon through the crevasse and amongst thick coastal vegetation. A track leads to higher ground, but my body has to crawl in many places to pass through. Whoever used these tracks was tiny. It is hard to see where the track leads but impossible to leave, as the scrub is impenetrable. Some places I am able to move more swiftly. Then once again, I bend and crawl. The day is still early.

I hear bird life, still gulls and terns of the ocean, but also forest birds now, and an occasional glance of bright plumage shows me an unfamiliar type of parrot. The hide of my lower garment allows me some comfort. Coverings of my upper body are torn, but the exposed wounds look healthy, and are healing faster than I would have expected, even with the knowledge of our own medicine woman. My only thought is to reach a point on this land where I can get direction of my people or see sign of smoke.

The sun is much higher in the sky, but the trees have changed and tussocks of grass allow me to move without stopping. The track seems to be running along the coast as I see ocean often now. From the top of a rise, the vista opens up of a sweeping coastline and some beach in the distance. I see no sign of human activity. I have no choice but to follow the trail. I suspect by animal droppings that it was formed by the wildlife of the island, if this is an island. The ground is stony so there are no footprints to mark the passing of people.

I am alone and hungry and frightened. Strange that while bound and in desperate trouble, I felt no fear. Now I am free and perhaps have hope of finding my *Nioma*, I am afraid. Once again, I have hope. Once again, I have a future to lose.

Fear puts strength into my legs, and I move off in a direction I think will bring me to the coast and perhaps signs of humans. The sun passes overhead as I reach a pebbly beach, which bears no sign of man or beast.

They will have travelled this way, as it is the direction of their journey. Some relief comes as I reach the end of the bay. I hear it first, then on rounding the headland, I see a crystal-clear stream cascading down the rocks and into the sea. I drink deeply and wash parts of my body. The rest will wait.

I will try to keep to the coast, going inland only when forced to. The coastal vegetation looks lower here and is interspersed with a variety of grasses, making travel easier. I wade past another headland and enter a bay with fewer cliffs. Here there are gentle hills that give me a long view of coastline. I see the land mass is curved so it is probably an island, and not large. Although I can see a great distance, there are no people. A feeling of sadness enters my body; I will not find them today.

The sun is low.

Then I find it. Hearths set back in an outcrop away from the wind. The coals are still hot in one pit. They must have left this morning. They will travel faster by sea than I can move through this country. Unless they settle here, I am lost to them. Fire may be my only chance.

I quickly gather dried grass and some small sticks. Flames appear immediately, but there is little smoke. A mixture of green grass, branches and dry material sees the sky fill with a grey cloud, but is soon gone. I keep going but feel my strength waning. There is little hope and night is coming quickly, so I find shellfish on rocks and a spring. The latter was probably what encouraged my people to stop here.

They may come back for water and a good camp, if this land looks promising. I will seek shelter and sleep. My mind does not focus on the risk of those who rescued and bound me. It feels as if they have abandoned any interest in me. My fire warms me and keeps me safe from animals. Perhaps someone may see it.

Exhaustion forces restless sleep and strange dreams until the morning light opens my eyes. Fear enters my body. I have a profound sense of lost future. Even when bound the touch of those tiny hands healing my wounds gave hope. Now I face despair. The fire finds hot coals and smoke is more important than an empty stomach. I drink my fill. All morning the smoke sends my message. It matters little to me if other eyes are watching. Without the sighting, they will have presumed me dead. They will focus on the interests of those that are most capable.

As the day passes the job of gathering fuel gets more difficult. When dark nears, hunger becomes the main issue. Sadness joins the gathering gloom with only a small fire to warm my being. Even the silence of the ocean birds is depressing.

The sun rises over the rocks with gentle heat and my eyes open. I have less hope, so I must see what I have to survive, and try to make decisions.

It is possible they will work their way around the island, then settle in a good place to gather food and heal the sick. Perhaps they will stay but something tells me this will not be the chosen land. There is food here so I will tend the fire for another day, eat and heal before exploring my isolated world. It seems hard to hear the words of the Mother Goddess.

I am alive! I know how to live. In time the answers may come. I must try to keep busy and not despair.

Two days pass with fire and food. Now I worry about the smoke only early and in the afternoon. Tomorrow I will seek high ground.

As the sun reaches the horizon, dark clouds gather. A storm is coming, although at present there is no wind. As I watch, I wonder at the power of clouds that are the opposite of my totem name. Perhaps a world I pay homage to is indeed angry with the one called White Cloud.

There is some overhang of rock behind the small spring. In heavy rains, water may cascade down like a waterfall, so shelter will not be found under this rock. I head for the largest tree canopy leaving most of my fire behind. The rain strikes before the fire has a chance to ignite. Even bark from the protected side of the tree will not light in the now strong wind. This will be a bad night and all thought of others finding me is gone. Only misery and cold will be my companions.

The rain continues, so my thoughts turn to my love and I wonder if she is on the high sea or land. For her own sake I hope she has not left these shores.

Eventually even drizzle settles in. Hunger joins with the cold of my body. I am glad when the light stretches along the now visible ocean horizon, perhaps bringing warmth of the Mother's new day. Her sun will give me reason to find better shelter, and a greater source of food. My thoughts have stronger elements of survival, and less of rescue. I have more will to act. I must draw upon all I have learned on the shores and in the forests of my homelands. I feel an inner strength, not for my love of Nioma, but for my knowledge of self, and awareness that self is all I appear to have.

The sun rises with a grey sky and the drizzle continues. My hunger is satisfied with more shellfish, and a good fish caught in a rock pool.

Now I shall find out what this land is and if I am its sole inhabitant. What beasts and birds share it with me? With my mind firmly on this, I seek a strong branch, which I grind on the rocks to produce a point, which I will harden with the help of my next fire. Now there is some protection. In that, small comfort emerges.

Towards the morning sun on my non-throwing arm, the land rises again making me more visible to the chance ocean travellers. As I move, I look at all things, plants, rocks, birds and animals. Even with the rain, small droppings of body waste are evident. The rain means few creatures will come out of cover. Even birds seem quiet. I am wet and uncomfortable with several injuries making my travel cautious. There is no track now but the climb is steep with only coarse grass and an occasional bush. Eventually I come out on high ground and cast my eye to grey cloud and endless ocean.

I know where the wind and rain comes from, so the valleys and headlands against the sea that give protection and food will be vital. I must find fresh water for the dry times to come after the wind and rain of the hot season. These positive plans lift my spirit and I thank the Earth Mother for her guidance. There will be time enough later to ask for her rescue, and other gifts, and perhaps her forgiveness.

I follow her ridges and lower valleys, always towards the high ground keeping the ocean mostly in view on my throwing hand. I will not return to the bay tonight, but seek food from the ocean. I cannot recognize seed or fruit that is food.

The light fades as I reach a small bay. The sun is an orange ball on the surface of a large ocean. Even in its fearsome expanse, there is the profound beauty of the Earth Mother. This is my strength for now. Shellfish are once again a too small meal. Tomorrow I will find milk nuts.

I have no fire so move in close to a rock overhang and pull the branches of thick bushes in front of me. Still I have seen no predators or snakes. Bird noises stop.

It is dark and the sound of gentle breeze and waves arriving on the nearby beach could not have brought me awake with my entire senses alert.

I move my back against the rock and reach for my rough spear. To my horror, a dark shape like a curved rock moves across the light, and I hear the sound of fear.

Instinct tells me I am prey. It is a reptile and very large. The point of my spear drives forward and deflects off a rapidly moving object. I stab again and sense it has retreated for now. The information becomes confused until I realize another creature has attacked the first. I can only hold the branches close and my weapon ready. The fight stops and I know they have turned their attention back to dinner.

The lack of fire in what I thought was a peaceful land is probably the end of my journey. The cover is thrust sideways and I must fight or die so I thrust again where I hope the eyes and the mouth of the creature, (or creatures) might be. The point sinks in and my arms are wrenched as the spear thrusts away from me.

I pull it free in time to thrust at the noise of another as it closes on terror. Again, it backs off.

Now another battle has moved back from me as several creatures fight amongst themselves. A brief period brings change and I hear what I think are the sounds of feeding with only occasional conflict.

For the moment, it seems I am off the menu. The moon comes out from the clouds, showing me many very large lizards, as many as the fingers of one hand. With spear in hand, I run down the beach not daring to look back. Some cliffs with low rocks appear out of the gloom and I drive for the high ground. I reach a platform, perhaps two men high, and a quick glance shows me they are to eat their own kind until gone. I have no doubt I will be the next delicacy for hungry reptilian bellies.

I remain wide-eyed until eventually the sky lightens and the Mother of all life brings warmth in a new day. Eventually I move down to the sand with new respect.

There is no sign of life, apart from birds feeding on a carcass picked almost clean. Quick inspection shows large crabs progressing up the beach, no doubt to take what remains back to the sea. I quickly retrieve several crabs and have food for the cycle of life.

Now I know, not only must I find shelter from the elements, but protection from at least one predator. I take a sharp-edged rock as I leave the beach and move quickly to higher ground. Now the search is on to find a temporary home until I have improved my weapons.

The sun reaches high then travels towards another fearsome night. This time I find shelter and high ground early, and light a fire. Dark arrives and hunger is now a greater reality. The light of fire and protection of the flame gives security so eventually once again sleep arrives.

My body wakes and all remains quiet. I stoke the coals of a diminishing fire and sleep to the sound of gulls announcing a new day. I push loneliness into the back of my mind. I will continue to travel and search, with the hope that my people have settled, and I will seek harmony with the Mother of this land, to gain food and strength before travelling. I am not sure I will survive without company, or without the wisdom of my elders, and the knowledge of those who serve the giver of all life.

With a sharp stone, I make a mark on my spear for each day I have been alone, and a circle below for the full moon. Once again keeping the ocean on my spear arm, I move out. As the day travels, the position of the sun tells me I am moving in an arc. At midday, I reach a bay and seek camp before hunger weakens me. I find food, with eggs in abundance. The tall tree supplies liquid and white meat. Fire provides protection and sleep comes.

Now the noise is back and I have only dull coals for protection. My sinister company moves past the light. Perhaps I am unnoticed. I feed the flames, giving me some vision, but beyond, nothing. I wish I had brought more wood for I will not willingly search within the scrub and fill these reptilian bellies; better they are food for me. With this thought I realize their meat on my fire and dried would sustain me for days on end. For now, though, I move back against the cliff and keep the fire in front of me. Eventually, welcome light shows a gentle sea and I presume the predators found prey that did not have the Mother fire for protection.

Now I know I have meat, and in time, I will learn to become the hunter not the hunted! To do this I must live. Above all, the hope to live with my love Nioma is still in the part of me that gives strength.

Several days pass with no sign of human, small or large. The notches on my spear say I have been here almost the fingers of both hands. The nature of the land is changing, fewer trees with scrub and grassland. Open rolling hills blend to sand dunes, then comes the sea. It is easy to travel but not easy to find wood for fire. I camp where trees are close to the coast from time to time. Then on the day of two hands plus the toes of one foot, life appears in greater numbers.

For a day, I have seen animal waste. Now on topping a hill, before me grazing on shrubbery is a herd of elephants the likes of I have not seen before. The tops of their heads would be lucky to reach my waist. Still, they have tusks and a bull stands guard. I guess the reptiles are his enemy or perhaps the little people if they come here as well. It crosses my mind that here also is meat, but I have no suitable flint or stone for edge yet so the meat would be hard, if not dangerous, to access.

The sun tells me now I am coming in a full circle. I have found no cave that I would choose to make a safe home. I need to stop and learn to survive using the ways of my people and adapting them to my new home. For now I fear I will complete the circle of an island far from other lands for I have seen no other on any horizon.

I have seen other campsites. They are not of this last moon so not of my people. They are perhaps a comfort as well as reason for caution. The country is heavy timber now and rain has sent me into the trees to rest at night. The predators are here but I can outrun them so fear them less. They will take me only if I am cornered or caught asleep without fire.

Another trail has appeared, and I wonder if animals or small men made this. Animal I think because man seems to be a visitor to this land. Eventually I come across a place I recognize and know I am near the camp of the little people. Loneliness turns my head in that direction, and what is the closest I have found to a safe haven. This is probably the reason they chose such a place on my now definitely island home. I am glad in a desolate way to be back. A quick survey tells me that with little effort I can block the narrow entrance and sleep soundly at night. This I will do after seeking food from the rock pools. I will look no further for my Nioma.

Now I must make a home. This is easy as the cliff comes well out giving good shelter from most of the rains.

That night I sleep and am left in peace accept for dreams that come each night to inform me each time I wake of all I have lost. My life was to be a discovery of the Mother's gifts and she seems to have tested me sorely.

NOTE FROM THE AUTHOR:

Fossils have been found on Flores and several other islands of both pygmy elephant and the tiny hobbits.

FOUR

SETTLING INTO MY NEW HOME

My first thought as the sounds of birds and gentle water brings my spirit back to the body is that I can be safe here for a time. Then I remember I have been around my land and my people have gone. Hunger and thirst as usual stop the sadness as I rise to face my challenges.

Luck produces two lobsters. This is a very good place and obviously well suited to those who come here. Will they be angry if they find me here on their return? They tended my wounds, fed me, and left me alive, so if they return I shall withdraw until I can gauge their acceptance of one so strange as me.

I light a fire on a well-made hearth of ash from many fires. For now, the food is good, and my spirits lift as purpose gives small hope. The first job is to protect the entrance as I think the creatures from the sea will not come up to the high ledge that is now home. Stones move easily into place and a dead tree supplies a barricade I can move easily to enter and leave. The rest of the tree I store for my hearth. I cover deep coals so they will burn longer and give me quick fire for food and comfort as dark returns. Warmth is not needed, as it is still the moons of the winds from the north.

Weapons to hunt and protect myself with are next. I must find rock that will flake to a hard edge. Then I will have good stone axes, knives and points for spears. The leaves from the tall food tree will give binding to attach, with perhaps help from gum of trees. I will quietly seek these things. With this in mind, I travel back towards the heavy forest using my old trail then moving inland to higher ground.

The rest of the first day gives me no suitable stone, but I discover birds eating fruit from a large forest tree. I risk eating a small amount and gather as much as I can carry. If my body does not reject it, this source of fruit will give health and sustenance. My medicine woman used captured fish in a rock pool to test plants. If the fish did not die, the old amongst us would eat. Thus safe roots, leaves, fruit and flesh are found. In time I may do that, as the spring of the little people's water supply has a suitable rock pool.

I now seem the leader of my own land. My long days to come must not drive me into despair, for that may be a greater enemy to me than the predator lizards. My body remains healthy on the trip home so I eat more fruit. It is delicious with oysters from the rocks. I feel better situated to live as each day passes. That is the immediate needs of life. If I can live without company is another thing.

Each day I rise, and make a notch in my original spear. I now have several far better for hunting. I enter the ocean to cleanse myself, then eat. I have found more fruit plus seed from trees that are food of my island creatures. Each day I move further inland by different routes in search of the stone. On the day of two sets of hands and three quarter moon, I find stone that will keep an edge and produce a spark when struck. If I can feel happy alone, this brings new cause. Much time passes, as I slab and divide suitable rock. When the sun tells me to return home, I have as much as I can carry to make tools.

For the days of one hand, I work on the stone. I am pleased with spear and knife and fire makers. The full moon comes and goes with my body gaining strength, as food is now plentiful. Even some birds are caught easily as they enter a burrow at night when returning from long days of fishing. My people would have eaten well here, but they would seek land not surrounded by endless ocean.

One morning the seemingly endless loneliness brings a deeper pain, so I set out in the direction my people made last campfire on these shores. I cannot reach my home base by nightfall so take extra food and weapons. As the sun lowers I have not found the cove. The track I took on those first days seems lost to me. Still, evening finds me safely in rocks by the sea, fed with fish and warmed by fire. It feels better to be on a quest, even if little can come of it.

Next day I find higher ground, but cannot identify recognizable landmarks. As the sun reaches its high mark, I hear running water and enter the location of the lost cove. I cast my eye to the sea for sign of life. As always, there are only birds seeking food and their own kind.

I turn back in the direction of the spring and come upon a sight that freezes my mind. One of my people's boats is turned upside down with support and other windbreaks, with covers each side of it to form a well-established camp. There are no other boats on shore and no people.

Then it explodes in my mind. They came full circle of this land and stopped at this original water to gain strength, before continuing their journey; my journey.

I rush to the hearth. The embers are cold but food scraps, shell and state of coal tells me the camp was in use in the last day or two.

They were here if I had only continued to search. My Nioma was here. I almost feel her presence. I can feel her presence. My head tells me they (she) are on the sea. With weight of a large stone in my chest, I search the camp for hope. The places of sleeping show signs of the gathering of supplies. Even bones of lizards, with drying sticks by the hearth, tell me they prepared for a journey. They took some of my predators, but also some of my food supply. Sense tells me there is more than enough for my life and beyond.

They were here, my people and my life. My future was here all the time. Tears flow over my cheeks and I sit under the boat. Then I hear the sound of my own voice as anguish bursts from my body.

Dark comes and despair remains. I light no fire, and seek no food. I have forgotten the thirst. If the predators come tonight, I care not.

I must have slept for my eyes open to a new day. Pain floods my body from feet to head. Thought seems separate and my body is a void. The light of another day has passed before I rise and drink then light a fire. I cannot return to the home that brought me small comfort. Now I think it deprived me of all that I think I am.

As a new day begins my eyes open and the mind begins to clear. I will eat as hunger drives me, not from the desire to live.

I move to the end of the beach behind the camp and see where they have loaded the boats and dragged those needed for fewer people back to the ocean.

There in the sand above the boat sign is a triangle of sticks with a spear attached pointing to the ocean. Hanging from the top, is the last thing I gave Nioma, shells and small bones threaded on the hair of her head and mine to make a decoration for between her lovely breasts. She is telling me where she has gone, and that she has not given up hope for me. The spear has always been the way to direct the travellers towards or away from our lives.

HUMAN JOURNEY

As he slept, I watched his love and the essence of Nioma in body travel far in the direction of the current and the wind. They have rested and are stronger now. The island gave them much, but not the home they seek. White Cloud's mind was closed to me as he thought only of his fight to survive. His mind was less accessible with the pain of his loss. The will of the body I share is strong so he may survive, but I fear for him, as the isolation will be complete. His people will not return. Much time will pass before more of his people travel this journey. His body will be dust and I will be awareness in the conscious universe, or look through the eyes of a new journey of the living flesh.

WHITE CLOUD

I have lost count of the days so have stopped making my mark. Many days I return to the beach, sometimes sleeping under the boat. Without my people, there is no protection here. Still the reptiles stay away. Perhaps those that inhabited this part of the island as their territory are keeping my Nioma from hunger.

Another moon has come and gone. This I have marked so the passing of time I know. The winds that blow from the north will become less in time with the cooling of the season. Then they will blow from the south for many moons. This will not affect me for I cannot put my people's vessel to sea with the arm of one man. I would be at the mercy of the Mother's great water. This body is not ready to perish yet.

One day as I near the camp the clouds grow dark and strong wind strikes. Haste brings me to the site in time to witness the protection of hide and bamboo torn from its supports and flung into the trees, to finally come to rest half in the stream. It will take more than I am capable of to repair for roof or journey to sea.

The storm does not abate so I seek shelter and fire nearby, until light returns. The wind stops but not the rain. I look at the damaged vessel and see now it would be possible for me to recover the hides and frame. I remove as much hide and part of the main frame as I can carry. Thus a new purpose is born, one that will keep me busy for the days of nearly two hands. I shall store this with care at my home. With these materials I can develop comforts. As the last journey finishes the materials seem to be both opportunity and perhaps the end of my connection to all that was lost.

After the passing of a full moon I feel a greater weight in my chest. Without purpose, loneliness bears down on me so I start to build by binding the bamboo with curves of ocean use still intact to give me greater protection. This job complete, I feel better and can store foods with greater ease. The fruits that have given strength and pleasure are rotting on the ground, and the trees are once more devoid of creatures.

Each day I seek a greater understanding of the creatures. Predators will become fresh and dry meat for times when food may not be plentiful. Still my days are empty and increasingly I sit for long periods. When the memory of the joys of my people and the loss of my hope becomes too painful, I empty my head of all thoughts. This gives a feeling of peace, and the strength to rise and do all that I need for a healthy body.

The passing of time puts the little people in the back of my mind. The moons of one hand pass and my new home of hide is a great success when the south winds come. The rains are less now but the fresh water is from deep in the Mother's earth, so I think will not depart with the dry times. Each day I take the remains of my meals and waste from my body out of my site and heave it into a steep little chasm close by. Thus reptiles have found some pickings and are coming closer to my home.

One day, there are three of them, directly below me, fighting over the scraps. My safe position gives me courage, and I choose a large stone and plunge it at the nearest creature, intending to drive it away from my base. It goes down, struck directly between the shoulders. The others move back as the body goes into what I recognize as the death throes.

Others move in on their own flesh without thought of danger from me. I think these creatures have no knowledge of other predators. I bring more stones to the cliff edge and rain them down on the unsuspecting cannibals. With one more dying and the other injured but gone, a new feeling enters my body, the age-old joy of the hunt. I have power over my land. I have new hides and flesh for my body. Cautiously I move in to gain my trophies. It soon becomes apparent that dark will beat me before I can skin both and transport them back to hearth. I cover one with stones against the cliff face as best I can and take the hide and most of the flesh of one to my hearth. That night I sleep soundly and my dreams of Nioma are mixed with the thought of new possibilities on my island home.

Next morning I reach the cliff top in time to see the injured one has recovered enough to return to the smell of blood, and an easy meal. This time my stone misses, but the creature moves away. Instinct for survival is learned quickly as is the law of the Mother. It leaves me to recover its brother or sister. Now I can dry food for several moons, and travel will be easier. I extend the hearth, and the next day sees most of my wood supply diminished. Stones form safe storage on higher ledges, and in holes in the ground. I store the meat.

My memory stores the story of the hunt for people who will probably never hear of my fine achievement. I give thanks to She, who gives all we have ever known.

Now as I travel this land I will seek other places where I have advantage over reptile, and perhaps even the elephant that dwells mainly in the hills beyond the tall trees.

As the next moon passes, I make many trips of two and three day duration. The elephants inhabit open country with only occasional trips into heavy timber country. One location is possible at a point high above a watering point. I have no need of more meat. Still, knowledge is strength. They are beautiful animals with a family structure that tugs at my emotions. I see the things lost in the behaviour of these herd creatures. Often I am drawn to the cove of my departing people, but always with a sense of sadness. In my only home I feel peace, for there one has comfort of some degree.

On the third day of the seventh moon and the second moon of the south winds I return, just on dusk. The stones and branches are not in place. What creature has invaded my safe haven? I move back to the cliff top. From here, it is already too dark to see below. I hear no sound or movement. Time passes.

I move quietly back down the path and enter the steep cavity to my cove. This place is all I have and now fear is deep in my being. Sticking to the cliff face, I move away from my camp towards the sea with cliff face beside me, and retreat behind me, if such should be necessary.

I reach the ocean and move quickly across the beach to the other steep rock wall. There are no boats. Too dark to see sign of landing, so I presume no little people. My body feels as if a creature will rush from the ocean to claim my fear. Now I move with all caution to the edge of my camp, for a long time staying outside the hide wall. Eventually all my senses tell me I am alone. I pass through the gap, and quickly reach the gate and block the entrance.

A new thought gains strength in my head. Perhaps my isolation is making my thoughts wander, and I departed this site, leaving the barricade open to all. With this in mind, my spirits lift and fear departs. The pounding in my chest slows. I deposit my new flints and dry material by hearth and the warmth of a small fire grows. I bring dry food, fruit, nuts and meat from stone cavities and seem uneasily normal. Eventually sleep arrives and I am glad to have the comfort of hide over grass and hide over body for the dreams that are perhaps the best life has to offer me.

My eyes open just as the sun casts its beautiful light over the ever-changing surface of the ocean; my joy, challenge and hope, but perhaps now my jailer. The coals catch in a small fire, for that is all one needs to welcome a new day. Then my mind returns to the night before. Daylight will bring some answers but I am sure it was the fault of my memory. After a small amount of food I open the hide with spear in hand.

They come from both sides, surrounding me. They are all armed, tiny men no higher than my waist; no sound from any. I lower my spear, as is the way of greeting a stranger who comes in peace.

They continue to look in silence. I know not who is leader so turn to he who appears oldest amongst them. I take some lizard from my belt pouch and offer it. He withdraws with a look of distaste and several clicks of his tongue. No words are spoken. A glance shows me many boats, some still at sea and full of women and children.

Amongst the fear, I am aware that regardless of danger they are human and I am no longer alone. The spears jab me behind the knees and I fall forward thinking the worst may have come. I lie face down but no pain follows. Slowly I raise my face and climb quietly to my knees. Words are spoken. And more clicks. They move aside and form a path to a tiny face that seems to be out of a dream, one seen from the water as I once before waited to die.

She is ancient and to my surprise, I think she is shaman. This tiny woman is covered in tattoos from head to knee and little else. She moves directly to stand in front of me, and peers up at the face of this kneeling man. The hand reaches out to the healed wounds on my body, causing loud chatter that I can tell is a mix of caution, fear, wonder and I hope not anger. Then her hands go to my face. I smile. She takes no notice. I think these hands have been those that healed me on days I had almost forgotten. She speaks then moves past me. I begin to climb to my feet but the spears jab and the message is clear. Stay where you are.

She returns to stand in front of me and for a time just looks. I can do nothing. Then with more of those strange noises, she moves back towards the boats with a strength and speed that surprises me for one so ancient in appearance. The men back away, breaking out of formation and moving towards the sea.

Now a new feeling is in me, fear of being left alone again. As the last of them enters the vessels, I move to the shore and try to let them know I do not want them to leave. I finally sink to my knees with open arms and a cry of anguish from a voice that has been so long silent.

They move out and depart in the direction of my people's departure beach. With only my spear, I quickly gain the cliff top and follow their directions. From hilltops, I can see I am keeping pace. Eventually as the sun descends towards mid-afternoon, they land and move to light fires near the flowing stream. This time I move far up the beach. I will not approach. Perhaps I am afraid they will attack or am I afraid I will drive them from my, until now seemingly empty, land?

As night nears, I light my own fire against rocks and seek shellfish.

The next day sees many depart to sea and three boats with small groups remain. They move out to a reef, and I see people diving off the edge of boats. They seek what can be caught by hand. As the sun passes overhead thirst becomes a reality, so with no tall palm for milk I move quietly towards the stream, but further inland so not to cause greater concern.

They have stopped their activities to group together and to watch my progress. After drinking my fill, I move back to my fire. The day passes and I seek more food from the sea. I wish I had brought more dried food, and tools to help. Then it strikes me. They do not want my meat, but perhaps the flint to light fire and stone for knife, spear and axe would bring me closer to these, who at least in appearance are close to my kind. I can reach my camp and the quarry site in one day, and be back by two, so decide to leave just before dusk.

At night, the beach has a line of fires. I think these people are drying what they catch for later uses. The next day passes and I arrive back just on dusk. Whatever the reason my spirits lift to see the fires and some shelters have begun to grow.

They intend to stay, at least for a time.

After a long sleep, I rise early and move closer hoping to approach as the men and young women prepare to launch boats. All activities stop as I quietly approach with samples of flint and sharp edges. Weapons appear. I lay my spear down from the sling on my back and move slowly in until no more than five steps from the nearest of them.

Choosing a sound stone surface on the beach, I start to demonstrate, first sending sparks into dry grass to light a fire, then breaking stone to form an edge and working it to both point and knife edge. They watch patiently. When this is done, I take the samples two steps closer and lay them on the sand, opening my arms to indicate that they are for them. Then I bring my hands to my mouth to indicate that I wanted to trade for food. I think they understand for one talks to all, then there is some commotion. Then to my relief I see much laughter, a sign that is universal acceptance, but perhaps never before by ones so different as I must look to them.

He who spoke first calls to those still at the hearth. Food is brought on woven palm plates, and drink in the nutshell of the tall tree. An older woman, who then returns to the fire hearth, puts them on the sand. I take the food with happy words, and I hope a friendly expression, then move back to the rock and eat fish to warm my stomach and perhaps food to warm my world, and to give me release from loneliness.

The one who appears to be leader removes my trade, and shows it amongst his people. I start to work on other tools. They move in, and happy, clicking tongues and strange language that, to my ears, is like the music from the bone flutes of our finest music makers, soon surrounds me. The younger are touching my hair, then jumping back behind their elders for protection. As the tools form good edges from stone, I hand them out: spear tops, knives, and points to make holes in bone or hide for decoration and clothing. In a short time, they move to their boats and are gone about their lives. Those at fires move to gather more wood and continue to process the various foods I can see. I return to my end of the beach.

That is a beginning. First contact even with a new tribe of my own people is always handled with caution unless at one of the Mother's gatherings.

That night, as dark approaches with a beautiful red sun near the horizon, a group of men and women approach. They leave me some more fish, along with what appears to be turtle meat. There is no conversation, but I am, if not happy, at least filled with a new sense of opportunity, which is giving me, I think, the first smiling face for seven moons.

Next midday sees me back at the cove to gather what I need to spend several days at what I now call *Departing Beach*.

After sleep, the sun is overhead when I arrive back. I have dried meat but spend time fishing in rock pools with little success. I think they have been fished out for a short time by my little friends.

As night comes, they return and this time they direct me to come with them, with much talking and laughter. My perhaps new tribe are a happy people. They show me a place with round stones for hearth just upstream from them and bring me wood and food. I am not sure if I am to keep reptiles out of camp or be food for reptiles. Fire will protect me, and I will happily guard my new tribe. As night falls, they gather at central fire. I see several guarding the perimeter, and perhaps keeping an eye on me. Their singing and I think story-telling gathers around the central fire. I am happy, if not to be included, to at least be in safety of tribal unity for this period. All quietens down and sleep comes sounder than I think I have known for a long time.

As the days pass, I move between my camp and Departing Beach, bringing some hides back, more stone and meat. They eat some of the dried lizard, and I think are much impressed when I draw the killing of the beast in the sand. Many gather around to look and that night I am drawn to the central fire where I think the story telling is in part about their new slayer of dragons. They seem happy to take all the firestone and cutting edges I make. They probably trade up and down the lands from whence they come.

On the second hand of days a new strange event occurs. When sadness enters my being, I withdraw to the other end of the beach to close my mind to all. Perhaps it is the thought of Nioma, usually a way to empty my mind and seek the strange peace that seems to come with such. After a time the sadness leaves me and I quietly think of the wonder of Nioma.

The blood flows to my member, giving the age-old need of the Mother some urgency. With eyes closed and an image of my Nioma, my hand moves and soon the seed bursts from my body. Laughter snaps my eyes open and a group of young women are happily chattering amongst themselves as they cast looks my way.

The ancient woman steps out from behind me and what sounds like anger is directed towards the youth as they increase their speed and move on. Ancient One turns to me and I see both fierceness and compassion in her wise old face. There is little I can do but quietly look upon her and smile. Regardless of the event, I feel relaxed and calm in the ways of the Mother. Eventually her tiny hand reaches up and closes both my eyes, then she positions my hands together on my lap (not my member) and with a touch of my lips, she speaks several words, and then touches my lips again.

I understand and repeat her words. This she does again until I understand I am to chant in unison with her, who is now seated facing me with her own eyes closed. This strange chant seems to take me deeper into peace until suddenly I sense I can no longer feel my body, or hear the wind, waves and gulls that are the sounds of this world. Then suddenly I realize I can sense this presence, and it is the woman. Age or body seem less, but her mind is calling me and I seem to be able to move with her. A blue circle of light seems to surround me and I am aware she is a shadowy figure within her own blue circle. We start to rise in this world without image, but fear of what feels like leaving my body behind seems to plunge me back, where for several eye blinks I hear the chant, then it ceases. I open my eyes to those of this one whom I now know is without doubt shaman, Lady to the Mother Goddess.

After a time, she bids me rise and leads me to the sea. She points at the sand and says a word then touches her lips. I repeat it. She points at the sea and a gull with more words for me to repeat, and a new door to another people's world opens up a little to me. I smile broadly and laughter bursts from my body for the first time for many moons. My new teacher smiles and reaches towards my chest. I bend to her and she strokes my face and pats my head. Then she moves back into the rocks from where she emerged.

I move off to find more peace of a different sort and in a different direction to the shaman lady, taking my spear with me. For the rest of the day I gather much wood and bring it to the location of the central fire, plus a little for my own hearth. That night I see these people are well pleased with me, but one of the stories is told by the young women which brings much laughter, and I am confused as to their Mother's ways or taboos. One thing is definitely obvious to me; my large body will never celebrate the joys that come after young women are recognized in the secret way of the goddess.

The night of the full moon arrives and another wonder enters my life. I see the young females have been gone from the camp during the latter part of the day. Torches are set on poles in a circle back from the main fire and lit soon after dusk. All people seem to have taken extra care with washing and grooming. Even I was taken by my now daily teacher to the place where the stream enters the ocean and taught the words for cleaning my body with more laughter from several of the passing ones who possess the catch of the day.

Singing and clapping starts, and the tapping of hollow sticks, which make an eerie kind of music. Then from out of the dark, the young females emerge. They are beautiful, with hair long down their backs, with ornaments on hair, wrists, ankles and the grass skirts surrounding their tiny swaying waists. For much of the night until the fire burns lower the dancers sway, and I presume tell stories. Eventually it ends and once again I am a little sad or lonely as the young disappear into the dark in couples. Older couples and singles also seem closer this night as most retire to separate hearths. My old shaman stands in front of me and I hear the quiet chant and feel her fingers close my eyes. Peace comes for a short time but not the blue circles. However, I feel at peace and even happy as I return to my hearth to sleep without fire.

The next moon passes without the shaman mother taking me into trance again. Although I concentrate, my own efforts do not bring the same results. The original camp in the cove is virtually ignored. My language is rapidly improving, and I am able to make simple requests.

Those who communicate take care to teach me more. Most are patient and seem to find it a novelty to teach one who is not a child. One day it strikes me that there are no babies or very young children, so this must be only a part of their tribe.

I cast my eyes over the ocean to wonder how these tiny arms travel boats only one third of the size of our own ocean going vessels overseas, and obviously do the trip often in order to re-unite with what must be another large group of people.

Where their homeland is has not been known by me or to my knowledge even to the ones of us who serve the spiritual life. Each day is like a journey into the light of a new life as their tiny clicks and musical voices begin to draw me into a world where I eventually will begin to get the answers to some of these mysteries.

I am increasingly found in the company of Sha-woman who now uses me to gather herbs, barks, bulbs and other products all seemingly to care for her tribe. Soon it becomes clear to me that all products, including medicines, are for trade and that at a time to come they will do just that - trade.

One thing is obvious to me; there is no room in their boats for a giant! With this thought in mind and a little sadness, I bend to pick up Sha-woman, so she can reach high in the trees. She moves behind my neck and a new purpose is found for me, much to her glee, as we move about the island at a far greater speed than the fastest of her young.

During the moon of the last finger of the second hand, the cool nights become warm and the south winds less persistent. All the goods are stored in the vessels, and I know I am about to be alone again. I move away to what I now think of as my end of the beach, and try to clear my mind, but the water moves from my eyes as I look into the journey my Nioma took, and wonder where it is these temporary people of words that I will no longer have use for will go.

A small hand brushes the tears from my cheeks, and quiet chanting with words that I now know have no meaning blend with my own and fingers I have learned to bond with close my eyes. Time passes and the pain in my chest begins to depart. The moisture on my cheeks cannot feel the southerly breeze and my ears no longer hear the sounds of this island.

The chant is gone!

Now there are only two blue circles and a peaceful wonder as this time her mind clears to me, and I follow her into an emerging world of silvery blue skies and seas with sparkling light more beautiful than even the Mother's most creative sunrises. We rise high and her mind blends with mine, and I feel her learn of my people, the warmth of Nioma in both of our chests; chests that are a shadowy form in a sphere of blue.

I ask her, "Where? Where do you come from? Where do you go to? Where have my people gone?"

We move higher and a new world begins to take shape with vast areas of ocean and lands that I can see both island and endless to beyond vision. She points at land like a ground turkey. I see my people, and I see my people would have reached these shores in not too many days' travel with wind and ocean current. Then she points to islands to the north-west and I am aware that they are those of her people.

We rise higher and I hear her thoughts with familiar words and unfamiliar but still clear to my mind say this Mother Earth is a beautiful blue circle but with much mountain land of ice to the south and the north. Her people have long inhabited what is to Shaman known as *Middle Earth*. She has known there are many lands and different types of people, all in the Middle Earth and northern forests.

She shows me an image of slim agile people of a size between her people and mine. She shows me a heavy people in cold lands with shorter bodies, but great strength and pale skins, people of many different colours. She says if I practise I may be able to find where it is that my people have settled, but she and her people will not see this land again until the winds return to the north. Now they will travel on the last of the south trade winds back to the trade routes and the rest of their tribes, which I can tell are plentiful.

That night I return to my hidden cove with a weight in my chest. I do not want to be there when they depart. Although I am strange in all ways to my tiny tribe, they seem to deal with a shaman's knowledge of the same living world called the Mother that gives birth to all that we need - the plants, bees, fish, animals and babies of my own kind. Babies of my Nioma that would bring joy my hearth. Now I must learn to hear only the stillness of my mind with lonely sounds of creatures that see me as an invader and predator within their lands.

A new day dawns and I rise to find my supply of wood and food is gone from here. In time I will return to the Departing Beach and gather what I have there, and perhaps what they leave behind. Memory serves me that the only thing they left behind last time was the coals of a dying hearth and one sick giant. At least this time I believe they will come again.

My mind goes to the ocean and the many oars that are required to travel the seas. Now my empty stomach becomes the leader of my thoughts and I climb the cliff on the small chance that my old enemy the island dragon will be scavenging. All is deserted so I return to fishing. I will not starve for the ways of this island have been revealed to me by my service as carrier of the one whom I learned to care deeply for, one whose words became both company for me and knowledge of food and healing I would never have learned amongst my own people.

As I turn to the entrance, my eyes cast to the beautiful colours of sun rising over a silvery sea. A stranger sight at first saddens then startles me. My tiny people in boats only one third of the size of our ocean crossing are spread out and fast departing with a firm southerly wind.

I run to the cliff face and stare, for a boat such as I have never seen is now the design of the two hands of fingers, two vessels that are travelling faster than even the fastest of my people with stronger arms and larger paddles. Their shelters of hide have been taken to their boats, but they have not been folded or used to protect from sun, wind and rainwater.

They are raised high above each vessel and catching the strong breeze. Even from here, I can see that small arms are achieving only part of the speed. These wonderful ocean dwellers have shown me a parting perhaps gift that I have never heard of before. Then it strikes me perhaps I could travel the ocean if the wind blows from the north. My heart sinks as I remember the condition of the only boat I have left. Still, now there is a kind of excitement in my body. Fear also, for no one of my people has tried to cross unknown distances without the comfort of all spiritual and tribal knowledge of my ancient people.

Food is forgotten and I rush to see what conditions and possibilities lie amongst the comfort I built for this isolated life. Apart from the sides of the outrigger, the entire structure has been pulled apart and now bends in all the wrong places. It will take all the skills of my boat building to put it back together. A boat builder, I am not. Plus, the bamboo gives the shape when green, but now dry will crack and break if altered. Only the outrigger could perhaps be put together. It is large enough for me and several other people but far smaller than what we consider safe to travel oceans. It is as large as those vessels of my little people. They travel the ocean. I need only an outrigger and the way of holding the structure to catch the wind to send me after my people.

New hope is in my chest and my spirits soar. Then I realize it is the time of the south east winds for many months to come, time enough to build the boat and learn if possible the art of wind and water. Now I will feed. Tomorrow is time enough for I have at least moons of the fingers of one hand before the journey can go south, a long time to be alone again. Two complete cycles of the seasons before I can follow my heart. Whose hearth will Nioma be at by then? This I cannot think about for loneliness and sad thoughts will drive me into the mental state that will ruin all chance of a future.

I catch food and sleep comes. Then my eyes open to a new day with at least a purpose. With purpose and work ahead, much of the dull pain of my misfortune can be ignored. Now I will be a boat builder and adventurer who if successful will be spoken of around the campsites of my tribe.

Food first then I take apart my cove home for the outrigger sides gave me the main structure. The hides remain attached, but they are not fit for the ocean. They are a start. I will need new hide or bindings from a plant. The leaves of the tall nut tree that feeds me and lines the shores should help.

By end of the day my shelter is reduced but still adequate, and the two halves of the outrigger are high up the beach and in the position to be brought together again. They in turn will need their own outrigger. Now I am sorry I never took notice of how Sea-woman's people built the wind structure. This for me is going to be hard to learn. I am fortunate in that there is much bamboo from the main hull that I will never build again. Even my little people would have trouble taking such a boat across the ocean, with its need of arm power.

The next days are spent stripping palm leaves into thin lengths and binding the hull. When I get fresh hide from lizards, I will cover these strips with fresh rawhide.

Each day the waste goes into the original site of my lizard kill. Almost one moon passes before the first creature arrives and on the third morning after this, I make a kill. I have a day to skin and peg out the hide that is left after cutting strips for bindings, then the next day for it to dry. All this activity is making me strong and determined.

The weeks pass and I achieve two more kills. Eventually, towards the end of the second moon, I have covered the front of the boat. Melted fat and sap from the trees keep the hide supple. Weeks pass and it becomes evident that I will have to hunt in multiple places if I am to finish the task.

Finally by the end of the forth moon a new vessel has taken shape. Not the most perfect craft but really for a simple sea trial. With much effort and some loss of skin, we float into the high tide. The outrigger holds the vessel at a slight angle but I think well enough. Some seams leak but nothing I can do will stop it so I pull it out and tie it to rocks higher up the beach.

I know not what to feel but most of the work is surely done. The old dry hide of the original main hull will make the wind catcher. With some trial and many errors, the upright pole is bound and tied to outrigger plus front and back of the vessel.

The hides will not support themselves so I bind a cross spar top then bottom and sew hide across the gap. It is not tidy but ready for a day with not too strong a wind. This arrives and I push out waist deep, then with some difficulty paddle beyond the headland and into the breeze.

Disaster strikes as the boat rounds. It begins to run with the wind. Then outrigger rises high and wind catcher and I plunge into the sea. Luck is with me as the current moves all towards the rocks and by dark, my undignified failure is secured on the next small rocky beach. With heavy chest, I return to my cove and am not able to bring myself back to vessel for part of the next moon.

Eventually, by removing the wind catcher and outrigger I am able to get all back to the hidden cove. Now I have an ocean vessel too large for one man to handle and not the great hope I wished to achieve.

Many days are spent trying to think but the problem seems too great. Life sets in and the boat is put out of priority. Tools comfort, and food becomes daily routine. With some clothing made I eventually come back to the boat with fat and sap to keep the hide from decay. My mind has turned to my small tribe for now I see the winds have turned. Many days they blow firmly from the north. When hunting and gathering my eye turns to the ocean and my body often passes Departing Beach. For the first moon of the north winds nothing happens.

Then one day, returning with the first of a delicious yellow fruit, I open the gate and descend into happy laughter and many new hearths. They have returned to their original site and with some inquiring looks proceed to ignore me.

My old mystic appears and it is soon evident that my humble home has a new tenant. She bends me down and with little care for my dignity checks my teeth, eyes and hair for obviously my state of health. With a look of disgust and the holding of her nose she voices her disapproval and in a loud voice for one so little commands me to the ocean to bath. As I leave, there is much laughter and holding of noses. My heart soars with a form of happiness or relief.

As I leave the ocean many are gathered around my mostly neglected vessel and I see if not admiration on their faces at least a kind of solemn respect. After several days, words become clear and clicks emerge into langrage.

Then lessons in boat design and what they call *sails* begins. My old friend who, with little effort to hide her glee, imposes herself as rider on this useful giant, who has so dutifully awaited her return, takes up my mornings. In the evenings when sea people bring the catch of the day, I learn and new work starts on my vessel. All is different with the sail easily connected and removed from the pole called in their language *mast*, even a way of making it larger or smaller according to the strength of wind.

Before long, language, both voice and sign with great expression for they love to act, is a large part of the evening entertainment. This is important for the passing down of knowledge from generation to generation, the old to the young. It is now evident that their knowledge is as great as, if not greater than, that of my own people.

One day as I am making new blades and points several men approach with the one I now consider chief amongst them. They explain to me that they will finish my boat and I am to make many stone tools that they will take as barter for the time they spend on the vessel. This I am happy with but work on my stone close to their endeavours, for much they do is new to me.

Another world is beginning to open to me. My old mystic never stops her chatter and so I learn the secrets of healing that only a few amongst my people know. She increasingly awes me. She has great wisdom and I am hungry to know all plants with the bonus of her at my hearth to see all types of preparation. Once again, I am to serve a purpose for her very critical pleasures. I am her cook and cleaner. To my disgust at first, I am much cleaner and feel healthy in a way that is superior to my past. The greatest bonus is that she has rid me of lice from body hair. The absence of itching, taken for granted by my kind, is a real bonus. I add this to my knowledge.

Towards the end of the third moon, the chief stands at the evening fire to announce that the winds should be suitable for sea trials of my now proud vessel. My mystic scowls and jabs me with a stick and many clicks that tell me she is annoyed that her transport will be idle tomorrow. Then she turns to another and several laugh with glee. Once again the joke is on me. It strikes me that I am happier amongst the little ones than the more serious ways of my clan's structured hierarchy. My body reminds me often of the pleasure of the hearth that I cannot know here, especially when I see couples happy in each other's gift and watch as they depart to privacy after the evening fires.

The next day I am fed before the sun brings the Mother's light. There are more good-natured complaints from my friend and teacher, and sometimes tormentor. Still she does not go to her herbs but leads the way to the attention of the day as if it is her achievement. Then she places herself in the nose of the boat. This brings laughter at first, then some heated discussion between Mystic and headman, who obviously thinks she is poorly suited to be a brave, strong, test sea explorer of this venture that is exciting to all. We are soon at sea, with several boats for escort and Mystic in command of an escort boat, or so she thinks. I think they would rather she stuck to healing and calming; the messenger of the Earth Mother.

The number of men being the fingers of both hands we soon reach open sea beyond the headland. With the gentle breeze, we turn to run with the wind and the waves. Now my vessel has three hulls, two for stability and one to hold my journey to come. It is exciting and we travel well through the waves with gentle breeze behind.

At word from the chief who sits astern with steering oar they call *rudder*, paddles are taken aboard and a sail of plaited palm leaves rises to catch the breeze.

We run before the wind. A new world of opportunity is now mine. I am both fearful and enthralled. With great cheer, I can tell they are well pleased. Without going far the sail comes down for I have learned the hard way it is easy to run with the waves but much slower to return from whence one came.

Other vessels join us and the day's industry begins. There will be no healing herbs or cutting of stone today for I am with this my proud vessel included in their ocean release. Life is good if the joys of my body's hunger and heart's love could only be met by the return of my Nioma.

At the fires that night the stories are told and I hear it said that now the tall man can follow the trade routes of the travellers. I see Mystic's eyes light up, and then cloud over as she becomes silent and retreats into her occasional quiet time. These thoughts, closer to the Earth Mother, I most likely will never know. I am not asked if it is my wish to travel with the little people but I know the journey and my life will probably be longer if I take that opportunity. Nioma is in the other direction to the strange lands of my now well-loved tribe. Regardless of the day's success I toss and turn on my place of rest. Mystic rises to make me tea that soon closes my eyes. This brings her peace, which I am aware is the reason for her kindness. My eyes close and peace is mine. If the spirit departs, I will not know for her herbs are strong. Her knowledge of the Earth Mother and perhaps what lies beyond is remarkable and perhaps beyond my people.

As the days pass, my boat and I are put to use. They like its greater room, but their vessels are swifter by paddle. Only a longer journey will tell when it comes to the power of the wind in sail.

The storm comes, bringing hot time rains that are a part of these northerly winds. These winds tell me if I am to follow my people. I am one man alone on what may be endless sea. Land exists out there but did my people find it and would one lone traveller on the back of Mother Earth ever survive? Perhaps fear or comfort and security makes me put off leaving on such a journey. So the days pass.

I am drawn back to my mystic. Her journeys around the island resume and my greater learning, more than mere language, becomes increasingly important in whatever it is that is the spirit of *White Cloud*. My travellers at first called me *White Cloud* in my own language, but on that night, they finally come to understand its meaning in their own language, and that it is my spirit totem name. One young humourist yelled with glee, "Not White Cloud, he is called *Head in the Cloud*!"

For his wit, he received a smile and a slap from my mystic, but everyone laughed and the name stuck. Now I am known as *Head in the Cloud* and sometimes it is shortened to *Cloudy Head*.

I guess it is meant in good spirit but I fear a little for the lack of respect. Mystic now calls me *Cloudy* and I hope she knows enough to understand whether the Mother is offended or not. Our spiritual leaders certainly could frown upon it. These small people are close to me, but my teacher and companion is more so. My need for a lover is put aside but on occasion I seek time alone and relief from the loneliness of my kind.

Time passes and one day I notice the return of cooler times has passed. Then when we round the headland, the wind blows from the south for the days of one hand and they continue from that direction. A glance at the marks on my spear tells me my chance to follow my people has passed, and more frightening to me is the now confirmed knowledge that these people are soon to depart and I am afraid of being alone again. My mystic seems aware of this and is kinder to me, but the morning arrives when all is packed in boats and ready to depart. Their load includes many tools of trade made by me. My boat sits alone and empty. Then I know for certain what it is that I wish. I would travel with them if they would have my presence. I quickly express this to the headman and much conversation follows. A short period of silence then a shake of the head and I hear words that mean I cannot be seen by the tribes.

Then my tiny Earth Mother climbs out of the nose of her boat and speaks at length. Once again, my fortunes take a turn, but this time I know not whether for the better or worse. They will hold the journey until the next day. However, if my vessel fails those with me will take to another vessel and I will be left to the creatures of the ocean.

During the day, my boat is prepared for sea and I noticed my mystic has commanded great comfort for her own now transferred position into the roomier bow of her new transport. She obviously considers me a great find in the comfort of how she gets around the Mother world.

Next morning sees me round the headland and after a quick glance after my lost love I head north into a new unknown adventure that is definitely my life.

The sails come up and I feel for the first time the wonder of a strong breeze with a trailing sea. Before long, it is apparent that by accident, not design, this vessel will travel faster than the rest of our armada. My new crew is well pleased and give a cheer as we move out in front. I see the paddles appear and other boats keep up. Mystic gives a look to all that seems to say this good performance is her doing.

I am of mixed feelings but mostly happy to be not alone and perhaps finding a new future on different horizons and strange lands.

After several days, I go to mark the passing of time and am sad to find I have left my spear behind. Now I am not sure how many moons have passed. Still I can count the changing of the seasons. They found me at the end of the north winds at this time of the seasons. Then they came and went, and came and now are going again.

I add two large marks for the full season. Now I will mark off each day during the journey. Then each full moon as it passes. The full moon arrives on the third night and the winds remained steady. The only paddle used is for rudder and occasional change of direction. All boats are within sight. This is done also with the raising or lowering of more sail. On the morning of the fingers of one hand, land is sighted. With much excitement, I realize this is the home of two of our crew and that home for many is on other islands. After sunrise, we round headlands into a beautiful bay protected by outer reefs. There I catch a first glimpse of long low dwellings and the smoke of many hearths.

As we come through the entrance to the reef, the chief draws alongside and I hear him say, Head in the Clouds will wait until he has spoken to the elders of these people.

All unload and go ashore and I spend a long lonely night on board while I hear laughter and celebration on the distant shore.

Mystic forgets me, until she has need of good transport. My mood is not pretty. Still, I would rather be here alone on my own boat and close to happy people, than trying to make friends with lizards that would have me for dinner. There are nights and days of wondering if I would live to see or hear the laughter of a woman who would grace my hearth and bring the laughter of children into an empty life. With the fantasy of such possibility, my body changes and I seek relief. With this and tiredness, distant sounds fade and sleep takes me to the morning sounds of gulls using my home for fishing.

My eyes open to a wise old face and I see several strong young men take paddle. She glances at me and says, "Do you expect an old lady to walk when the Mother has sent such as you to give purpose to a worthless Cloudy?" With this, her laughter comes and I am happy again.

On shore, there is a large crowd; as many people as I have seen outside the gathering of the clans. I see weapons so presume not all are pleased to see this large man from a distant shore. Wide-eyed children hide behind mothers and an occasional father, who are probably ready to kill me if I attack and eat all before me. However, I have not left the sea when Wise Face, who must be obeyed, informs me of her wish and arrives once more on my shoulders. My burden she may be, but protector and teacher she definitely is, and when it suits her perhaps even friend. Perhaps!

She directs me to run up the beach and back to many astonished looks. The thought crosses my mind that now all the leaders of such little people will want transport like me. The thought makes me laugh to which I receive a jab in the ribs and pulled ears. Apparently, I am not to lower the dignity of my esteemed passenger.

When she tires of the performance we retire to a smaller dwelling that I have to bend low to enter, but I am much impressed once inside. Tables, chairs and beds are all too small for yours truly but a space is indicated that I may make comfortable for myself. Once again, I am left alone as night falls, but my mystic is not one for late nights and returns before long with several maidens bearing plates of fruits and flesh from the ocean.

Next day gives me time to explore a little and children slowly come closer as curiosity overcomes fear, one even producing a pet monkey for my inspection.

It is the dwellings that give shelter which most impress me for they are communal. Long houses are well-built and all clean of waste that has its own separate location. The buildings form a square around a central area that has provision for entertainment and I can see trade. The goods of not only my tribe are displayed but items of art and body decoration and tools (some of my making) and weapons. I have an understanding of many objects.

The objects that most impress me are what they call woven cloth of a material I have not seen before. There are also nets of a design for fishing that I have seen them use, displayed here in quality and design superior to any I have seen before.

The people are, although small, graceful and appealing to look at, especially the young women with hair worn long and decorated, their wrists and ankles adorned. They are firm of bust and full of smiles, although when looking my way expressions are somewhat more serious. Their young beauty brings movement to my groin, causing me to look away and focus my thoughts elsewhere.

Three days pass and we move back to sea. Trade has been successful and my boat now sits lower in the ocean, but they are obviously pleased to use the extra room. The lands are closer now and most nights see us, if not in new settlements, on sandy beaches. It is a happy and busy journey. Some new foods and many different ways of cooking make my life enjoyable. Everywhere we go my mystic demonstrates my usefulness. She also trades and swaps knowledge with others of her kind. I learn more and each day my desire to heal increases, but I am not encouraged to touch the ill or the healthy. Only Mystic rides my shoulders although I see the more than occasional envious glance as we go about these lands at direction of other Earth Mother priests or healers to obtain that which now we both treasure. It is easier to talk with my mystic as knowledge increases, and I see some admiration for me in the knowledge I am retaining.

Many of these lands are large enough to support many settlements with other islands that I have not been to. We are ocean traders and stay close to our transport. These people have long used this trade route. On lands with multiple settlements word of a giant travels overland with longer crowds gathering for our arrival. Apparently, I am good for several reasons now, not just transport, although this is not mentioned.

My strength allows me to break and carry flint and other suitable material from these lands, thus I am soon creating a small following to view me making knives and the like. This activity is lightly tolerated by my friend, teacher and tormentor.

After the land mass of the fingers of one hand I observe the number of boats travelling with us is greatly increased. At the next island, virtually all able people take to vessel and with little to trade, we travel on. More boats join us all the time. We are moving towards a large gathering of the clans. Mystic tells me I am to see the central settlement of her kind. There is anticipation in this and more ocean people than I have ever heard of before. Now I see that colours and different banners tell one who they belong to by tribe. We pass another two islands but this time we spend the night at sea.

When day breaks, land is only about a finger of two hands away. On rounding the headland, we drop into an area the wind cannot reach and so all take to paddle. With this, my vessel, being larger with fewer people, soon drops behind, and is left alone as vessels round more cliffs. Soon more are arriving from behind. The smoke of many fires appears, and it is evident I will soon know what lies ahead.

We reach a huge bay with dwellings stretching the full length and on cliff tops as well. I see a fair sized narrow entrance but we are still far out. It is almost dark when we arrive. The decision's made that I will again spend my night in the boat, but this time my mystic remains with two others. They inform me a good campsite will be hard to find; best to seek it at daybreak. I think that by then the giant will be known of as word at gatherings travels fast. I toss and turn so Mystic gives me herbs. This time I know what they are and how they are prepared. I am pleased with myself.

The sun is well up when we move into the mouth of a substantial river entrance. The dwellings follow the river well inland past turns and out of sight. The land opens up and temporary windbreaks take the place of long houses. Still more people live here than I have ever heard of. Size of body does not matter when it comes to combined industry. I now know it is by working together that they achieve so much.

We establish a site that is amongst those known to my group and I am left with instructions on how to make my teacher comfortable, while she goes about her day's less tedious tasks. She is back for evening meal then on my shoulders to move to a large gathering in a natural depression that gives many seats with good view of the evening's entertainment.

Fire torches light up a large area and are placed on tracks across the hills. It is an impressive sight with light of many campfires outlining the winding path of the river as it moves to the ocean.

I learn that language is similar amongst all the clans so knowledge and trade is no problem. My mentor guides me to an area that is for those who heal and guide in the ways of the spirit. After much talk of the stranger amongst them, I am moved aside to become a curiosity to many who pause to stare.

This interest in my difference does not please me as it soon becomes clear that I will be alone amongst many. Among more people than I have ever known I feel desperately lonely. My heart calls out for those of my own kind.

Several days pass and some of my island people bring me into their world for food and stories. Finally, my teacher becomes aware that her triumphant worker is not happy and spending increasing amounts of time off in the hills alone.

On the third night, she brings me into the circle of those that serve. I smell the herbs and soon hear the quiet rhythms of chant. She has made them aware of my ways so they accept me sitting quietly beside Mystic. She is a comfort and part of what life I have so I feel a little better and relax to the pleasing smell of the smoke from their fires.

HUMAN JOURNEY (YOU)

White Cloud has come to an important circle of knowledge, a place where the birth of a physical glimpse of the mind of the Universe can take place. It is a gathering of numbers of these humanities that can spread truth for harmony on this life-giving creation of the conscious-ness of all that can be glimpsed to exist. The body of White Cloud, with Small Mother's help, will blend his mind in conscious state with his spirit; that eternal tiny part of all that is in spirit connected and as one with all other individual spirit, but complete as one.

This is the profound gift and giver of all matter from a single point infinitely small to everything that can be believed by the mind of the observer in whatever part of the Universe they may exist. An existence that in reality does not exist without the ob-server and as all spirit is part of the mind entangled from the single point then each container of spirit is, in part, mind of the creation. It continually brings about its own White Cloud and all else, with an inert knowledge of the combined entangled profound gift.

The Living Universe…a conscious universe.

WHITE CLOUD—HOBBIT OF MIDDLE EARTH, 148002 BC

My eyes close and I begin to feel light in my body, as if I am drift-ing. The strangest feeling of all develops. I feel I am a spectator and that another conscious mind has control of my senses. I hear the words my body speaks but it is as if they are thoughts in my head, and I am not saying them.

All others of the circle are quiet now. They stare transfixed at my form as it seemingly takes control with no help. How can one person be two people at the one time? How can I know wisdom that is not mine?

As I listen, I think not of my people or my world or time. The blue circle is not only a shadow around each of the Mother's guides but a blue circle that seems to encompass all. As I look further afield the circle expands to encompass all surroundings in a kind of semitransparent dome.

I see stars brighter than ever through blue mist that is both haze and an entrance into what may be a world that exists with and somehow beyond the world of my body.

HUMAN JOURNEY

They can hear me. I am no longer an observer, one set free of the physical by the body of White Cloud entering a state of un-consciousness sleep. There are eight of them, five men and three women. One is younger, with the rest the old of their kind. I see they are all aware it is another presence in place of the one Mystic delivered into their presence.

As *Human Journey*, I carry a message across time which is far beyond the Mother's people, White Cloud's people and the simple spirit that is Human Journey.

My ordinary qualities that exist in ordinary physical bodies in many lifetimes make me a voice greater knowledge has chosen to use.

I say to them, "You are the messengers and bearers of knowledge of what you call the Earth Mother Goddess. You worship all life as the birth of her living self.

"You are the observer of the sky above, which during the day holds what you call the son (sun) of god. At night, it shows you the light of vast numbers of stars that you think are in the house of the Father God, but are the living presence of those that have lived with the Mother and passed over to afterlife.

"The moon that comes with the same rhythm of the blood of the Mother's human children you call the daughter of the Mother Earth Goddess.

"All these things are good and in total are the existence altogether of the one thing, that is the result of the mind of the creator, who is neither male nor female, but all things and the creator from the beginning to infinity, of all that can be conceived of.

"In the beginning everything that makes all that you see was far smaller than a grain of sand. From this tiny point all that you know expanded and came into being.

"Through meditation, what you are and the world around you disappears. The mind of the universe is in tiny part you. When your mind becomes clear of all thought your contribution to matter reverts to particles of energy. For all matter is particles of energy, positive and negative in equal parts, no energy from the simplest to the most complex can touch.

"For these things will come to be understood by science at about what I call the Time of the Writing."

WHITE CLOUD

Even in my state, or because of it, I understand all this until the final statement. Then, at a loss to understand the spirit called *Human Journey,* I find I am alone again in my body. Now all chanting stops and I feel discomfort by the attention I have created in this inner self, an inner self that now I remember, but which baffles me.

Questions follow and I wonder why I know few answers. All I can say is I was almost, but not quite, like them; an observer or spectator. I think the communication was not for my ears so much, as for those trained in the ways of the Mother. I see they are in great awe and even Mystic looks at her mode of transport with a different kind of respect. For me this only adds confusion. For the moment, depression has been set aside. There are too many questions, too few answers.

As I get up to leave, they say they wish to have me return to seek more knowledge of the one known as Human Journey.

I sleep deeply with few dreams. Perhaps it was all dreams brought on by herbs and I am all dreamed-out for this night. In the morning, to my surprise, a youngster from the clan does the cooking and removal of the rubbish. Apparently, life has had a small change. After eating, Mystic again climbs high and we seek company of others of her learning to seek the secrets that lie in the river valley and the surrounding hills. I think my Mystic has gained strength of position by contact with me. I feel this shared insight will not become general knowledge to ordinary tribal people. Such learning will be held close and distributed discreetly in ways that will not be divulged to me.

For the next two nights I am to return, but these times, I emerge in the lovely blue circle and am called back to the sha-person circle. They are well versed in blue circle and find some frustration that the voice or persona of Human Journey does not return. Still, the servant remains and my treatment with all Mother guides is apprehensive once the surprise of it all fades. I find my interest greatly increased and ask many questions about the meditation used to reach the journey of the circle and perhaps others.

With much practice, it gives me a sense of bliss and peace, but without the help of the Mother guides I do not yet have skill to achieve the sense of body departure.

After the time of one moon, we pass on. The main island has been first a place of celebration, then a place of trade. For the young it is a place to meet partners, and as we travel I see new faces have joined us and some departed. The clans remain strong with new blood. Those with coming babies and new children have remained with the central people. They are complex and complete people.

The outer islands supply a ready supply of material for trade, thus, I am with a main area of travelling traders.

The next three moons see many small settlements, and then we move slowly on calm days toward the south again, this time on a different course. I think we visit the same islands on the opposite sides. It is a good life but we are all pleased when the weather gives us time on good sheltered land with fresh water and diverse food. There are more travellers here amongst what I now know are central islands to these people, and more competition for product of sea and land, both in the obtaining of resource and the trading.

Now there is less curiosity about the giant for many people were at the central gathering. A greater curiosity exists with the Mother guides, as the story of Human Journey seems to have spread amongst sha-people.

Eventually the north winds arrive and the supplies are laid on for a long ocean voyage. I am keen to return, perhaps to follow the path of my unforgotten love. I tell Mystic and see her settle into deep thought.

The sails go up and days and nights pass into a full moon into the ocean. We are all tired but one late evening we round a headland and I arrive at the closest place I now have to call home; Hidden Cove. It brings first a sense of happiness, then all the lost people (especially my Nioma) are once again close to my heart.

As days pass, I work on stone and travel with Mystic, but keep busy and laughing with the story and songs of the night fire. My longing, and a sense of loneliness for my kind, remains.

One afternoon upon finding me alone with wet face Mystic once again closes my eyes to the gentle chant and takes me into the realm of silvery blue world to rise again. This time we travel high and move south to the land of the turkey. Then we go south again at blurring speeds, following a coast that perhaps only one tiny band of tall people has ever seen.

I feel Mystic's thought say we must return but far off a thin stream of smoke touches an approaching sunset. My heart soars with the possibilities. We flash towards a winding river and there below lie the almost forgotten boats and simple dwellings of my love. I am drawn in a flash to the hearth of a small family and there with child on her breast and swollen belly is the centre of my youth, the hope of my future.

In a flash, we are back in our bodies and I sit quietly as the tears flow on my cheeks. I feel the tiny hands of my friend trying to bring comfort to my lonely body but the pain remains. She departs and it is quite late at night before I return to my place of rest. She rises and moves around the fire, then brings me a hot drink of comforting herbs that brings a feeling close to deep meditation, then sleep.

During the time of the fingers of one hand she keeps me at peace with her knowledge of such plants of the Mother. I have lost track of time, but my love's growing child and perhaps other children tells me the season has changed at least several times.

Slowly the pain in my chest becomes bearable and I return to the activities of my now- people.

One night Mystic raises the discussion of a great land to the south. She speaks only briefly of my small clan, telling to eager ears her stories of vast resources and adventure that bring both entertainment and some fear. For such an event would see travel over the Mother's back for more days without land than they have known. This also is a land they have never known. I see Mystic talking long to the headman and the elders.

My emotions are torn. I know not what awaits me with a people where the hearth of my youth cannot be mine, but my love for her remains. Though she has become a mother of the clan, she is still in my heart. They are still my people, although in the back of my mind I think they were quick to say goodbye to one lonely White Cloud.

With so many deaths, my survival would have seemed un-likely to them. Their own dangers were far more important to Swift of Foot and those he was charged to take to a doubtful future.

Now I have seen with my own eyes the new life of my people in a land rich with animal and probably plants of the Mother. A new sense of hope stirs in my chest. Peace with wonder returns.

One night I enter the quiet conversation of new land and explain my desire to travel on.

If such a journey took place it might be hard to return in a span of one wind to the centre of our people. Trade would perhaps take the passing of two seasons. This would be for a land they would have to share with the tall people.

Still, it is said such a land is bigger than all the lands of what they call the Middle Earth, the lands of the little people that seem endless to their mind.

I see much awe in the faces that have become dear to me. Nowadays it is not only Mystic who rides my shoulder but children who run down the beach to be first to be lifted so high and travel so fast. Their laughter gives me joy, and thoughts of my own hearth children can be put aside in a hidden part of me.

Another moon passes with the advent of one of the great storms that bring terror to us all. I see why they favour Hidden Cove for it is comfort when the full fury of the Mother sweeps over her world. After the winds, the rain is unlike any seen for at least the time of two hands. My position is crowded for it gives best protection with overhanging cliffs. They add to it and it becomes a communal long house. This I find pleasing but after several days the desires or perhaps boredom of the young lovers take over. I wish I could be spared the unsubtle pleasure this brings to others. It turns my mind back to a journey that in this weather seems even less likely to inspire my companions or me.

Eventually the sun emerges, bringing with it a new discomfort as the air seems full of water. However, fires emerge and hot food with Mystic's wonderful brews brings life to all. Fish are less prevalent but the shellfish and the crawling creatures are if anything more abundant with food washed from island to their ocean floor homes. At the evening fires the clan puts talk of travelling on to a strange land aside.

Three hands after the storm Mystic talks to four elders. They call me to their hearth and tell me their decision. The new land should be found and it will be announced at the celebrations after the change of the winds. Our clan will send two boats as well as Tall Cloud's. Other clans will be invited to send a vessel if they wish, although it will mean opening this clan trade ground to others. This journey will take place early on the south winds, before the likelihood of the great storms. Then perhaps they can return within one season. The large part of the clan will remain on the ancient trade route so life of the people and all they know remains secure.

They fear conflict may arise with the tall people, and that life may be lost. They ask if I will make contact and bring them word of the tall people's response to sharing the land. My heart soars with all these words. I will keep my new tribe and find the beginnings of my old. I see the way of their wisdom, and I will wait. Fear of travelling into the unknown would take more than the courage of an ordinary one such as me.

Once again, the winds turn, and I have to struggle to remember the changes of the season.

With hope of a future that includes contact with my own kind I gain a new strength of purpose. As I absorb the ways of healing and mysteries of deeper beliefs, I have a desire to take this knowledge to my own kind in a new land. I hope they might accept strange ways, but I will walk quietly upon first contact.

As for Nioma, if the dream travel is correct, in part she is lost to me. If she abides at the hearth of another I must respect the laws of the Mother Goddess within the structure of the tribe.

The winds blow true from the south and I enjoy the ocean with greater knowledge.

They teach me to observe the direction of the ocean currents.

They teach me to observe the stars that guide them by night.

They teach me to observe the birds that return to home bases at the same time, each time of the receding sun.

They teach me more than their own clan's people. Such is the connection I now have with Mystic and the stories that circulate through the elders, from clan to clan and island to island.

As Mystic and I travel together, it is almost as if we become one.

By the fire one night a question enters my thoughts. She is old and travel to new land and great adventure may not be for her. When I ask, her expression saddens and she makes two quick clicks.

In the language of these tiny people, one click means yes, with two clicks for no. They are so much a part of me now that a return to my language will take concentration. In many ways, their manner of communication is more precise, and so superior.

The thought of parting with Mystic saddens me. She sees this. I think if she was of my age and in a body of my kind, it would be far easier to give up the loss of my hearth with Nioma.

Amongst the many strange ways of these people is one that fascinates me. Their tiny arms do not have the power to throw spears or stones, as my kind does. Instead, they have devised a throwing stick that is light and sloped like the light of the new daughter moon, sharp at both ends and sides that turn quickly and travel high into the sky. They alter the angle so it will travel straight or turn in a long arc, almost returning from its beginning.

On land, it is of use, but in a long sea journey, flocks of birds fall prey to it with both birds and weapon floating on the ocean to be recovered.

The moons pass and the proposition is put to the gathering. The communities are divided.

In many cases, the young seem excited at the prospect. The elders are cautious. Many argue that their lands were given by the Mother. To break with this bond may bring displeasure down upon all the clans. Quiet talks take place amongst those of influence.

Sometimes I am brought for whatever input I can offer. Eventually it is decided that a small party of three of our boats and several from other clans will make a quick discovery journey.

That is close to the decision of my clan elders, so I am content to let the journey unfold. I settle to enjoy the nightly dances of their beautiful youth. They are as lovely in miniature as the finest beauty of my own kind, but can never to be hearth mate with me. This part of my heart and loins remains for my own kind, but now with some hope. With a possibility of greater happiness, the human spirit will strive for a future no matter how vague.

Many of these clans are nearly as seafaring as my clan. They are the ones who travel the greatest distance with older knowledge of ocean currents and stars. Although there is much talk with many questions asked, only one crew from a travelling clan seems certain to go. A few in pairs and alone make a crew from a number of tribes and another vessel is found to travel first over a long trade route. Time will tell if they are willing to risk the final step into the unknown. Many from my own people were not and experience showed that many died. This makes me think about the risk we are taking. These I have come to love may face death in my quest to find my people, who also may have met death. Are the spiritual journeys to be trusted? A large part of me is glad my ancient Mystic will remain safe with her own kind.

The celebrations end and the north winds finally come. A different sense of excitement enters me. The closer to leaving, the more divided my fears and desires become. I fear the others may falter too. This creates quietness within me. Others who have expressed bravado become less enthusiastic as we move towards the Departing Beach.

Upon arrival, our supplies are depleted. I am secretly glad we will have to spend perhaps a moon before we travel on. The Mother has taught her people that great storms are more likely with the latter moons of the north winds. The decision is made that only one boat will depart from other clans.

My original vessel is still the largest. Much work was done on it at the central site where the river people were known for skill with ocean craft. We have settled on Departure Beach, but they say after one moon all will return to Hidden Cove for the moons of another one hand, and the south winds. I see a growing excitement, even amongst those that are not going.

The day finally arrives and Mystic brings more products to my ever-growing supply of all she considers necessary for a journey with the Earth Mother. All listen quietly as she says I have learned much knowledge passed down through her people, and that the spirit within all people has been shown by the one that resides in Tall Cloud to be connected to the one conscious mind of the world below and the world above.

This confuses them, so she says, "You all have the way of the Mother within you, but White Cloud has listened to the healing, and will carry her ways with you."

A new leader has already been chosen, and is now renamed *Horizon*. The sun shows the way once again as I follow three brave boatloads of clever journeypersons out unto unknown waters. The travel lines go in and soon we pass through a school and fish rise from the depth to keep everyone busy. This is a good sign from the one who protects us. The rest of the day passes and eventually it is my turn to rest in the care of a strange tribe on a new sea into an uncertain future.

FIVE

ON LEAVING

NAME OF ISLAND, KEP. TANIMBAR

HUMAN JOURNEY

Once again, White Cloud sleeps and a part of me speaks from that ever-present consciousness that I call *From the Time of Writing.* For three years, he has lived apart from his tribe and travelled the circular trade routes of the little Hobbits of their lands. From his island, to be called Kep. Tanimbar, the most eastern and isolated north goes through Seram, then east to central land on Sulawesi, then south to Bali Flores and eventually via Timor back to Kep. Tanimbar. This is their vast ocean world.

During the vast ice ages, what can be perhaps called Middle Earth was, because of the nature of the Banda Sea, one of the few paradises on Earth during these cold times. After a quiet observation of these brave physical bodies of the conscious universe I use and observe a journey that I am pleased will not be without great distance as long as currents don't push them past land contact into what will be the Indian Ocean to be lost forever.

With this in mind, I do not blend White Cloud's mind but move south to find the fires of his lost people. Here also are the spirits of many who now reside in slumber. I settle into union with the ultimate bliss that is the many separate minds of the creation. Here I shall place a powerful subconscious message into the minds of the leader Swift of Foot, and White Cloud's still loved and loving Nioma. In wakening, their dreams may prepare them for one who will have to search a vast land. Then I shall return to become the subconscious mind of White Cloud and perhaps with his developing skills blend with his consciousness to give him knowledge of his journey to come.

I see Nioma's aura merge with her awakening body and quietly watch to see if she has experienced any waking change. She moves to the hearth and a small flame brings life to her still lovely face. Then comes stillness. Eventually I hear her say, "He is alive, I am almost certain he lives." Then she turns to view her hearth mate and child with her hand on the one still to be born. A slow tear runs down her cheek and it is all I can view.

White Cloud's eyes open to a new sea, but with the same clear thought; that his love is aware and that regardless of the complexity he will find her.

WHITE CLOUD

The ocean is calm with the beauty of the dark valleys between rolling waves and crests reflecting the beautiful sunrise. I feel at peace as if some sleeping journey has brought me greater insight.

It will have to suffice for now as, although the sail is billowing in gentle winds, it takes work to keep the boats together.

I take my position on the steering oar for my extra strength on a paddle creates imbalance with the efforts of my remarkable crew.

Our food is good and all are healthy. Day three passes and I sleep in the afternoon only to be woken to a different world of dark skies with black clouds stretching to the horizon. Our leader has brought the boats together, for a bad storm at night will see us lost to each other forever even if we survived.

Far to the east great streaks of lightning strike the ocean surface. I hear weeping of a young lady, who is quickly taken in strong arms, and then all is quiet. Lines are run and for better or for worse we are bound together with only tiny sail. The rest now prepare to create shelter and keep water out of the boats where possible.

We move on. There is little we can do. I hear quiet prayer to the Earth Mother. The sun reaches its low point, only a glow with the lightning taking over from the starless night. Eventually visibility is reduced to the hand in front of the face to be instantly changed with each stroke of the Mother's fury to a vast strangely still, ocean world. With no stars to guide us we can only hope still gentle winds blow in the right direction, and that the storm passes in the east.

Time moves by swiftly and I feel the change coming. There is a sudden chill in the air and louder claps of thunder. The dark becomes daylight and lightning strikes the very ocean, seemingly even between the vessels. In this strange surreal darkness, I see the ocean rolling towards us and grab for the rudder, calling to all as the wind strikes, then the waves. At first, they are high but then the wind is so strong the ocean is cast into long rapid swells that the vessels can ride. The lines grow taut but all boats hold, taking water but not foundering.

People bail frantically and work the oar to hold the rear of the vessels to the onrushing wind. In this instant, I wish we were back in protected Hidden Cove, and understand why they would not be out in the season of great storms.

Then as quickly as it comes, it passes and there is almost instant calm. All settle down to handle an ocean still coming to terms with the new lack of wind. Water in vessels is removed and some food eaten. All have survived.

We move on and I hear quiet thanks to the Mother. The lines are broken and fishing starts. There are no stars to guide us or wind to tell us the direction. Only the ocean currents will guide the next part of this journey that I think all are too tired or stunned to fear. I steer with an occasional glance at the dark. No stars or moon means little to see. Only the calls of the people in all vessels that are used to keep us together can be heard. I am lulled into a quiet peace for we are all used to our boats as ocean homes. I think of my lost people and all this new tribe (more especially Mystic) have taught me in what has become a strangely interesting life.

Slowly new sounds lull me from a dreaming state and I hear excitement in a growing number of voices. I cast my eyes to many pointing fingers. There in the distance is the glow of an unmistakable fire. Far off is a glow over the horizon, but obviously a huge fire for one so far away. For fire like this, this must be land and much of it.

The storm has done us perhaps a lifesaving favour. Earth Mother has not deserted us for on the course we are taking the ocean currents would have swept us past this world and on into perhaps starvation and oblivion.

All hands man the oars and the sails come down. Two vessels, more manoeuvrable than mine, cross my bows and we swing to follow. The work is hard for now we run across the ocean swell, perhaps without help from the movement of currents. The young bail as water comes in. If progress is made it is hard to know but we stay together and eventually a soft glow spreads across the horizon to join the diminishing glow of dying fire. The light brings hope of new direction for the two types of man. Smoke becomes the beacon that leads us on.

The ocean settles down and the wind becomes a gentle breeze. Our maker and provider is felt to be with us. These intrepid explorers are once again eager to find opportunities never before seen by their kind.

The risks of new worlds and creatures are put out of my mind. Sounds of encouragement from boat to boat travel across the ocean. The sun rises and once again, blue sky becomes our inner warmth. My people seem closer to me again, but will they welcome my return? Can I ever find them?

As the sun passes overhead a new fear of not finding land before dark enters my thoughts. Blue sky should lead to a starry night and the knowledge of small wonders will tell even me how to hold a course. The smoke is gone now, and small swells make travel unpleasant and slow. The world of ocean turns to a moonless night with no sight of land. I take my leave of the rudder to sleep rocked by waves moving sideways to our direction. Tiredness brings oblivion with few dreams.

HUMAN JOURNEY

He sleeps and thanks to the power of nature's storms, they have escaped death in the expanse of an ocean that would have been without break until it found the great ice continent far beyond human endurance.

WHITE CLOUD

My eyes open and the great star cross tells us most of the dark hours lie behind. The sea is dead calm so we move with slow ease towards the coming dawn. The nights are cold this time of season, another reason people normally do not travel long distances in the middle moon of the North Winds. Sun breaks with a beautiful orange orb and clouds on the horizon are all we see. Slowly we realise one cloud is in fact the first appearance of an island world. The whole day passes before more points of land appear along the ocean surface.

Dark arrives again. This time I work the rudder from side to side to keep the direction. It is late in the night before I sleep, so the sun is well up before they raise the sail coverings from me. My tired eyes open to a new land stretching as far as the eye can see, the new land of my people. It is the one I am excited to discover, but not, if the journey of inner spirit is correct, one where I shall claim the hearth of my hoped-for joy. She is on my mind constantly now, as if a part of me has already found her and bonded.

NIOMA

My dreams are now full of White Cloud. During the time of birthing, I became happy with my hearth mate and new life at my breast. For reason beyond my knowledge, the love of my youth has returned to haunt my sleep and waking thoughts. My face is turned downriver towards the sea, now more than a day's journey away. How can he live? Is it only his spirit that haunts me? Do the carers of the Mothers have the answers? Is it against the ways of our people for me to bring absent love to a hearth family blessed by the laws of the tribes? I fear, I yearn, I still love. I am lost, for my body wants to return to ocean front to search for what seems to be approaching destiny, or disaster for one mother of a tribe's future who wishes to seek probable taboo.

Six

White Cloud

These tiny heads, so beautiful to my eyes, now are quiet. The immensity of arrival at a new land has perhaps taken their breath away. Fear, excitement and wonder of new discovery will have filled these fine intelligent and brave people. I wish Mystic could be a part of this moment and quietly express this thought to faces that turn to my words. I am astonished to see tears on the cheeks of some faces. Although I know them for three years, still their depth is outside of the ways of my tribe.

We round a headland and a beautiful beach opens the way to the mouth of what appears to be a splendid river. Large two-legged creatures the height of two men leap away on legs supported by a long tail. Birds, all strange to the eye, run on long legs with flightless wings.

Our vessels touch a gentle beach and tiny men fan out to protect all from what may be dangers new to the hearth tales for all the time to come. Apart from the squawking of birds, nothing appears. Boats are turned back to sea and we move into a river that has several entrances. A delta system will provide much fresh food for hungry mouths. Within little distance, we find cliffs with good shelter and safe harbour for boats, a new camp in a new world, in Nioma's world.

The passing days of one hand are spent setting up camp and finding food from the ocean, which is nearly all familiar to my people and theirs.

Then with comfort and food taken care of, I ask if they will explore this new land. I find little enthusiasm for more than the coast and some river trip, so the following day I gather half a boat-load to crew my vessel and move upriver with the incoming tide. Quiet travel brings a new world to life. I have never seen plants in such abundance. Upon our rounding of each bend of the river, new birds cry to warn all of our arrival in their world. Small animals are swift but the large graze with curiosity and observe our arrival with some interest before either lumbering off into tall grass and sparse forest or leaping in the way of huge tree rats at greater speeds. I suggest the fur hides and meat will be of benefit, as they seem easy to hunt. They are not wary of us.

As the sun climbs overhead, the river enters tall red cliffs with increase in water flow to the sea and tide of no use. Small arms tire and we decide to turn for home. I realize only I have reason to search this vast land, which is empty of people except for those I seek.

On the following day, I announce my wish to take supplies for travel and explore the coastline. No one offers to come. I explain that I seek medicines and new knowledge. No one offers to come. I prepare weapons, food, and all I hope I need. I have seen no beast that seems a danger to a man; no giant lizards of my island home. At daylight, I say goodbye to those who take the trouble to notice me depart.

By day's end I have moved north with the sun setting over the sea opposite my throwing arm. There are only sand dunes and scrubby grasslands now, no high country. I have kept to beach for fear of beasts that may dwell in hidden cover. I will learn this land at a pace that should ensure my survival.

I build a timber and grass mound to light on the sunrise. Each day I will seek smoke and create a signal that I hope will be seen by those of my Nioma. The nights are warm, so I light only a small fire for comfort and perhaps protection. In the night, I hear animals. Sleep would be easier if another stood watch. I wish I had been more persuasive.

At daybreak, I am alive and well. The smoke rises high in still air and a clear blue sky. The days of one hand pass and I discover animals of many varieties, from tiny mice to small elephant-sized creatures. None moves in large herds, but I have seen mobs of three hands full of fingers. Fresh meat has fallen to my spear and the fire serves two purposes.

Each day I light the fire then stay by it in hope it will draw attention. Each day I go towards the high ground, but see no smoke. Even the little people, whose fires I suspect are built so as not to attract attention, are unseen. As sun moves overhead, I return to the beach and move as far north as possible. The ocean at least gives me what I hope is safety on one side of the night's sleep.

As the day of two hands arrives, I turn for home. Lack of sleep and no sign of humans have depressed me. I need the sound of Hobbit voices, the smell of cooking fires. A new fear enters my mind. Maybe Horizon will take his people to another site or worse return home without me. The return takes less than the days of one hand.

For a time I settle to gather many new wonders that I now see they will trade well. There is excitement amongst them and the stories at evening fire are full of the promise of wealth from this land for their clan at central gatherings. They tell how the North Winds will blow them to this land and the South will return them to the old trade route. Now I realize this time is approaching. The South Winds. Can I return without searching far for my people? Now I cannot travel on land and hope to survive. I realize I must move with my boat south with the winds, then north again, if ever I am to find them. My days have been so full of activity I have not stopped to contemplate the wisdom and ways of Mystic. White Cloud must seek her ways and place faith in the generosity of the Mother.

That night, as the stories end, I stand and move to the light. All are quiet. They too, have been wondering what is to happen to White Cloud (Head in the Clouds to them). I tell them of my love for them and try to say what they mean to me. I tell them of my lost people, and my yearning for the woman's hearth I cannot have with small beauties such as them. This brings gaiety but it is short-lived. I tell them I would take my boat south and north to search, alone, if I must. I tell them the boat will not be ready to travel on the first of South Winds and maybe not the last of the South Winds. Excited noise erupts. They need my vessel. It will carry much trade and some people could have to remain behind without its use. For the first time in many moons, I see anger and resentment on faces that have learned to trust me.

Horizon enters the firelight with no acknowledgment of me and calls and end to these words. All leave.

I stand alone. I realise this may be my only future. Sleep is full of dreams. I seem to see my Nioma with her face turned to search and water on the cheeks.

In the early hours, I rise and move downriver to find the company of surf rolling from a still familiar sea. I follow the ways of my mentor but am perhaps too sad to reach the state of calm needed to enter trance again. I miss Mystic for she could take me from despair to spirit in a manner that is only vague to one, still in early training, such as me. The sun rises and I heat water and try new herbs for tea with little success. I set out to find medicine that may exist in this land. That at least I perhaps can bring as a gift to people I owe so much.

The Mother is not with me. Her plants and mosses are mostly strange to me. Much time will pass before food and medicine is commonplace from what will I suspect be a homeland greater than all the Hobbit islands of Middle Earth together.

YARGREY

I am the second last of my kind to come into being. The last has also been restored and we stand together to await the presence of Betrana, the one amongst the long-lived who brings knowledge to new revivals of our kind. Twice before, I have woken to observe our arrival at one of the life systems. Zeeta has woken to observe and learn of his first arrival.

We are at one end of the vast space cylinder that is home. The other end is beyond vision in this vast world that has travelled the habitual zone of this Galaxy for time greater than the stories of the oldest and wisest amongst us. Here the gravity is slight as we are far from the curved walls, covered with grasslands, forests, lakes, and our buildings, which serve multiple uses.

Betrana approaches and we gesture with our minds to acknowledge our readiness to absorb new vision of both space and our world. All is quiet. How long is not relevant. Time for a spacer is not measurable, not continuous. Her words come as thoughts that arrive complete in our minds.

"What is it that you see? What is it that you are a part of? What purpose?"

I turn to Zeeta and minds move to conclusion. Our answers come as expected from those new. We see a living world that has given us a place. We are a part of our home. It serves the purpose to nurture our makers and us.

Her answers come.

"Within all life are billions of cells that hold the designs of all matter that reaches both simple and complex consciousness.

"You see the shape of all cells and the centre of this your Galactic moving world is the holder of the designs of the living universe.

"From whereas life emerges from division of a single cell, your lives emerged complete. The purpose of this Galactic centre of universal designs is to be part of the evolving life that is like all matter part of the living universe."

We turn together and look up to where there is no gravity and sea machines moving between huge protein factories. Others are moving in and out of the gateways to the Nucleus and centre of hidden knowledge of our world.

Betrana answers our inquiring minds. We are the result of the existence of knowledge you see, not the makers. In part, we are the caretakers but none of our kind knows the age or from where this came, except to say all matter is affected by the mind of the universe.

In the process of our thought communication, we are an infinitely small part connected to this conscious cosmos.

We enter an enclosure high on the end of world, and doors close behind. Another opens in front and before us are the beautiful metal vessels that take life (including us as crew) to and from the worlds we awakened to service. A small craft appears which takes us to observation and control centre for this part of Galactic world. I am profoundly privileged to have come into being as Yargrey, Myself.

WHITE CLOUD

Night arrives and the mood is quiet. Eventually people leave cooking fires and gather to the community hearth. The few elders of the tribe enter the light with Horizon. I see they are serious. Much discussion has taken place and a decision has been reached. The vessel of White Cloud (Head in the Clouds) is vital to the future of this journey. Tall man's need to find his love and people is, however, understood. A crew will be found and they will travel south on North Wind until they find what he seeks. Then they will turn north on South Winds to return to this site. Then all will go north on the coast for one moon before returning to the trade routes on the Middle Earth.

My heart soars. I think they have great wisdom. Tears flow on the cheeks of my smiling face. Little people do not notice for now they are all keen to take the adventure. As evening closes, those who are to travel have still not been chosen. Horizon calls a hold with knowledge that the coming day will bring the decision to evening fire. Thus, we all sleep with much on our minds.

I am up early and bath before the sun rises, staying clear of the riverbank because crocodiles have been seen there. A new respect of coastal waters enters my knowledge; these creatures are known to both of my peoples, in all of my memories.

I am surprised and pleased to find the number of two hands and more gathered at my vessel, with supplies for the journey being stored. A quick glance tells me they are good workers and women who will dwell in harmony with men. I select six men and two women without their knowledge and go in search of Horizon. He is up and agrees with the eight. The crew is ready and we will leave the next day.

The wind is strong in the morning and the sun has passed overhead before we depart.

We travel no great distance before the delta is behind and high cliffs give a site for my signal fire. If possible, I will travel two days then stay by my signal fire for two days, giving any who may be in range time to reach us before we move on. It will also give us time to gather trade to keep Horizon happy and his people wealthy.

The country changes between red cliffs and vast delta plains with many coastal mangroves. Crabs, turtle, and shellfish are in abundance. From time to time, we see game, both large and small. Supplies of furs, shell and flint grow in volume. There is little time to dry flesh, but we eat well. My crew seems happy and eager to help me contact my people.

When I tell them I am not tall amongst my people they laugh and I think I am not always believed.

As the time of one moon passes, then two, I start to lose hope and all become quiet. The North Winds are less now with days of calm and occasionally south. I see they wish to turn back. I think the women are especially tired of the lack of laughter and song around the evening fires. I hear talk of wanting to return to trade route to tell off adventures that will make small people walk tall amongst an ocean people.

NIOMA

At night, my dreams are full of him. He seems to be passing, growing away from me in my sleep. I wake to memories of running after him, almost touching him, only to have the image fade, then disappear. Then I wake. What do these things mean? My waking hours are sadder and my partner has grown angry that I am not foraging for food and items that give life to our tribe. We are healthy in a fat land with no tribal competitions. Although some are lonely for lost people the memory of many deaths in the crossing keeps us focused on a future in the Mother's new land. We raise stones and place offerings on stone to give thanks.

None is as lonely as I am. My strength seems to be gone. Now another helps as my milk is drying and my child is often at another hearth. My man reaches for another at night and I hear her cries of pleasure while little inside me seems to care.

At times, when I can, I go to high ground and look down-river to the ocean where my heart yearns to seek one who seems still so alive. What is happening to me? Why am I not following the laws of the Earth Goddess, the laws of my people? I think if we were many in number their patience would have expired for one as seemingly useless as me. I am one who refused to take the name chosen for me at the passing of maidenhood. What is it that will not let go of a perhaps forbidden past?

WHITE CLOUD

They have turned with good winds from the south. No more fires are lit and the time of half a moon sees us back at camp, full of trade and for all, much excitement. My quest is almost forgotten.

The next day sees everyone ready to move north and it is only after much talk I am able to remind Horizon of his promise to seek my people as we moved north. They are all anxious to return by the shortest time and route to old ways, with new story.

He gives me one moon, so we can travel two days, then light a signal fire, two days more, then another signal fire. There are no returns of smoke, no people with heads in the clouds. Some look a little sad for me, but all look impatient. Still their trade grows. As the moon passes three quarters, and the daughter of the Earth Mother begins to light night skies and ocean views, I am told we sail for home in two nights.

That night my body seems to soar high and move north to a great river then inland to many lights. There my people rest in peaceful sleep with few guards. Only one sits in isolation by dying fire, a thin tired-looking one, who is only part of the image that was my love, but is the entire woman who is my heart.

I wake and we move north. A great river opens up with vast flood plains. I beg my people to search inland. It is as if I can feel her presence. They refuse. I beg and they spend extra energy building a great fire, which I pile with green branches to create white smoke that sails high. All day and into the night, I tend the fire. Eventually exhaustion, then sleep, comes. In sleep I find the same events of the previous dreams. She seems near. They are leaving while the moon is still full. The earth daughter gives support to the children of her own Mother Goddess, the Daughter Goddess.

NIOMA

As evening nears, the cooking fires are full, and the smell of food makes my now meagre body heave what little nourishment remains to the waste of my life. I move slowly out of my camp and the one who shares my hearth mate's pleasures feeds my children, and he who will place life in her body.

Eventually, as the sun sinks I reach the cliff top and look as always to seek nothing but sadness, a thin line of blue grey, almost white in an unbroken line raised high in the area of the distant ocean, almost two canoe days from sea. Only one creature can create this and my heart tells me only one has. Consciousness rushes into my senses only to reward me with the slender weak and dismal looking creature that I have become. It is too late to raise a fire and I am too weak to travel. I must try both. I must reach Swift of Foot and tell all of perhaps more people to give us strength in this lonely land.

YARGREY

A vast wall rolls back, one made of almost pure ore. That is the shell of this our travelling home within the inhabitable zone of the Galactic plain. There, through the window, is the star that gives life, still distant, for this my ancient world always remains outside the systems that circle each solar system. We ask how in such vast space we can find the one that holds the lives we have come for.

BETRANA (SPACER)

As you hear my thoughts, we of this world will open our minds to the complex organism that is life in this system. Such is the signal point that guides our world on its many journeys.

An unseen adjustment is made and the ball of energy rapidly increases in size. Swiftly a tiny blue world with a moon about one quarter of its size begins to grow until they are the only two images in the view. They are beautiful. Our minds centre together and the vast array of conscious thought that is life comes from the blue cloud-covered world.

We ask how is it that life such as this exists in so much space that is sparse of matter?

All life in the universe is by design, whether it is evolving or dismantling. There is neither destruction nor creation in all we see, only the bringing together of particles of energy into atoms or the dismantling.

Are there similarities of all life centres, such as this world?

Before you, the star is exactly four hundred times larger than the moon which is one quarter the size of the blue circle. The moon is exactly four hundred times further from the star (the sun) than from the planet. This will tell all who see such as a world both spacer or one who reaches high intellect on said planet that their existence is by design, not chance. This similarity is found throughout the inhabitable zone of this Galaxy and, we believe, all others.

Is it the only similarity?

There are more than twenty different essentials for each world before it can have conscious life such as us. Some are water, and position both in solar system and Galaxy, atmosphere hydrogen, oxygen, carbon dioxide, iron core, moving tectonic plates to form the planet crust and of course, a large moon of the exact proportion. That tells all of wisdom, that living worlds are by design not chances.

If it was chance, how rare would such worlds be? They would form less than one thousandth of one trillion of all stars. In other words, many Galaxies you would search before you would find another.

Amongst this world how rare is high conscious intellect.

A world such as this can be billions of years in development before intellect arises. So by chance, the number of planets with intelligent consciousness could be vastly less, so if one arose it would be a profound gift beyond comprehension.

Is this so? Is this as it is?

No, the profound gift creates the condition of life to be part of design in the living universe. This becomes the eyes and ears, the taste and feel, the infinite parts of a complete conscious universe, the Profound Gift.

What are we, this Galactic world and its inhabitants? We are older than our knowledge. We have a blueprint to aid in the chance to bring evolutionary improbability into the profound gifts, requirements for observation and understanding of all that is by design observable and understandable.

We are moved into transport and the wonder of entry to such a world is to begin.

WHITE CLOUD

The next morning comes and I see they will not stay; boats are manned and I climb in. The sail rises for the journey to continue.

Few look at me and I realize I must leave with them or face a hostile tribe in an empty land of nearly all people.

One of the older men quietly says, "You would search this land for many lifetimes and never find your people. That is if they still live in a new world such as this."

I resign myself and the day passes with some conversation. Tomorrow we sail for our old lands. That night I light fire on high ground again and sit by it late. Sleep comes full of the same dreams.

In the morning, Horizon calls all together and we ask help of the Mother to guide us. With no Mother representatives, it is all we can do to place our minds together in her favour.

My mind goes to the day this journey started and the trouble my distraction caused me. In looking back, I wonder if it was not a sign that I was to avoid the journey. I wonder now if that would have been best. What have I achieved for my people, my love? Have I achieved for these my now companions? They are eager to depart this new beautiful land. If I remained alone I would almost certainly perish. Will they return on the next South Winds? Loneliness tells me to stay with them, to return to Mystic and forget all else, at least for one season. Perhaps I can return.

The waves break on the shore as the wind is slightly to the west. Once again, I am reminded of another journey. I take my position in the rear of the boat and we row for the break in the surf. As we clear the worst of the ocean and move to catch the wind a clear picture of a brave and loving friend casting herself to the surf to abandon her people and face the world alone with me impacts on my thoughts. I know without a doubt what my destiny is. I must find her or perish.

I rise and with quick word of gratitude and luck to a loving people, I dive and catch the swell that will cast me once more alone on perhaps an empty land.

The sails are soon out of sight. Even so, I move towards high ground to watch for as long as I can. My emotions are in turmoil. Is this good? Is this the end? At least my body is well fed and time has taught me how to survive. But all resources are moving away under sail with my spears and tools. I have a pouch and fire flint plus sharp edge, though, and the rest can be made. First, I need a spear for creatures that will not fear one alone.

The boat is missed almost as much as little voices, smiling eyes and songs that will not be heard to hold back the dark by evening fires. By the time the sun is overhead I have a good signal fire and am working on fire hardening the point of my new spear. An axe and knife can be found. Large logs are easily found and an old dead tree makes a base by a rock wall. The fire will burn well into the night with stone behind for some protection.

Sleep comes and this time, for whatever reason, I sleep deep and wake ready for this world. I am alone but I have purpose and hope. I may find Swift of Foot's people. If not, I have survived alone for the season of winds. The little people, I think, will come again with the North Winds. The trades will add prestige and prosperity. Perhaps more will come and this will become new land for two peoples.

The next day I set out for the river that seemed to haunt my dreams. I will search for all I need as I travel.

NIOMA

It is dark by the time I return to camp. My frail body is exhausted, but I make my way to the central fire. Song rises as story ends and I have difficulty attracting attention. Eventually I am spotted and all grow quiet. It is, I realise, not my attempts to speak but the mere presence of one who has become like a ghost amongst the people of the evening fires. My voice is heard.

"I saw smoke in the direction of river mouth, a single column. Only a signal fire makes such. We have company. More people have arrived to give strength to our tribe." (In my heart, I think *one person has arrived to give joy to my life, a reason to live*).

All are silent. I think with dismay they do not believe this woman whose mind has left to be replaced by wilful spirit. Then Swift of Foot asks questions. The answers are quick and simple. After brief times he says we will investigate on the coming light. I say if fire is lit on high point perhaps they will see it even at night. Perhaps their light from their fire can be seen even as we speak. Perhaps there is no need to wait until light.

No discussion occurs, but I see several warriors leave camp. The songs do not return. Conversation is reserved and many glances are cast my way. Now I have reason, so return to the cooking fire and force my lonely body to take nourishment. Then I go to the river for appearance and strength are as one in my tired mind. Then sleep and hope mix with dreams of much confusion.

The next morning arrives. The men who sought the high place and stayed long saw no fire. They lit no fire for Swift of Foot says, "first we will see these strange ones then we will make contact."

Perhaps others have reached this land from our own kind or the others from far places. I am dressed and ready to go. Dismay strikes, for no women will travel. Boats are launched and strong arms make swift progress. I can only wait.

The day passes and a night of little sleep. On the arrival of the following day, I sit high and boats appear with sun overhead. I am stronger now and hope seems to have put vitality into my meagre body. I arrive in time to join all as the men reach our landing place. The news is not good. No fire was found, and no smoke has been seen. It is not said, but looks say it all.

This was the wishful thinking of one who is now close to being shunned by her people and definitely shunned by her hearth mate.

All backs are turned to me at the evening fires. I depart and sleep with lonely furs and lost hope.

New day brings new determination. Something in my sleep seems to have renewed my own belief in what I saw and what it can mean to me. The day passes. Nothing changes, and even the young hardly notice me. I attempt to speak with Father, Swift of Foot, head of tribe. He looks at me for a time then moves off without a word. I see him stoop to enter the dwelling of Medicine Woman. After some time, they both emerge and summon me. Is this better than being ignored? I enter her world of herbs and mysteries of the Earth Mother. She sits me and goes about making tea and burning plants to ash which in turn is added to hot brews and small leather pouches. The sun sinks below the horizon and evening songs bring comfort to most in this tribe.

I am told to drink. For a time nothing happens then the world begins to blur and the sound of voices becomes much louder, with a sense of distortion. She sniffs some powder and shows me I am also to breathe this strange mixture. In the state I am in, no fear is registered. I have a sense of rising and I view my body then, in an instant, the tribal area with circle of cooking fires is below me.

I see the Mother priestess. I know it is she, but she is young now and her thoughts are clear to me. They are kind and seek what it is that sickens my spirit. She sees clearly my needs. She sees clearly my belief that White Cloud is the one of the smoke. She sees clearly that what I saw is truth in my mind. She tells me with clear thought that White Cloud is dead. No man could have survived. No man could have followed. She rises with me high into the night sky until ocean fades and coastline becomes vast with islands and huge lands to the North. She says, This is our land, these are the islands where the lost one perished with many of our people. Others have had to let go of their loves that perished. The strength of the tribe depends on such acceptance.

In this state, I feel calmed by her. There is a power within her that I can feel taking control of my beliefs, placing doubts and putting strength into a sense of new direction. Then I know with absolute certainty, without seeing, that we are being approached. A new spirit is coming. It slams into my mind with absolute clarity and there before as in a blue sphere is the presence of White Cloud. He is older. We register clearly, I am here. I am coming.

Earth Mother's mind attacks his presence, "You are gone over. If the Mother Earth was pleased, you would no longer have earthly presence."

Then we are back in body, and I see she is angry. "You are being haunted by the soul of a departed one, one who has not been received by the world of those who find favour in after life."

I remain influenced by the secrets of the Mother's ingredients. I know not what to believe. She leads me back to my empty hearth. I think my hearth family is with new hearth mate. I know this to be so. As my head clears, I drink water and eat a little. Then I remember, and I believe, but not the one I should believe, the guide of our spiritual ways. I believe White Cloud.

The moon is up, but night is dangerous to travel alone. I will gather spear, food and sleeping hide and leave before dawn. I doubt any will miss me. Not even the ones who gave me life will follow one who has defied the Spirit Mother guide.

Daybreak sees me well clear of the riverbank and moving west away from the rising sun.

HUMAN JOURNEY

I have seen the anger of the Earth Mother priestess. I have not felt the anger of the world of spirit that I seem to know so well. Her skill is evident but I am surprised she could not recognise that I remain connected to the physical world. For an instant, I merged with joy in the soul of my physical love. On the morrow, I will seek the body that perhaps only I can heal. Then they are gone, the trance broken by one skilled in the old ways of my people. My people.

WHITE CLOUD

Once again, I wake from strange yet familiar dreams. With wind and ocean behind, greater distance was covered by sea than I can match in two days. So it is that on the morning of the third day I start my journey upriver. The delta soon gives way to a single, wide river with low banks, but in the distance I see the red cliffs beckoning me into the depth of this unknown land. Why is it I feel I can find a tiny tribe in such a vast land? It must be the Mother's guiding hand.

I am strong today, with an inner strength. My spear strikes from rock and I eat a large silver fish without fire. One eye is always kept on the movement of the huge crocodiles that are abundant in this land. With a stronger tribe, they too may become food for hungry family and hides for greater comfort and prosperity.

The cliffs soon rise so I move to high ground but keep the river in view. This water is tidal so people will have moved inland to find water to drink free of ocean salt.

I come across five large fur-covered creatures almost as tall as a man. They are slow moving. They show fear and seem to recognise me as an enemy. This makes me believe ones such as I have hunted them already. It is a sign.

At midday, I seek shelter from the sun and dry the rest of the fish. I find fresh water. I feel hope. This land is full of promise. Something within me feels the promise of that which has given all life.

With the sun lowering behind me, I move on. If possible, I will come down to the river and find cliffs or cave for night shelter. Well before night, I have a fire and a high ledge against cliff for safe sleep. The river is still deep with ocean tide.

NIOMA

All day I have travelled. With food to eat, I feel stronger. My mind is clear in only one direction. All else is sadness and despair.

The cliffs are higher on my side of the river but easy to pass and view both water and high country all around. No smoke appears. Some light rain and springs fill fresh water that has already become familiar to the evening stories of the clan. As the sun moves lower, I am afraid with the sudden realisation I have never spent a night alone in my entire life. Suddenly doubt grows stronger and the words of the Mother are in my head. How could any creature such as us survive alone? We are a people who depend in every way on the strength of the clan. Even two people I can hardly believe would survive alone. Who will watch over me tonight as I sleep? Who will keep a fire burning to hold a creature at bay? Who will find hides and food when one person fails in the hunt? To be alone is alien to all that I know. My mind must be truly damaged. Perhaps it is time I passed over to the Creator. For it is only those who go to death, that sometimes are alone at the last.

I find a place that seems safer than most to sleep and seek wood and branches to place around me for extra protection. From here, I can see the river. As dark approaches the sounds of parrots and creatures I know not seem louder than ever before. Then I see it, first smoke, still far off and on the other side of the river. As the sun sleeps, there is a tiny spark of light in a moonless sky. He is with me. I know it. Somehow, the one who governs all has created the impossible and delivered White Cloud across time and distance to a huge land, to a lonely woman on the river that holds her clan and his. How is this so? It can only be from the worlds understood by the ways of mystics.

How is it that our mystic could be so wrong? I know in my heart it is he. Now he is here I am afraid of losing him again. Before dawn, I will rise, but sleep comes with difficulty. If he leaves the river, he will not see me. How can I cross the river without a boat? If I enter the water, I will almost certainly be lost. Strong tidal currents will sweep me away if I survive the giant predators that rule below the surface.

To my horror, when my eyes open the sun is up. Exhaustion had its way in the end. I could easily have been food for a hungry belly.

After drinking my fill from a rock pool, I am away. There is no smoke and in the morning light, I am less sure of the location. It seems to change as I move. There is a lot of game along this part of river, from the giant hopping mouse that is as large as two men to a tiny version of the same thing.

Some huge four-legged slow-moving creatures stand as high as a man's head. None of these is a danger to me and they have proved easy food for the fires of our people. This land has seen us fed and clothed with luxury not seen in the world of our birth.

The thought enters my mind that the banks of the river on his side are lower. He can travel close to the river course. As he has come from the smoke I saw days ago, the direction of travel is obvious. I can conserve energy and move, not in his direction, but directly to the riverbank at a place where he may see me. There I will light a fire and put up a signal. My spirit lifts. I feel sure I will find the maker of last night's fire. The spirit within me tells me who the maker is. Then I can clean and feed this body and try to present it in a form that will please one who has come so far.

WHITE CLOUD

Before the sun reaches its high point I see it at a distance; a place I will reach by early afternoon. Smoke, smoke, not made for cooking but as a signal. Perhaps they saw my fire from the night before. The fire does not spread but as I travel grey clouds rise into the sky in the manner of green leaves being cast into a single hearth site. I am no longer alone. If it is Swift of Foot, will he welcome me? Will my Nioma still be there for me in body and desire?

I come over a rise and see a tiny figure trying to strip more green branches of bushes. I see only one single figure, too far off to know if it is a man or woman. The river is about fifty steps across, not wide where the fire is, but deep. There is no means to cross but easy to call to the one. Now I will find my people. Why is one person alone? Is this one lost?

The figure is sitting now and from where I am, I see a small group of the large four legged creatures moving away. They will reach her before me as they move through brush and pass under trees just upriver. In an instant, all changes; the creatures scatter very quickly, some almost overrunning the lone figure.

A noise I have not heard before erupts from the trees. Then I see it as I close at a run, and I see her and I know her. She is running downriver and the striped terror has emerged from the trees in pursuit of those it lay in ambush for. It is not fast and it will not outrun its prey, but it will outrun Nioma.

As I reach the river, and would enter a huge reptile slides of the bank. Striped one is not the only hunter to see my love. She is in mortal danger on land and also in danger if she enters the water.

The tiger is closing. I call, she sees me and there is no choice, I plunge into the river and strike out for her. A glance sees her coming my way. A glance sees the striped one angry but unwilling at first to follow. The current is strong and the tide must be running out. If I can reach her, I must bring her to my side of water. I pray to the Mother the reptile is well fed.

I hear my loved voice, the first voice of my people in many seasons. In a moment, she will be in my arms. In a moment, we may be lost. The striped one has entered the river. It swims well. My heart sinks but the fight remains; I have not come this far to lose her. Now the three of us are closing together. I try to prepare my spear to strike. I reach her and spin her behind me with the words, *swim for your life for far bank.*

She stays. The eyes and huge sabre teeth are terrifying. It has no fear. With little strength in water to thrust, my spear reaches for its heart.

SEVEN

REUNION AND SPACER COMMUNION

(THEIR GALACTIC HOME, GALACTICA)

YARGREY

Time has passed and the three-sided transport has reached this beautiful world. The clouds pass and large landmasses give way to vast oceans. In the ways of our kind the thought waves of many species comes into our consciousness. Speed slows until we are moving over ocean at minor speed to allow wide view of the approaching landmass.

The thoughts of those we seek are not here. I see Betrana is surprised.

Animal, bird and fish of many species are present, but those that can change their world with brain and hand seem to be absent. We look to Betrana and she says the planet has developed form. It will be on the other land. We pass on and I see wonder on the face of our teacher. Dim thoughts filter through. *They are here but in numbers so few it is impossible or improbable that so few can be all for such vast land.*

All together, we sense the intense fear. There is struggle. Some dramatic event is playing out below us. We move in a great grey shadow cast over river and land. There in the view two huge predators are converging on the one we most seek. With courage beyond capacity, one ancient weapon reaches for fearsome fur-covered predator to be swept aside.

A blue light flashes down and the drama seems to be frozen in time and space. Even the river covered by the light ceases to run. Then they are swept up.

Now only two beings remain. The light withdraws and another drama unfolds as the unseen enemy of the fearful tiger strikes and twists in violent roll. Great strength emerges and the creature breaks free. In turn it strikes. We move on.

This is the way of healthy worlds. We are not to interfere in the nature of the Profound Gift.

I turn to where the two creatures we lifted from the water lie quietly in an unconscious state. They will stay until all we need are gathered, then return to Galactic world. Some will be returned to bring a greater conscious capacity to this evolving by design in this world, one of thousands we visit in the service of the living universe.

Ten times, we circle slowly around this world from icy wilderness to tropical forests. Each time we take a different course until knowledge of the geography and diversity of life is complete, all the time gathering creatures and plants from the simplest microbe to the most complex observer. Now we return to set a new environment in our world, of this world. There some will dwell with minds controlled to avoid trauma.

HUMAN JOURNEY

I see the well-loved body of my physical world at peace beside my form. I see those of which I have long known. Those I think of as galactic caretakers reach down and prolong the life of two primitive creatures that are to me the present. The spirit of Nioma departs her form and joy, bliss, is felt as once more immortal unity is experienced.

WHITE CLOUD

My eyes open to meet those of Nioma. I hear birds singing and the flow of water. My glance moves around to observe fruit on trees, grain with plants and fish in the river. This is a land of plenty. I see an eagle strike and it eats well. Another follows to score large silver reward but drops its hard-earned meal on the solid ground.

We move together to retrieve it then turn back to dwelling and hearth fire that although I don't remember lighting seems normal and comforting to me. I am completely happy and completely in love. The nights, although seemingly vague, I am sure are full of the joy of Nioma. We eat and once more, I believe, once more, she enters my arms and the wonder of her welcoming femaleness gives the completeness that only this can bring.

The light returns and I rise to find enough fire to return heat. The weather is good with a gentle breeze. In each direction I look there is fog in the not too distant world we dwell in. I see another small group of people and go to investigate. As I near it becomes evident that they are very different. They have strong heavy bodies, but they signal friendship and lay down weapons and all they are holding. This shows open hearts; the sign of freedom of approach.

They are one male, two females and three children. They are almost white in skin. Even their hair is pale. Although coarse of feature, in my mind the expression is kind and the laughter of children brings warmth to my chest. Food is offered and it is good.

A glance shows Nioma has risen and is approaching. The women go to greet her. Words are spoken, but they are strange. Signs are made, and the tools of stone, shell and wood and some kinds of hide are shown. They have more than we do.

I would like to ask how many seasons they have dwelled here, and then it strikes me that I do not know how long I have been here. As soon as this thought emerges and anxiety raises its head something calms me and my mind turns elsewhere.

My love enters and there is happy laughter and much chatter. The ways of women and children seem to be the same regardless of differences in appearance. We stay for a time and learn by sign that they do not need to hunt here. Food is abundant, in fruit, fish and grain.

There are other people of the slender build and those of tiny statue. None of this seems strange to us. Even the few of all people is if unusual not concerning to any present. As days go by, we mix with all four species of humankind. Each seems to have an area where they are comfortable. None approaches the fog that appears as a wall that never fades.

Another day ends, and we leave our fire for happy union and sleep, which seems strangely dreamless.

HUMAN JOURNEY

Our spirits depart in this Galactic world and I am instantly aware that although free of the physical body that brings such contrast between joy and a painful struggle, we are under mind control and very much in the presence of a very powerful part of the profound gift that is the living conscious universe. Now there is no fog and I see all that can be witnessed from this place. The centre, or nucleus, of this world is never still. It is creating and recreating life in all diversity, as it exists in abundance in the inhabitable zone of this beautiful spiral diversity. In this state complete awareness of purpose is with Nioma and me.

As we observe, the body of Nioma rises, gently at first, then with increasing speed. It moves up and disappears into the complexity above. Other forms - animal, insect and plant – ascend, including a child with an adult of the heavy set of people. We evolve naturally in this universe but we also evolve by design.

In this form, I know that if the mind of the living profound gift ceases to exist, all life and matter down to the tiniest particle of energy are no more. We are at peace with what takes place for it is in spirit that we are unified with conscious immortality in its ultimate form. The bodies come and go. The spirit endures. In body we struggle to comprehend this complexity and though vague in concept do our best to serve the Creator of physical life. We have only dim awareness that it is the Creator of the spirit. Not in the beginning or in the end, not in a location for time and space is the concept of the living universe. Therefore, every aspect of matter is a concept of ultimate mind.

YARGREY

Once more, we flash into the solar system and emerge through atmosphere onto a pretty blue planet. Other vessels veer off as life returns to continue its journey of evolution with this living planet. Time passes and once again, we are over a river where the start of the purpose of this journey began. Light fades from the surface and our great craft peels off on its timeless journey of ancient purpose.

WHITE CLOUD

With both total fear and anger my spear flashes towards the great beast. In an instant, it snaps from my hand and I know all is lost. We are food for predators of land and I suspect water. A blue light surrounds us and instantly we are alone with current pushing us towards the distant ocean. A large reptile moves off the bank a hundred steps upstream and I push my love towards the bank away from this frightening creature. No time to think what happened.

We reach shore and move rapidly out of reach of the reptile, and of the striped terror. I have found her, and we cling to one another. All the sadness, loneliness and fear seems lost in the joy of her in my arms. Her body is so frail that for an instant I think it will break and gentle my hold.

I hear her words. "My body will heal, now you have returned. I have reason to live. I have reason to love." She is wet and exhausted. I must make fire, bring food and create comfort and safety for her. We will plan for the future later. Her immediate needs now are all that matters.

My chest swells. My love for the Mother that provides for two such simple creatures in such vast lands and seas is complete, is awed and humbled.

We work together for dry matter in shelter of the cliff with the high edge. Flint strikes and fire appears. I leave her to gather food but am mystified that my own body feels well fed. It takes little effort to find shell, fish and crab. I cannot take my eyes off her and watch as she eats without touching my own food. She tells me of those that exist and in time, I start to tell her of all that has passed for me. Her eyes grow wide as the stories unfold. I am happy in the wonder of her approval. Extraordinary events have delivered us to each other.

The question arises. How did we escape from the striped terror and giant crocodile?

She suggests the reptile attacked and it was dragged into the depths into a fortunate death.

It seems strange, and dimly, something nags my subconscious. I think something else occurred but what it may have been is gone from memory. Only the blue light that surrounded us remains a mystery.

The days of one hand pass and we remain in the ledge. Then the weather changes and we know it is time to return to what I now think of as Nioma's people. We find shelter for one night and after high noon next day, we come over a rise to see my people (Nioma's people) for the first time in many seasons. Now will be the test of a tribe's reaction to perhaps broken taboos.

By the time we reach camp all are gathered who are not out hunting. Swift of Foot and several men, including Nioma's hearth partner, are not present. Part of me is relieved and part wants to face the challenge of acceptance at once.

I can see amazement on the faces of most adults, and a little fear. They are asking the question; how can a land man have come over sea alone? How can he have survived? I am sure some think I have returned from the dead.

Nioma takes my hand and quietly says, "He has much to tell and all will be clear at evening fires."

Swift of Foot and the heath partner return. I saw a runner leave earlier so I guess they were sent for. Nioma has approached the one who feeds her child but the reception is cold so she returned to sit at the fire we have taken a little apart from the clan.

Just downriver, I see Swift of Foot talking with Earth Mother priestess. He does not approach until the light begins to fade. Then he addresses his daughter and ignores me. He says the songs of the night fires will remain silent. Earth Mother will ask for guidance as to the place of one who has left her hearth mate for one who may have returned from the dead. If it is the wish of that which gives life, then White Cloud's story will be heard. Then perhaps the wishes of hearth partner and Nioma will be considered.

Food is taken, then, when all are gathered at the central fire, we approach. Hearth partner sits with the one who feeds the children. His decision has obviously been made. He has shunned Nioma who left him for one who perhaps returned from the spirit land.

Swift of Foot speaks. The clan will remain silent while Earth Mother speaks for the good of all. Plants are added to a tiny fire in front of her seated figure and a chant familiar to me is heard. Now I feel another presence by my side. Perhaps it is my imagination but it is almost as if the image of my beloved Mystic is taking the place of the clan priestess.

I begin to quietly chant in Mystic's ways and soon the world around me blurs and the familiar sensation of being drawn from my body begins. The silvery blue light brings clarity to the dark and I am above the scene with the image of Earth Mother only now beginning to leave her form. Another blue shimmering beloved presence is definitely with us. My Mystic is here. Now we are three. Earth Mother priestess is stunned. Even in the world of the Mother she never expected to encounter the reverence of a tiny image that can only be called pure spirit of the creation.

We are now communicating in pure thought.

I register, "What are you doing here? Is White Cloud from the land of the dead?"

Mystic communicates. "He is of the living and has found and been cherished by a new and different people. He has travelled far and learned of their ways and more. He has learned much of the healing ways of the Mother. He has brought our people to this new land, a land large enough for all to dwell in harmony."

I can tell that Mystic's thoughts have deep effect with clan belief, and feel my teacher and friend begin to withdraw. Then the memories of complete surprise begin to flood into the conscious thoughts of all three through my mind, images so clear and strange that all time seems to stop and observe. An image emerges as if from behind the stars. Then from out of that, three sided images also emerge. The clouds part and one settles over a river that is here. Blue light descends and bodies rise. Then there is an image of creatures both human and non-human, looking down upon silent forms that are my love and myself. This fades to a scene of moving objects that seem to be in the sky of an enclosed world.

Then all disappear including my Mystic, and I am back beside my Nioma. All eyes are on Earth Mother priestess. None seems to have observed any strange event involving me. Her chant stops and eyes open to observe Nioma and me with what can only be called an expression of awe, if not fear or bewilderment.

Swift of Foot approaches and asks, "Does the Mother give her blessing to this clan if it takes White Cloud and Nioma, who has deserted her hearth for one whom we know to have departed for the land of the dead?"

The priestess's words can hardly be heard, but she says, "They have strong protection, and must be given sanction within our protection."

I can, for an instant, see relief as Swift of Foot glances at his daughter. He turns to hearth mate and says, "Speak your wishes. Would you ask the return of the mother of your children?"

He states with, I think, some resentment, "She has given up her right to hearth and children. My new mate will seek the blessing, and bring warmth and wisdom to my hearth."

Swift of Foot gives the verdict. The children will grow with knowledge of both mothers and be nurtured in the ways of the clan. New stories will be told in nights to come and now we will say goodbye to this day and sleep for tomorrow to come. Singing breaks out briefly, then all disperse.

For the first time without the Mother's blessing I feel the joy and safety of a hearth within the acceptance of my old people in what may now be all our new land, one I can truly rejoice at being a part of. Right now though, even the confusing vision of trance is put aside for later as exhaustion seems to overwhelm me and sleep arrives without the wonder of Nioma's gift.

As days go by, it becomes evident that our mystic is not keen to communicate with us. The events that were witnessed seem too remote from everyday life to deal with. I wish my tiny

Mystic were here in the flesh. She would not fear the unknown. Even for me it is to strange to deal with, so I am happy to let it go. Perhaps friendship with the one who holds the ways of the Mother will come later. For the time being, I am happy that life has at last become close to normal.

EIGHT

WHITE CLOUD BECOMES SHAMAN AND ARISE

BEGINS TO EMERGE

Three moons pass with the changing of dry season to wet. Nioma's body is now healthy and happy, starting to swell with the evidence of growing life. She is happy and seems to have found peace with the women of other hearths. Her children of her previous hearth spend time with us and the other mother feels no tension. I hunt with the men.

With the coming of the North Winds, my thoughts are drawn to my tiny people. I remained silent on the events of my isolation and strangely, few have asked. Our tribe moves farther inland as the large game we hunt have become wary and few in number. We are following for they provide easy meat and large hides for dwelling and clothes.

I know my little people will perhaps travel the river some way, but will remain on the coast. I feel I will not see them again and am saddened. So it is that one day I sit quietly with Swift of

Foot and simply state, "Another people have come to this land; ones we have long spoken of in our legends, the little people. They inhabit islands across vast seas, and are skilled in the ways of ocean travel. It is with their help that I survived and their knowledge that enabled me to find your people, my people, and the love of your daughter."

I can see he is happy Nioma is normal and productive to the future strength of tribe. He asks where they are, and I tell him much of the stories of their travel routes and trade. I say I think they will soon once again arrive on these shores and continue to come. He thinks for a while, then says, "It is half a moon travel back to the coast. Our boats become less important to us in the ways of the new animals that we follow in this land."

Some part of me is saddened that the knowledge of how to sail with the wind will not become knowledge for my people.

Several seasons pass and one event occurs that changes the path of my life from the happy normality I was grateful to have. Our shaman woman becomes ill with a sickness that she seems to find no cure for. As the weeks pass, it is evident that she will die. She is in increasing pain. I have been quietly collecting the plants that I think heal and help with pain for my own hearth family, which now number two children, a girl and a boy. I send Nioma to our shaman with tea that I know will dull her senses and help with the pain. I think she knows these plants but is no longer fit to help herself.

From then on Nioma administers treatment from me to her, and the clan takes notice. At the evening fire just before her death a young girl asks how is it that White Cloud knows the Mother's ways of healing. I look to Swift of Foot for permission to speak. He nods and I say quietly the story is of strange events.

So it is for the first time my rescue from near death and healing by tiny people with and old Sha-woman is told.

The fires are long that night as all listen in stunned silence of a world over the ocean where tiny people have knowledge of things strange to our legends; sailing boats and wisdom of the stars to steer by on the darkest night. Next day the elders come to me and ask if I do indeed have knowledge of the ways of communicating with the one that creates all and gives life to all; that which brings the light to our world each day, and the moon so we can tell the passing of the seasons.

I am not sure how to answer for what one experiences in trance is often of such nature that I am not sure what is real or not. If I say yes, that is what the clan will expect of me, to enter trance and seek advice or direction for my people from the ways of creation. Therefore, I sit quietly and tell them of the teaching that Mystic gave me, leaving out the journey she created for me into another realm.

I tell them I will take up the ways of healing if they can find another for the communication with the Mother. They tell me what I already know, that one who perished on the journey to this land was in training to be a replacement. There is no other. My answer is I will not promise results but I will help where I can until one grows amongst us with such ability. They seem content if at a loss or saddened to be so far from our past knowledge now far away, and in a rapidly receding past.

Now my role has changed without much choice on my part, the men ignore me when they go on the hunt. This I understand, for I am expected to advise on what will best reward the hunters, and tell of coming rains, supply of fish and other game. This does not involve in their opinion one carrying the spear. I should sit alone with the strange herbs and brews that show I am doing my job.

I think Nioma is slightly amused but not so pleased that she has to forage for food, and ask others for parts of a beast at kill. They are happy to supply these, for traditionally the Mother's contact is not far behind Swift of Foot in a choice of much the clan gained. Even position of hearth at new campsite is left to me as first option, although it is Nioma who has the quiet demand, and I am happy to follow.

Another shelter that allows me to go unobserved when I please is always built for me. Even here, I am rarely asked to haul log or supply hide. I should be pleased but in truth, I am distressed to have lost the companionship and good-natured rivalry of the men on clan activities.

The time I have on my hands leaves me much of the day alone. As a result, I return at times to quiet meditation, and am soon aware that much of my beloved Mystic's teachings is still with me. Without the need of herbs, I quickly seem to enter a state of peace. Although, not leaving the physical body behind, I have discovered what I can only call a state of near emptiness, where the body and all other of my world dissolves into nothingness. I am left in a circle of blue light and when I return to my body, I feel elated, in a state of bliss. This I practise and the procedure becomes important to me. I hope it is on the way to becoming a state of trance that will help my clan, who fortunately are in good seasons and still finding a ready supply of good game by moving camp every couple of moons. In this land, we are becoming nomads, wanderers without a permanent base. It is new to our ways. All seem happy with only an occasional sadness at loss of community trade and ceremony of the old world.

Our numbers are growing and it is obvious that if the Earth Mother continues to smile upon us we will soon be a number of clans in this ever-expanding land. I expect the population of large beasts will expand in the lands we have already passed, so it will be many generations before such abundance passes. With luck, my expected great gift will not be needed, as it usually is called upon in bad seasons and times of great storms and other natural disasters.

So, apart from boredom, our family is happy and two more seasons pass. My first daughter and eldest child is now nearly four seasons and already showing signs of being interested in much the children normally don't observe.

It is Nioma who with a half-smile first says, "Perhaps the little one shall bring the female back to the Mother Nature and let you depart on the hunt."

I glance at the tiny face; the one I have perhaps favoured over most of the children in the hearth and clan. I am astonished to see her intense expression and we turn and stare, stunned when she utters the words, "Those that come for me at night during dream time will teach me the ways of those who dwell amongst the stars." She points to the Orion belt.

I quietly ask her what she means and am stunned to hear a story that immediately brings back a flood of memory. The look on Nioma's face is one of near shock.

Our child she says her body can fly in dreamtime and in a blue light she has been able to rise above the land where we live and look down upon the home of the clan. She meets people who say they are stars' spirits and like all else formed from the mind of a supreme spirit that is the Creator of us all. She has been shown an image of a world that travels amongst the stars.

She has been told that her mother and father have entered that world and in part from their bodies and in part with help from Star Clan she was formed in that world.

"You are right to think I will grow to be knowledge to your people. For it is for that reason I have been told I have been placed amongst you. You who are to be a new people in a new land and in time will be one of many ancient people in this new land, for many will cross the sea. I have been shown those from Middle Earth, those from the clan land, others from the snowy north and alien species from a far southern land. Many types of people will come and some will stay for time into the far future."

As quickly as she speaks these words, the young face returns and the child is back and soon asleep on her mother's lap waiting for the time she is always put to bed. Now we quietly stare at each other and I wonder at the profound mysteries that exist and the amazing events that had brought grief, hardship then joy, mystery, and finally this extraordinary child.

Where has this child spirit been, and where does she go now? How has this story that matches my own astonishing experiences come into our lives and how did she come to us?

As the moons pass, she becomes my companion more and more. At first, I worry about her lack of interest in other children and their games. In some ways, she returns to a normal child. The plants and mixtures have to be taught to her young mind and at times, she forgets. It is in her observations that I am most surprised. She will observe for a long time the effect of a plant on fish or the habits of insects in their journeys through Mother Nature. When I return her to her mother, she becomes a child with other children of our own and many hearths. Her childish laughter brings me as much pleasure as any gift she may possess.

Another year passes with only some success at the changing of season when we celebrate the sun reaching its lowest point in the sky. The clan seems to accept my part in the ceremonies but I can see they miss she who was trained from young age to represent the Mother in such times. Arise is five seasons now and we are saddened when Nioma becomes pregnant but loses the child on the fourth moon. At times like this, I realize how little I know about real disease of the body.

I regret the loss of contact with Mystic's people. The child asks me many questions that I do not know the answers to. Then one day I realize it is amazing that a child of five season changes can grasp the depth of questions beyond the thoughts of the average of the clan. I soon discover that what I cannot tell her she endeavours to find out from nature, other elders, or any who will listen.

As the moons pass, I realize Nioma does not appear to take child into her body, and I wonder if all is well with her.

The child tells me first. "She is not eating a lot, and is in pain that she does not wish to bother you with."

I move quickly to her side for pain I can help with. That night I take greater care to observe her and discover the area in which she suffers; those places that are closest to the Mother in all females.

In the following moon, contact of any sort between our bodies ceases and it becomes clear to me that I can do little to save her. She seems to be shrinking before my eyes. I can see Swift of Foot is aware, so I talk to him. We are a long way from the coast but one day the hunters return with news that they have reached a new river larger than our own, which is now no more than a tiny stream with large water holes here and there.

That night at the central fire there is much talk of moving to the new river. I see Nioma is not fit to travel.

The child's small voice enters the quiet that follows my word. "It is this river that flows to great sea where the South Winds will take Mother to the one who heals, she who knows the mysteries of the little people."

Swift of Foot looks at her in amazement, then me and asks if I have told her that his daughter is to return to the ocean, and what journey is it to be.

The small voice simply says, "The old one calls for me to come and bring those that gave me hearth with me."

My old boat and those of our people's great pride are long behind us, probably beyond repair. It is Swift of Foot who says, to the surprise of all, "Two new boats will be built on the banks of great waterway, and my daughter will be taken there to start her journey."

With dread in my chest, I wonder if she can survive such. Then on reflection, I know that Mystic must still live and be calling to the child so I will place hope in such mystery.

NINE

CHILD BORN OF SPACER WORLD

ARISE

I have seen the change of five winters so my father tells me, although I am much smaller than the other children of the same number of seasons. They are very different to me in interests. At first, I thought it was my tiny size that made other children rush off to explore and play the games that imitate the ways of adults.

As I grew, I realised to my surprise that other children and adults do not see and hear as I do. It is not only that other world, the dreamtime, which is evident to me. It is in the night, those large periods of quiet, when my world seems to dissolve and images with sound enter to compete against the reality of my hearth. Images of far greater complexity that have, through thought language, given me a capacity for comprehension that I think already matches that of my father, who is wise amongst the ways of our tribes.

One thing above all that seems unique is the transfer of my young awareness across space and time, to observe through the eyes of other beings. The world seems so accurate that their vision is mine. The smell, taste and sounds of their world are mine, along with the joy of pain, pleasure and sorrow that the different bodies feel. At first, I thought these were random effects, accidents with no control or reason, but as I have grown, a beginning of reason is surfacing in my conscious mind.

Sometimes they are aware of my presence and now for the first time I know I am called, and it is more than the dread of my dying mother that has been the reason for the profound events that are to come.

It is also more than the ancient one who says she is Father's Mystic. There is a shadowy presence, close to Mystic, who also calls but who has not appeared in clear form. For whatever reason, I feel drawn across space to this presence and feel it is a young male, but in some way, of my substance. A kinship seems to be calling that should not exist outside my hearth. I question my father on this strange calling and ask him if those of his hearth exist in the far land of little people. He simply says he did not think it possible to mate with those of such statue. None welcomed him to hearth mate so no kinship exists.

Another I know as *Yargrey* has seemingly called and I have seen strange sights and learned mysteries still beyond my comprehension. Those images seem to bring to the surface strange memories for he who sired me. The questions arrive more and more but the answers recede into unknown worlds of creation beyond understanding.

We have reached the big river part of one moon back, and boats are already taking shape. If it were not for my fading hearth provider, I would be excited about the journey to come. Nioma is in pain and sores have broken out on parts of her torso. There is much to sadden Father and me. White Cloud only leaves her now to offer advice on how to set boat for this sail that will call the wind to take us safely over sea; to take us to Mystic's cure for one who, regardless of quiet ways, is deeply loved by many of the clan.

Food is brought so all are strong who walk without sickness. Father is eating less so I take him food, and quietly say his strength will be Mother's strength to hold her in the weeks to come.

TEN

ANCIENT MAN MEETS HOBBITS OF FLORES

(2004 discovery of 12000-year-old new species, Homo-Floresiensis, less than one metre tall).

WHITE CLOUD

The wind has gone round to the South. If my tiny friends still come this far they will be making ready to return to trade and ceremony. I know not where we were located in this vast land. I will pray to the Mother that I remember this map in the world of the Creator above that can guide me to land. I will ask the Nature of birds and clouds to show me signs so swift return to my clever healer can be found. If my heart was not so heavy with sorrow and fear I would be alive to the challenge and opportunity this return to trade route for my people could open up, new knowledge, new ways and friends for two separate peoples.

Finally, vessels are moving downriver in rapid water, once more into unknown lands. The large crocodiles give wide berth but all are careful to keep arms out of water. Large carcasses here and there show even the biggest fall prey to stalking reptiles as they come to water in the cycle of life.

Day seven sees us with great care trying to run surf, as it breaks on two different waters as they merge into ocean. Nioma is taken on a stretcher to the beach with many foods that would perish in rough seas. By sun overhead they arrive, and beach for the night. From here for some days, we will follow land north until I hope to recognize old landings, then the ocean for a quick crossing and perhaps solution for my love. Only the tiny one, daughter of great mystery, travels with us out of our hearth family. Others remain with hearth of Clan general, until our safe return, when winds once more turn to North, as I now know so well. I take great care to wrap herbs for pain out of ocean's reach and do the best for a body now slowly slipping away from my world.

A part of me is almost angry with those that give life. For such struggle to find such love and then to be lost is confusing. I must struggle to understand the reason behind all in this great world. It gives with abundance, and then seems to take with ruthless aggression.

The wind is gentle today, so it is good to raise the sail for the first time. There is much interest and some disbelief that the wind will replace the strong arms of men. I let the other vessel draw ahead for the rising of one finger of sun into the sky. A sail made from hide new to our people, from giant hopping creature, takes the wind and soon strong arms are moving more rapidly to keep pace with the surge through water. Then some cease to row. Eventually all oars are raised and quiet voices marvel at new sensation as we begin to overtake the forward vessel. Excitement begins to raise the tempo and I call for care as I see a restless form stir in the bottom of vessel. She sleeps with help from the Mother and Mystic's ways that I hope wait on a distant shore.

We pull alongside and soon another sail catches the wind and as evening brings a full moon to give direction to stars still to appear, people give thanks to all around them with a confidence perhaps greater than is normal.

I sleep and will rise when the cross is overhead to point the way to those who know stars that at times my tiny girl seems to feel such empathy with. This is beyond ever my connection to distant objects of such mystery. Perhaps as some say the souls of the departed ancestors returned to the body of our Creator. I wake and am slow to rise. Seeing Nioma is also awake, I make broth and a time sees her eyes close. Her movements show pain still holds command and sleep waits till exhaustion overcomes all feeling.

My head rises to clouds and I see for the first time that no moon or stars guide our way, only the wind. Several are on watch, with the rest in some state of sleep or rest. As I move to the rear to reach the tiller, I am surprised to find tiny Arise tucked in beside an older lady, the only other female amongst the two hands of people that crew each vessel. I say the wind will blow in the direction we seek and daybreak will give us the sun to guide us. A small hand touches the strong hand on the tiller and boat moves in simple correction. The warm voice hugs her close and simply says, "Your daughter talks to Earth Mothers always and guides us to one whom she says you are returning to."

The small hand rises and in the dark, I vaguely see her point. "The cross you seek is located here and it points our way as you have taught me." I ask her how, and she says, "The heavens are clear where another gazes upon a cross. If I clear my mind, their thoughts become my thoughts and through distant eyes, I see vision of what you and others from distant land have taught me to comprehend."

Now many of the words this child uses are strange to me and I find the answers between unknown verses.

The winds stay steady and the gentle sounds around me bring peace to the dark night. They call goes out from our boat in a female voice, answered not far behind by a male voice. This way we keep close, so daybreak will see all on the same course. The wind makes a gentle hum in rope overhead. Below, the ocean parts with sound like a stream tumbling over rocks in mountain valleys. The only light comes from a green blue phosphorous glow at the rear of the boat stream.

I return to Nioma and listen to occasional sounds from the one in whom I have an increasingly humble trust. If all else was normal I would still find this tiny girl's complete lack of fear and absolute certainty amazing.

Slowly the sky lightens in the east and bodies stir. Food is passed around with some inquiry as to the way of the journey. A little girl lifts the arm of her companion and moves to lie beside her mother. I see her thumb go into her mouth and a mother's hand caresses tiny curls. Then her eyes close and I am not surprised she sleeps, seemingly peacefully dreaming of all children.

I move forward and take the tiller with quiet thanks to another remarkable female.

The morning light creates dark troughs between waves, creating an illusion of more dramatic waves. This will settle as the sun rises. Fishing lines are checked with some success and fresh bait returns to seek company in unknown depths. The Earth Mother below and around us has nurtured us well so far. The Creator above has returned the son to bring direction and warmth to our journey. My namesakes, white clouds, roll back and blue gives confidence to many in a vast and seemingly empty ocean.

On the third day, we see them. From out of nowhere come sleek recognisable boats numbering the fingers of one hand. For the first time two people of vast difference in appearance, but many similarities of emotion and belief, are to come together. Once again, I marvel that tiny people in vessels only half the size of our two can be in the middle of this vast water world.

They are travelling faster than us and by movements of approach I can see caution. I stand forward and call greetings from White Cloud. At first, there is no response then I hear a voice say, "No *White Cloud*, only *many Heads in the Cloud*."

At first, I am the only one to laugh. Then I hear laughter over water, and I call, "Welcome little brothers and wise sisters of Head in the Clouds."

They move in and now I know there is hope.

My first words are to say that we seek the ancient mother of mysteries, my friend and teacher.

Now I recognize Horizon and we fall into formation with tiny swift boats on either side.

I call men to oar and we are able to keep up. I hear over water another voice from the past, saying, "He still builds boats that are more suited to make shelter for hearth!"

More laughter at my expense follows. It only now dawns on me that none on my people has understood a word I have said, that I had naturally returned to Mystic's language. Then a small head looks up from Nioma's side and smilingly says, "Who is one so tall he has his head in the clouds? My father is not so tall."

Late the following day, clouds appear and, with daylight as my friend, we enter the tiny cove that I know so well. Small faces greet us and then part for the one so old and tiny but still a leader of men, my Mystic. She moves to me, instructs me and takes me to her. I feel a desperate hope.

With swiftness and wonder, my love is moved gently to a place by a fire already prepared for her. I am given instruction but little is required of me. I tell her the plants I used. Then in a short time I am moved away to the central fire and only one works the mysteries of the Mother of this living world.

It is a long time before I even begin to register the others. They seem to be talking quietly as if aware that one is close to departure. Eventually the fire shrinks and they drift away to sleeping places on land and vessel. I am aware that many will depart tomorrow and that all were intended to go. Nioma is an un-foreseen holdup.

I slowly register that I must take care of Arise and am surprised she is not beside me. I rise and take a burning torch and move to the healing site. There, in front of the shelter, sit two children, so still that I almost fall over Arise in the dark. They are not talking but chant in union and I doubt they are aware of me or any living creature.

I sit and close my mind and chant to myself for I am afraid to break the strange bond that is in realm not normal for the untrained or so young. A small hand that I know and love moves over my face and quiet sound brings my chant into harmony with the young. Then as only Mystic could do for me I feel the world fade and my spirit rising from my body to the almost forgotten silvery blue world. There above the form of my love Nioma is a blue sphere that is neither a part of her body nor entirely separate from it. I feel the presence of Mystic and see the other two, which are almost one, on either side of the struggle for life that is so close to lost. I am made aware that they are calling for the life force from somewhere other than this space. I am aware that it is not the Earth Mother they call back, but something far and beyond our beautiful living world. I am aware that they are holding and delaying the departure of mother of child and love of father of child.

Mystic is gone and in a flash I am back in body. To all intents and purposes I could be alone, as the healer is gone behind the shelter to tend Nioma. These two, daughter and stranger; are somehow almost joined, only part of my understanding. At some stage, I fall asleep only to wake and find furs have been placed over me and a tiny girl sleeps curled up beside me with thumb in mouth. My child daughter has returned, but who is it that she really is, and who is one who she has found kinship with from amongst those with whom she should have felt little affinity?

YARGREY

When we gather together and our minds blend we become as one mind in the life and consciousness of the profound gift. It is not possible to put into words the level of joy. Under the aura of Alpha on one side and Beta on the other the inner sanction of Galactic world fades and the circumference of star people becomes a blue circle of light. The healing and creating becomes one with the tiniest particles of energy that constantly explode and reform to a design that knows no time or space.

Across this cosmos of light, we hear messages that come and go from our journey. Then two minds come almost as one that registers from the minds of tiny forms from a world we have not long departed, a call for help from bodies of light that took form in our Galactic world and left in the womb of two very different mothers. A blending of species with the gift of the living universe brings value to an evolving organism that is their living world.

An image forms within the blue circle, two tiny humans from Sol less than ten Ly from our presence. The mother who came from the river is at the edge of death. These children are aware. These children were asking us to channel the gift of life to one who should pass over. They are as we created them, remarkable for their world in its time. They have found each other as those of a kind are drawn towards their like. The unanimous decision goes out and I see the woman's soul draw back to her body. We are aware that the tiny cells that multiply to give her life are invaded by destruction.

As we watch, strong cells begin to dominate. It is not for the woman we involve our healing purpose for she has served her purpose by Galactic world. It is for these young who will see a glimpse of possibilities for their evolution on a new society in a young world present. They will, by this mother's healing, gain spiritual confidence and grow in the way chosen for them, in the way chosen perhaps for their children's children now that they have found each other.

The circle fades and there is harmony amongst us as we prepare to observe the gift of energy at the tiniest level of matter where the design of the mind of the universe exists. This energy will transform Galactic world across what appears to be empty space to another designed planetary system. It is good to be in existence, an infinitely small part of the living whole.

NIOMA

My eyes open to a tiny ancient face, one as small as my child who is small for my people. They are eyes of immense kindness and wisdom. For an instant, she looks confused and I think surprised to see me observing her. Something once again is taking place in my body and life that is of the like to make me wonder if I have entered the world of the Earth Mother, my journey after the end of this life. I feel as I watch the little one my body begin to grow stronger. I feel for the first time in many days growing hunger for food and thirst for water.

Without I think knowing my first words (but perhaps she in this world knows our speech) tiny ancient one understands. She brings broth liquid with vegetable and meat. I consume it all and it stays down. I can almost feel my body growing back.

The look on the tiny face tells me she is watching the change come over me. This change she apparently did not expect. She makes many signs then begins to chant and soon it is as if I am alone. Then exhaustion comes and sleep that I know will not be clogged by nightmares and pain; the sleep of recovery.

My eyes open to faces full of wonder, my wonder in life. They are faces I seem to have not seen clearly for a very long time. My arms reach out and Arise leaves the side of a strange boy and moves under cover with my seemingly strong body, definitely hungry body, and one that wants to rise and relieve itself.

My hands touch the face of White Cloud. Fingers tender and alert to touch wipe several tears of his face that seems exhausted, older and relieved.

Confused but happy, I tell them I wish to go to the privy and they move to help, but my body is able to rise. Although unsteady, I move out of cover and into the warm sea in early morning light. The water washes over both body and dirty cover, which quickly depart my slight frame. Waste is removed and I look to my changed world with eyes that almost seem to see for the first time. Everything is covered in a pure light. Even the early morning breath seems to have particles of light like water with the sun shining through it. The tiny cove is protected from the four winds. It is beautiful.

I turn and there before me are many people. Most, like the ancient one, are so tiny that they do not reach the top of the legs of our few people. On the faces is much wonder. Some I think show a little fear. On the tiny faces, words I do not know are spoken and the universal language of laughter is heard. With this, a kind of tension is broken and laughter and happiness spread. Many leap into the sea with play. A space is left around me. A lone figure moves down the beach to stand by my White Cloud who without thinking reaches down. She moves unto his shoulders in the place Arise so after commands. He seems to know this ancient one. They blend as one.

Then I see Arise, only six seasons, and holding the hand of one who appears young but is her height and as tall as adults of the little people. They seem surrounded by light and that light I can almost see flows from one to the other and back. If I have passed over, then I am happy with the Mother for in this world all that I love also exist. Something tells me though that I am still in my world but full of healing that has brought life to every tiny part of my being. This is an extraordinary event that for a moment I fear is a dream. I am awake. I am alive. I will watch my children grow. I will perhaps now grow old with the one who has many answers to provide, for his stories were not often told of his time alone when he crossed the ocean to find me. There seems much that is strange in the ways of the Earth Mother Goddess. I think there is much that is strange in the ways of the one that commands all that exists that is beyond the world we dwell on.

As I leave the ocean the sun shines down and warms my body. I take White Cloud in my arms and am amazed once more for I feel the need of that which brings the gift of life. People part and he picks up weapons and with a smile for the ancient one, his strong arms lift me and the camp is left behind. He knows this place of so much beauty and life.

WHITE CLOUD

Nioma is with the women who seem to have adopted her as their miracle one; one who will bring good fortune for the Creators smile upon her. I sit quietly with Mystic. I am surprised at how happy I am to be back here, a part of the ocean and all that I discovered amongst these wonderful people. There is little communication between those who travelled with us. Our camps are separate and only Nioma, Arise and I join both central night fires. My people have seen the life return to my love and they are restless to return to our tribe. The winds remain strong from the south. They will not travel until the seasons change.

Now Mystic is telling me it is time for all to follow the trade route and celebrate with the gatherings of Middle Earth people. I have a yearning to follow and see great things for both people in the way of ocean sailing and the trade that it brings. The hides and bones of large creatures are of great value to the Hobbits, for creatures so large are not hunted by ones so small. I tell my people of my wishes at the night fire and am greeted by silence. Eventually, several questions are asked and I tell of details of trade and the many islands and busy communities of the little people. They are not impressed.

In the background, the two children that seem bonded together sit with Nioma and I hear quiet conversation pass between them.

Several days pass and successful hunting of the island elephants occurs. That night all gather to feast on fresh meat and both people for a time are content. But language remains a barrier and division occurs after the meal is finished.

The next day Horizon begins to pack the vessels and I am left with the prospect of unrest of my tribe as they wait at least two moons for the winds of the north to return. That afternoon, I deposit Arise to the ground and the company of her shadow, Estra. These are two little people whom I now know have both just seen the change of six seasons. Another is to take her place and I can tell that the bond between my Mystic has grown during the absence. Both sadness and joy come in the return of two souls to one.

She mounts my shoulders and old instructions become new, bringing warmth to my chest. The day passes quickly and many plants (some unique to this island) are gathered for both peoples. My forgotten knowledge is returning under her wondrous gift and she asks many questions about plants of the new world with advice on how to prepare and test them for results with animals then humans.

Now more than ever I feel the need to return to the ocean and the trade routes. The evening fires arrive and there is no sign of Arise or Estra. They do not return for food. I rise to look for them and Mystic's hand reaches with determined strength to return me to the quiet gathering. All are aware that we must be alone to wait in this, to them, strange land.

Once again, I tell the gathered that there is need to learn this trade route and perhaps with the help of sail even reach the lands of our own people from whence we came. This raises some excited questions but then the death of so many is remembered and the questions stop.

I say I can take my one boat with a small crew and still return with the new winds at about the time that all will be ready for the return trip.

Discussion occurs but I can sense that the overwhelming feeling is to stay safe and return at first winds. I tell them the early north winds do not last and all could be lost at sea. This they know and I see some young ones looking at me with interest. The woman asks Nioma if she is keen to follow White Cloud. Her answer comes as news to me. My child is bonded to little Estra. She does not know how two different people can come together, but that she only lives because of them and that if they have their future on the trade routes so she would follow White Cloud, as long as they return to the other hearth children on the coming winds.

This I say is my wish too, although I had not considered Arise, and regardless of my bond with little people am startled to find that I saw her future with a hearth mate of her own people. Or, more to the point, I saw her become the voice of the Mother Goddess for spirit and health of new people in new land.

My feelings seem to be confused and driven into two directions.

Nioma senses this and her voice rises, out of character for her. "We were brought here to seek my healing, which has occurred in manner not told in the central fire stories for all memory. It was Earth Mother's wish that these events came about. It is the wish of the Creator from above such events came about. Such wonders will not have come to our people without reason. We are to follow White Cloud and the children to give new meaning to the lives of our own people, perhaps to bring the old world back to the new world. This is to include Middle Earth and for us to live in peace with its Hobbit inhabitants."

Now it is my turn to speak but I can say nothing. Who is this woman I love? More to the point, who is in the child adult that is both and only six cycles of the season old? It is the other woman who turns the tide. Her words are simple. "I will travel with White Cloud and I have faith in the child Arise."

Then another hand of youth rises followed by several others. I say they will leave early in the morning so there is much to do. Water for everyone with coconut and food to take that is already dried. Nioma kisses my cheek and I move out to speak to Horizon. My words are greeted by a toothless smile and I return to hearth as two little shadows melt away into the moonlight night.

All are up before light and it is beautiful, perhaps a gentle breeze. Colours merge in all their wonder, to slowly dissolve into white cloud and blue sky.

Only one boat is loaded and ready and perhaps one in three stand by it. We are enough. I simply say we will return to guide my people home on the best of the North Winds.

There is fear mixed with resentment but all are quiet.

I tell Arise to sit up front in the bottom of the boat and two children move almost as one to take this place. Another touches my leg and points. I lift Ancient Mystery, who promptly takes her place in the nose. I think we have a new commander of this vessel. This is a strange crew indeed; one never seen before.

With all aboard paddles are soon in hand with our new lady adventurer on the rudder. We move out to open sea. Small people form up on either side with much laughter and some rude remarks about Head in Cloud to slow the journey. I hear Mystic chuckle and am pleased that her enlightened mind is happy.

The sails are set but with gentle breeze oars continue to drive the ocean and song breaks out. I feel good; excited that not only new lands exist but now with Mother Earth's help we have continuity of the old and the strange. Gulls gather and dive into the ocean towards the horizon so we divert for this food source to take to deliver on the first of these island homes to come.

Some fish come to our vessel and the call goes out for we have no hands free to clean and store for drying. We move in; transfer occurs and we set sails with a slight lift in the breeze. I am happy and see excitement on the face of crew. Those that are left behind will not suffer the isolation I knew but without hearth mates they will be restless for signs of probably the fourth moon to come.

As the sun reaches the horizon the small fast vessels fall in with us and enjoy the calls that travel over ocean to keep us in formation until the moon rises. Stars appear and the small voice of Estra tells me we are off course. Now little surprises me that emerges from these two.

On the next sun overhead we reach the first of the islands, and although we have little to trade we create great interest. As we leave two days later the number of vessels is greatly increased. Now it is not only Head in the Clouds they stare at but Nioma and friends. I am full time answering questions that come my way.

The time of a new moon passes and we are nearing the next before we reach the central ceremonies. If any doubt existed amongst my people it is now gone. The sail has given great confidence and all feel with these islands to connect we can reach the old lands and gain wealth with knowledge all the way. Now on many landfalls it is the strange combination of Mystic, Arise and Estra that collect plants. More and more I think I am transport only, for the old one devotes an intense (or happy) learning curve for these young minds, much of which is already outside of my knowledge and I think at times outside the knowledge of Mystic. For amongst her teachings are many questions, sometimes followed by periods of silence that I can see have left Mystic deep in contemplation.

One day she says to me, "The children tell that the stars are the home of many worlds of living creatures."

She explains the stars were not, as she thought, just the world that the ancestors inhabit in between lives but also the dwelling place of travellers who have the wisdom of the Creator.

"They say that all we see is a part of a living one. If that one does not exist there is no Mother Goddess world and no stars."

The son (sun) of the Creator and Moon daughter of the Earth Mother would also cease to exist. Mystic thinks for a while then says, "In the central ceremony, when we ask the son (sun) to return from its low point in the sky, we should ask the living one to bring forth the sun and moon to bless the Mother and all who dwell upon her goodness."

Eventually the winds change and we return with the feeling of safety of many small vessels. As each island passes there are fewer until at last, with few vessels remaining for companions, we reach silent Hidden Cove.

The only inhabitants are two giant reptiles feeding on the bones of another and the bones of two people. Events have not been happy here and survivors have moved away, not by many days by all appearances.

The reptiles are driven out and an old gate is put in place. Five days later, we depart with the intrepid travellers; Horizon leading the way. This time Mystic waves goodbye with less interest in one, but a tear in her eye for two children who won't be parted. I do not know what will happen when we part company with Estra's hearth people and travel the big river to return to our people.

The winds hold for two days then turn against us. Now I am well aware that five vessels are holding for we do not have the arms to drive us through waves that now come on our nose. All are exhausted by evening light but as the sun sinks, the clouds clear and the breeze drops. With tired arms, we begin to make distance and take turn to sleep. For a time I see two little people with our lady crew member on the rudder.

Then sleep overtakes me and I open my eyes to a new day and no sign of another vessel. With wind once more behind us, spirits lift and at day's end clouds give way to what appears as a number of islands. There are many smiling faces. We still have risk but this is living and Nioma seems ready to ride the ocean again.

On the next day after sun high, we find a vessel on a beach behind the reef and move in for rest and fresh food, water and shelter. Fires are lit, bodies are washed and evening finds songs sung in words that no longer seem as strange to my people. Two days later, we depart alone and move south to seek the great river that will lead us home with new stories and trade goods not seen or heard of by the clans before.

Finally, we see smoke and arrive at a busy campsite some distance upriver. All look sad for there is no sign of another vessel. News comes quickly. No one has returned so we fear for the worst. The Mother's back offers a great journey of opportunity, but danger is greater than those who are happy with what this land has to offer. It may not be so easy to get crew for the South Winds when they return in four or five moons. Meanwhile we have a new hearth son, and I suspect the clan will gain from the presence of one so strange to them.

Estra is growing taller than the others of his kind. It is almost as if they were designed for each other. Whatever or whoever it is that controls this world is a constant marvel to me. It takes so much and gives when you least expect it, sometimes far more than your greatest expectations. Nioma and hearth, even without children, would have been adequate for happiness in my life. Although older in appearance each year she is still beautiful in my eyes.

Clan life settles down and the loss of three hands of our people begins to be a part of the past.

As time passes, I notice that few tend to the boat and only occasionally it is used to fish. No long trips to the coast take place. When the winds change, no interest is shown. The moons of one hand cycle past, then another. Now the youngest medicine people in memory tend the tribe and their health plus their spiritual needs seem to be in remarkably good hands.

Another cycle of the seasons pass and with the arrival of new children our numbers grow. Now I think it unlikely that I will see my strange tribe ever again so I settle down to clan life. At the fourth season of our return, the clan splits into two and we move further upriver, eventually coming to rapids, which cause some to resist taking the boat with us. After some discussion it is left in what is hoped will be safe place from floods that come late in the North Winds. I am pleased when large game that we follow show in abundance and the clan settles, only a part day from the vessel.

So many days I travel and continue to work on changes that I hope would make those who jest about Head in the Clouds proud of me. When the wind is right, I travel down the stream with strong currents and am able to return alone on paddle and sail. A new vessel is designed that suits the river above rapids and many return to fishing. The young find pleasure in these vessels that have no sail but move easily with several people. I feel that these people will follow rivers inland after larger animals as our numbers grow whereas boats for the ocean will be forgotten. Still we are happy as we watch children grow and we grow old together. At night when we lie down together, no words are needed. Our world is complete. So I put the ocean out of my mind and believe the memories of little people of Middle Earth will be lost.

Eleven

ARISE AND ESTRA. NEW JOURNEY TO OLD

CONNECTIONS

One day I watch my beloved Arise approach with a tiny baby tucked into her hides. My life proves that not all surprises are to be denied me before I make the last journey into another life. She sits quietly and tends the baby. Nioma joins us and together we watch the approach of Estra with four other young couples.

Now my ageing interest is on full alert for it is not often a diverse group of the future tribe seeks our company. Nioma's hand slips into mine and her lovely smile greets an enquiring glance. They gather in a half circle around hearth waiting for what I do not know. A jab in my ribs with soft word says, "Elder, where are your manners?"

With silent laughter, I say, "You are welcome. Please state your purpose."

It emerges that Estra wishes to return to his people for a visit and the young who have no memory of ocean crossings wish to know about the journeys that are now only songs of the central fire.

For a time no words come from me. Then Nioma turns and says, "Head in the Clouds is so old he is of little use to an old woman such as me."

I look at her. "Do you wish to go once again, where others have perished?"

The answer is, "If they go, you must go. Who will remain of my hearth as your other children are grown now and will be part of the crew? Do you wish me to grow old, alone amongst my own people?"

From deep within me, I feel an excitement I have not felt in seasons. As one looks upon these young faces there is renewed hope for forgotten dreams - old and new worlds together again, trade through Middle Earth. Now I know why I had continued to develop an ocean-going vessel long after all talk had ceased. It took new people for new belief.

I suspect these two, who still after many seasons are almost as one, have always known and quietly influenced my mind. That night at the central fire I stand and say the young have a request. The two who are so small amongst our clan stand tall in the light of fire and moon.

There is some argument, but I sense they fear the loss of medicine woman and shaman, for that is what they have become. Eventually they are told it is the will of the Creators and will bring blessings with good fortune to the future of our people.

The next day we set off for trials that will teach them new ways for ocean wind, ten strong young people and two old. When we leave, there will be four children plus two babies. As the moon comes and goes new hide with tree sap and animal fat seals the vessel and it is the sleeker and stronger, I think, than any vessel I have known.

When the day of departure arrives, our numbers of young have grown to three hands plus one. It is perfect for strength if the sea turns against us.

The days pass and old knowledge blends with new. As we move up the coast we find many more little people and great courage is found as we move out to an ocean world that they seem to have mastered for time beyond the songs of their many island homelands. This time the sail rises in a steady breeze and we surge forward, surfing on the downward side of the waves. I feel quiet pride as I see our place amongst other vessels hold and many glances cast our way tell me my years of work are being admired.

We are well stocked with water, fruit and dried food of variety. The bottom of our vessel is covered with large hides that will be rare and trade well across all lands. Old sites come and go on a journey I remember so well. Little is asked of me for the two that for some reason I call star children, guide with a knowledge that seems a match even for the ageing Horizon.

There is no sign of Mystic and eventually Horizon shows me where her body was laid to rest with honour amongst her people. New mystics are met, sha-people of different clans, but star children now adult are the ones to seek wisdom. I occasionally gather herbs to trade and on one occasion a child of my child's hearth rides high on my shoulder. For some reason this brings a tear to my eye. I see laughter on the face of Nioma, followed by a gentle smile I love beyond love and probably life. I see joy on the face of Estra as he reunites with his hearth people and laughs amongst his own. He is a tall man now and above all of his kind, one of the many mysteries that no longer seem so important to me. My pleasure is in young strong arms finding knowledge in their own mysteries and perhaps the courage of Swift of Foot who so nearly changed my own journey, plus those brave people who had the courage to walk with him.

Few events apart from normal problems of all people occur and with company for all the journey we eventually reach the shores of New Land with its great towering red cliffs.

After many moons we are greeted by the clan above the rapids once more. This time there is a change; a new camp is built about two thirds of the way upriver and we become three clans in the new world.

Over the coming moons, another vessel is built with a simple acceptance that this clan will take the winds and trade the goods of our three clans to Middle Earth. Much talk of our old worlds takes place around the central fires and with time, it is decided if the winds and Mother Earth favour her people we will try to complete a round journey. The only advice I can offer is that it may take the cycle of two seasons.

Star children consider this and say with less time at each trade point it can be done in the cycle of moons of two hands.

Once again, Nioma looks at me as if to say you should have known better. Sometimes I think that this old woman who only looks pretty in my eyes should show me more respect. Still once again after evening fires I feel the soft breath of her love on my cheek as I drift into sleep and the dreams that bring insight that perhaps helped birth the knowledge of the spirit.

Time has passed and two proud vessels join the little people. Trade takes place and the journey reaches its extreme without stopping for the central ceremonies. Now all eyes turns towards a world that only three of the six hands of people remember. Only three remember the loss of life. Perhaps only two remember the survival of one who has brought all back to this point in time and location. Only one feels the responsibility if some or all are lost in the journey that is strange to all.

As the night fires set on the land, there are few Hobbits for they are still at central ceremonies. We are now as close to the edge of their world as Hidden Cove once was. As morning son (sun) climbs into a new dawn for an old journey, I see two lone figures descending a cliff path to fires just now gaining new life. Eventually all are gathered and some discussion takes place. Then two voices speak almost as one with a life of practice. We will turn to the setting son (sun) for it is there that the lands we seek, lie.

Now I speak, for such direction places the wind on our cheeks and the currents of Mother Earth on our face. Now the journey has new risks and difficulties not before considered. For the first time I have fear if not for myself for those I love and the one beside me who means all in my world. I raise my concern but the discussion comes that the journey will start and if the world turns against us we will turn back. This I say may not be easy if wind blows against us.

Arise looks concerned as she holds young life in arms, but Estra says we will ride home on the currents.

Days pass and brave arms help a wind that we learn to use by new direction for the sails. Some days are calm and I wonder if we are making progress against ocean flow. Our food and water is good so confidence remains strong. On the day before two hands, birds become plentiful with many clouds on the horizon.

As dark arrives, the wind becomes strong and we lower the sails. They now close around us for warmth and protection from waves that may become large enough to swamp us. The stars disappear but the voice of Arise seeks her old ways and guides us forward. Wind remains on the cheek. Few sleep. All man oars.

Eventually age takes Nioma and me to exhaustion and we sleep in the centre of a now unstable bed. My eyes open to daylight and dead calm. The ocean is beautiful with sun reflecting behind us. Half now sleep and the rest quietly paddle across this peaceful scene. To the south are dark clouds covering from horizon to almost overhead. There in the west is land. Now it looks like five islands but soon I think it will become one land, the land of our origins and our stories, and the birth of my dreams and love. My soul feels great joy and wonder at our achievement with no loss of life.

I think our Hobbit sea folk have much to be thanked for this journey. It is to the Creator however that I hear two voices giving thanks.

The day passes to sun overhead with land now one long strip. With luck, we will arrive before dark to find safe landing. Then a new day will arrive to tell us whose lands we are in and where those reside that we departed from so long ago; my hearth parents that could not seek new lands. My mother cried tears as I followed a tall girl with a lovely female form into the wilderness. They, I think, will have departed this world. Will their children be able to believe the wonder of giant hopping rats and tigers that raise their young in a pouch on their stomach? Even more so, a race of intelligent seafarers that stands tall at below waist height?

The wind lifts and white caps form on a rapidly changing ocean. There is no gentle increase from breeze to strong wind.

It arrives in force almost instantly and I am glad the sails are still down. We are forced to change direction and run almost along the coast to avoid being swamped, moving towards land at every chance. Now after coming so far there is fear on all faces. The other vessel holds close but with increasing difficulty. I pray to the creation who gave us life that the storm will be brief. Lightning strikes and before long is all around us then rain arrives swept along in the wind to eliminate any sight of land. We have no choice but to run with the wind. Now we have no idea where the other vessel is. It is each for its own.

I move to the back, take the tiller and call to the rowers on each side to help hold the boat straight. If we turn side on, we will perish. Several begin to bale water out. Eventually Nioma joins me. I can see she has no more strength. We are moving very fast, surfing down the waves and swept rapidly to the top of the next.

Time passes and to my stunned eyes, land appears, close but with cliffs to be avoided. Through the sound of storm, now I hear waves crashing into rocks. Swiftly an opening appears and I pull for calm water beyond what may be reefs before, I hope, beach and safety.

The vessel lifts high. I glimpse rocks and below them, the rudder collides and is swept sideways from my grasp, lifting Nioma and launching her into the raging sea. In an instant, I call for another to steer and follow my love. As my body enters the water, she is swept into my arms. All times seems to slow and images of life sweep through my consciousness as I feel water enter deep into my chest.

I see a beautiful young woman dive from a vessel and sweep towards me as I stand alone on a beach before a long journey.

Then I feel and see her again, young and smiling with a profound sense of love. The world has changed to a silvery blue and somehow we have risen together over a lovely bay of calm water where I see two vessels moving onto a sandy beach lined with dwellings of a people of our birth. I see a small woman's face; our Arise clinging to Estra. My love leads me down to them and her hand moves to wipe the tears from her cheek. It passes through and we know they cannot hear or feel, then for an instant I see them both turn to us and a sad smile enters her beloved expression. We have passed over but with the gift of these star children, they can see our continuity. With love and acceptance, we turn to an age-old journey that I can now see will return us to an existence beyond death that is the consciousness, the beginning and a continuation of a profound gift.

TWELVE

RETURN TO INDONESIA. THE OLD COUNTRY.

AFTER DEATH OF WHITE CLOUD AND NIOMA.

ARISE

One moon has passed since they departed. Each morning I look to the other hearths before the memory descends upon me. It was not until White Cloud was no longer that I realized how much his knowledge gave us all strength on the journey.

On the second day, we discovered an old woman who had met her hearth mate at the gathering of the clan of this region. She remembered White Cloud and Nioma as part of her clan. Those that went to the new land came from several clans over a distance. The story of their departure is well known over a great distance.

By the end of the second day, people are arriving from neighbouring clans. Questions are plentiful, some even asking after ones who still walk in the clans of the new world. A feast is set and stories told. I am unable to tell the wonder of my hearth parents so listen as Estra talks of all that has gone. There is much astonishment. There would be more if Estra and I spoke of our mysteries that still travel with us, although the visions of star people seem to be now a fading memory. However, when we look to the heaven knowledge beyond the little people's ocean travels remains strongly implanted in both our minds. We are keen in time to speak with those sha people and medicine ones of this land.

We trade hides but the mysteries of creation and health will be kept for those we may discover with greater knowledge. On the fourth day, we departed with a number of boats keeping us company. As we rounded the headland, our sleek White Cloud vessels raised sails and caught wind. It was as if the clans were standing still as we move gracefully away and lost sight of others over the horizon. I felt a worth in the rewards that he who has gone over gave to so many people to come. I felt reward in the feeling that the many that remained in both vessels would travel these ways in the future.

We now reside with the people of White Cloud and Nioma. Many hearth related people are present and each day more arrive to hear the stories that will become legends around fires for a long time to come. Already I have heard the song of those that sailed away, Fleet of Foot greatest amongst them. Great care is taken to learn of our vessels with sails, and work is already taking place to achieve the same. Talk is of others joining us on the long journey back when North Winds arrive. Still I hear the voices of fear in their thoughts when the losses of those who travel are spoken of. When my hearth mate and sometimes the sha ones seek the ways of the Creators we hear all that will journey on. Few will go so no vessels will have crew enough. We, the clan of The Cloud People, will remain for a time, the only ocean goers to cross from Old to New and back again. I see that in time children will grow and become ocean people, born to that world.

On the second week of the next moon an unexplained event occurs. Estra hears them first or becomes aware at them first. It is as if they are similar to star people but closer to this land. We are astonished those who have Estra's and my ways are present and coming this way in Old Land. We can only sit and stare at each other in wonder. As they near, we feel the presence more and more.

Half a moon passes and we go to greet them on a rise over the village. There must be three hands or more. It is not possible to tell how many have the gift, but all are of our statue. Neither are the size of hearth parents of Estra or Nioma. We know with absolute awareness that they are our people. They approach and quiet words are spoken from them to us.

"We have come for you as we have found the others. You have the gifts of the travellers."

We know of whom they speak, although the memories are no longer fresh in our minds.

We share food and all are made welcome amongst the hearths of the clan. It is to our stories quietly told that they listen. The next day they simply state which we have already felt in their minds. We are all born of travellers from beyond imagination. We have wandered far to find others. They will travel to ocean with us, new blood for a new race to find mates with and blend amongst other people.

Strong trade has given us the goods for the best of clan vessels and one is soon adapted to our knowledge of wind and ocean. With North Winds, we depart with three fine vessels. The seasons pass and our tribe grows. Only three more of the gifted join us. Several are found entrenched in the clans as givers of sha knowledge for the health of those that are across all the old land as well as those that are slowly spreading in new lands. Only our ocean tribe visits the Hobbits of Middle Earth lands. Estra and I grow old with good health and our children's children spread over many hearths.

Estra leaves me first for a journey that I see in complete joy as he leaves his body, but the space around me is no longer complete regardless of the efforts of loving gifts from those who sprang from my loins.

Upon the departure from the big river I simply part from my people and with their mind gifts they know my choice, and mixed emotions travel the wind until many vessels cross the horizon.

Time becomes still as I seem to blend with all it is that creates me and all that exists. I sense that I have departed my body when the one that needs flesh for new life arrives. So the cycle of existence of animal spirit and small mother of new tribe for several lands moves forward for new arrivals, new joys and new sadness, that which seems to be in some balance by design from a profound gift, living creation that perhaps knows no limit in space and time.

Thirteen

White Cloud (Human Journey)

is born again

I hold hands with the one I love. He stands tall in my eyes but is one of those that are gifted travellers. We have many ways that are strange to the hearths of those peoples larger and smaller, whose lands we pass on the journeys from Old Land through Middle Earth to New Land. The songs have stopped now and we are content with full bellies. Our journeys make us a tribe who bring goods from far places, sought after by many.

We are known and spoken of by those even beyond our journey's reach. Some come for knowledge and the blending of minds gifted in the Creator's way. Hearth Mother stands, for she has been asked to tell the story of White Cloud and Nioma, her mother's hearth parents, long gone from these fires.

All become still for even through it is part knowledge to me and others it is a tale that stretches back to new beginnings for our young clan that is almost unbelievable to me. As the story unfolds, I reach for the hand of my love to be and our minds begin to blend, as is the way of those who are close in these people. The voice of Hearth Mother remains clear in the telling of journeys, but as I look beyond the fire into stars lost amongst the ambers of a clear night, images of the story begin to take on a reality beyond that of mere words.

Then the words become distant and I am listening to a group gathered around an altar to Earth Mother and I know we are gathered to ask guidance for a journey into the unknown, to search for land beyond knowledge, land only known to those who have travelled beyond the living body into the mystic way of the Sha-people.

My eyes travel over the people and I know my mother and father who are apart and will not travel this journey. Then my eyes reach a lovely smiling face; it is *Nioma* of the stories. As I look upon her I am astonished to feel change come over my body and look down to realize I am in the body of a young man. Then I am certain it is a past life. The past has become for the telling of the story the present. I am aware the group is breaking up and I am being shamed. I have shown bad form and perhaps brought the anger of the Earth Mother upon us all at a time of profound importance. A life flashes in images through this young man's mind and all is both pain and wonder. As the story ends, new knowledge of the part of star's origin is partially clear.

Then I am back in young female form and smile upon one whom I know has taken a shared journey beyond conscious existence into an existence where time and space are one thing. We hold hands and give thanks with shared minds to the wonder of what seems to be the immortal soul.

FOURTEEN

FINISH OF WHITE CLOUD - NIOMA

HUMAN JOURNEY

C ountless thousands of years pass and I am born and reborn on Earth and other universal gifts until at last I am
born into what will become France at the Time of the Writing.
I am an ordinary part of the living universe. Many lives are cut
short by the difficulties of the worlds I encounter. Some are
long lived with great love. Sometimes, drawing into my life from
many previous physical existences, are those whose sole experience of unified field existence was on similar plane of existence.
Many I have seen of the rare knowledge that has gone far beyond
my rebirths into a universal knowledge that is beyond my enti-
ties' journeys but all are bound by physical joy and pain.

It is 27,000 years before the Time of the Writing.
Small girl sleeps in her mother's arms.
Mother listens to old master.
Human Journey observes the story as told.

NOTE FROM THE AUTHOR:

DAWN OF THE SON OF GOD (SUN)

Sun reaches lowest point 22nd December in North and rises one degree for its birth in ancient time on 25th December, the oldest continual ceremony on the face of the Earth, a ritual that took place through vast periods, over perhaps most of 200,000 years of Ice Age Earth.

The next part of the journey gains inspiration, with fiction as base from the work of the French cave painting research done by Chantal Jaques-Wolkiewiez.

DAWN OF THE SON OF GOD (SUN)

I hold my breath, and as evening closes, towards the end of the moon of both hands and the thumb and pointing figure of another hand.

We join hands and pray that the son of the Great Spirit will rise again and bring the Mother Earth and her daughter moon the cycle of warmth.

We join hands and pray the son will rise and drive away the ice from the land and snow from the sky.

We join hands and pray the son will bring life to the Earth Mother so trees will grow leaves and flowers will bring seeds and the bulbs of the earth.

We join hands and pray the animals and birds will rejoice as the son warms our land, so bringing forth the young of the Mother goddess.

We join hands and pray the son will give life to the giver's insects so fish will live in the rivers that flow again.

As the orange ball of living warmth reaches its lowest level on the horizon, it once again enters the realm of the spirits who shine forth in the night sky. Only now at the coldest of moons does it die on the cross of the south that rises in the new dark.

We join hands and pray that it will rise again in three days on its ascent into heaven to bring the Mother all the gifts of this our living earth.

We return to the fires of our hearths and feel sure that once again our circle of stones has told us the time to give praise to the son of the father, who nurtures the Earth Mother goddess and her daughter the moon. Who nurtures those that give life to all that I am.

FROM THE TIME OF THE WRITING

I am a Heterosexual male but for the integrity of the story, it is realistic that reincarnations (consciousness) will merge and re-emerge in both sexes.

SUN IS VIEWED BY THE LIVES OF THESE FICTITIOUS PEOPLE AS THE SON OF WHAT THEIR IMAGINATION OR SHA PEOPLE CONCEIVED TO BE WHAT BROUGHT ABOUT THE CREATION OF ALL PHYSICAL EXISTANCE. THUS IT IS SPELT SON IN PARTS OF THIS BOOK.

FIFTEEN

SMALL GIRLS SLEEPS: MOTHER LISTENS TO OLD PRIESTESS

HUMAN JOURNEY

I look upon the body that holds my spirit when in the physical form. Her tiny body rests in the arms of her mother. The tribe has gathered with other tribes at the gathering of the greater clan. People stretch in large numbers around the base of a series of cave openings. Dwellings and temporary shelters stretch across the plane towards the river.

It is the start of the fourth moon; the time when life emerges in all its joy from the depths of the cold winters we are forced to endure. While my body sleeps, I am free to dwell in the world that is close to all that we are, one with the universe. I see the energy force radiating from all who are present. It is a feeling of good will at this time. All nature of this living planet is coming alive as its cycle brings it closer to what these people have now come to call the Son of God. This is the ball of energy that thaws their frozen world so that the flowers and insects emerge from new earth to feed creatures that feed the others, which in turn sustain the one who is my tiny self.

I have heard the words spoken by those revered by hunter gatherers, once more free to roam. It warms my conscious entity to hear that from such harsh condition for life.

They worship the world they walk upon.

They worship the world above. They think of this as the home of their ancestors and the one they will dwell in when their lives depart, which can happen all too soon in frozen winters.

They worship the son of these, in the form of that which warms their world.

They worship the moon, which cycles with the womb of the mothers that brings life to the bodies that gave substance to our conscious existence (the daughter).

In essence, they are close to the truth and it will be a healthier co-existence with the reality that is beyond their waking thoughts. It will come, in emerging civilizations that once again will rise on this planet when the seemingly endless cycle of ice releases its grip upon this beautiful world. Even the Human Journey is happy to call this world the Mother Earth and revere it as a special part of the conscious universe.

It came into existence from singularity to the present, to eventually cycle once again to singularity and onwards, the immortal soul of the living universe.

The people are dispersing now but my form sleeps on. It will wake when hunger comes and seek milk from a mother who will guide me in a new and valued life of all senses.

It is the ones chosen to serve I look upon for they sit now with hands joined at fingertips upon their laps, with legs folded under straight backs. I see an aura that is conscious existence cycling around them in what I know is the shape of the universe. The energy expands as it rises outside the physical form then contracts as it enters the vortex at the back of the head to emerge from the organs that pass on life, to cycle throughout this life's journey.

WILDFLOWER

I am seven seasons old now as we gather once again to celebrate the return of in part the carpet of colour that gives me my name. All across the river flats and surrounding hills, new life in all its wonder is emerging from ice that becomes water that feeds fish on its rush towards the great ocean, which my hearth parents tell me does exist. Those travellers who gather at central fires give drama to dark nights. I am glad to have the safety of strong wisdom from ages past.

It is in part the stories in song we sing at the evening fires that are the source of courage and knowledge. Emerging knowledge is my wondrous life. It is the turn of she who is most respected amongst those who serve the Mother Earth moon cycle.

This is the start of the fourth moon. I know they count the days from the birth of the son of all else that is home of all life, that which is gone before and that which is still to come. I feel drawn to the Mothers as all young girls do. It seems to me that when the blood of the moon flows from the female bodies and new shape emerges, young women stop thinking of the beauty of the priestesses. They turn their eyes to the strength of young hunters as they take turns to demonstrate feats of bravery that have occurred to bring food to hearth of sometimes frozen winter's nights. All these things bring me fascination but days are filled already with fewer childish games and more softening of hides and weaving of plants into baskets and garments that help hold off wind and cold, or the gathering of grains and sometimes bulbs or fruit to give variety to this young body.

My eyes are beginning to close before the one who holds the central light stops talking. My last waking thought is if they will wake me to see the sunrise on the day that is second in importance to all our people, the celebration of the start of spring. It is then when, in truth, we emerge from frozen existence to live again. This is the time and reason to celebrate life when all creatures mate and bring wealth, when young lovers renew pledges and couple to give reverence to all the gifts that return as with the love of the giver's gifts.

My eyes open to the smell of cooking at our hearth and I realize the son (sun) is already bringing his warmth to this new season. They have risen without me to usher in this day. Young lovers will have little time for children or the old in the moon to come. Hot food and cool water brings contentment and soon my friends gather for I am free of work on this day. A gentle shove from Hearth Mother and smile from Father sends me on my way.

Laughter on the flats below our dwellings calls to young ears and we take flight down well-worn paths to seek adventure in the valley where tall hunters have driven away creatures that would end young lives. The sky is blue this morning but distant dark clouds on the horizon send a message that it will be wise to stay close. Storms can be wild and cold, still intense at this time of the spring celebrations. The dark clouds remind me of the stories of herds of the mammoths that hunters say block out the stars when those brave enough seek to send such giant creatures to the givers' door.

Riana and Bluebird are my best friends who carry baskets to gather berries and other goodies that may have come early. Though I think, we will be lucky, for many plants have only just found new leaf and life-giving fruit is a long moon or more away. Still I am happy and something will turn up to fill the baskets and please the hearth.

The water thunders down the river giving a beautiful light, and a rainbow of colour, as the sun strikes spray. Snow melt bursts high off stones down the rapids to large swirling pools below, where some older hunters seek fish to keep their place amongst the clans. This site will feed people from far places for the coming days until we are sure the Earth Mother is happy with her people. Then, once again, they will disperse to follow her new life in the age-old cycle of her profound gifts.

As we reach the top of a rise, I crash into Bluebird who in turn tumbles Riana who has come to an abrupt stop. As we gather our undignified youthful forms together again I see them on the hill by the fast moving stream. At least five hands full of fingers move in a slow column. They are beautiful and my breath catches.

"What shall we do?" I hear Riana say.

"Stay still and bow your heads, move off the path only so they can pass."

We remain silent and my thoughts stray to our early morning appearance and empty baskets. It is customary for one to lay an offering on the path of those who serve the Mother. Still we are only children and have little to offer. As they near, the sounds of melody arrive, and it is the voice of only one who sings in a clear lovely voice like that of the wind and a bird at the last light of the dying day.

Eventually, we hear soft footsteps and a new voice joins in at chorus in the song. Then all is quiet with the approaching footfalls. We do not raise our heads and I see feet begin to pass by.

Suddenly an object falls at my feet and without thinking, I bend to retrieve what has been dropped. As I rise to hand it back with still bent head, all movement stops. A hand touches my head and my face is raised. My eyes lock on those of the deepest blue, almost black, so dark in a face of pure wonders.

We stare at each other and images flash before my eyes of what seems like many faces over eons past, but all come together in the one who wears the blue circle on her forehead, and seems equally mesmerized by this state of absolute awareness. I believe she is seeing the same journey. It flicks across my mind; is this what all Mothers achieve? Is it a power that one gains when chosen?

Her words come to me. "Who are you and from what hearth or clan do you arrive?"

I am surprised to hear my voice. It is as if I hear myself speaking in slow motion with the words from the body of one much older than my seven years. It is as if time has stood still. The others, both friends and mothers, are present but in a time and world apart.

She leans forward and says, "I have found you my love," and I feel her lips brush my cheek, then she is moving away.

Sound returns. Stones on the track, birds in the trees and the river rushing towards an ocean perhaps closer than the strange events I have just experienced, closer than a world that was both here and somehow that of a dream. I stare after her receding back until they disappear over the hill then I become aware that my friends are staring at me. Many questions follow and I cannot bring myself to answer, but I know that my path has been chosen and at least a part of my future is with the ways of the Earth Mother Priestesses.

We move up the track but my thoughts have turned away from the happy laughter that was ours as we set out on a morning of adventure. They ask me who she was, and how I know her. My answer is I have never seen her before but the rest of my words make no sense to me or my two friends, for I also say I have known her always. Now I think they are a little in awe of me for the ways of the priestess are felt with both joy and fear. We find some bulbs and we gather plants for weaving then return for the gathering.

That night the fires burn brightly. Young lovers slowly return to the firelight, new love given permission with the dancing of maidens around the fertility pole early in the day. There has been much talk in quiet voice of the women who arrived early for none had seen them before. They withdrew to the company of those who serve and have not been seen since. I can feel the expectancy of all that they will appear to give the blessing at the close of day.

The snow has held off, and cold winds are silent so it is a good night to feel confident about the warm times to arrive with longer days.

They arrive and take the place reserved. New torches are placed and I am able to see Blue Circle. I am in the semi dark, well back amongst the place of children so beyond her vision.

For a time she looks and listens to the words of the revered amongst us, then words are spoken by one of the newcomers. They may be words I have heard before but make little sense to a mind that has seen the changing of only seven seasons. Then her gaze travels and she looks my way and it is as if I am bathed in warm light of morning sun shining through raindrops. I feel the colours of a rainbow surround me and I know she sees clearly where I sit. I feel a calm I have not known before enter my young body. I am aware that the other children are unaware that change has come once again with the presence of this woman.

They come for me the following morning. Tears flow down my mother's cheeks and my hearth male turns and walks away with quiet respect. My heart tears in two directions. I hear my mother's words. "She is only seven changes of the seasons."

There are no explanations. With calm faces the Mothers withdraw, and wait. I know they will not wait long. With loud sobs, my mother wraps my clothes and few possessions. I hug her and turn to see Bluebird and Riana wide-eyed at a nearby hearth.

"Mother, I love you and will return."

She leads me out and I fall into place in front of Blue Circle whose serene face gives me some comfort but not relief from the pain in my chest.

The journey is not long. I arrive at the first of the caves that I have heard are the domain of the Son of God. Here, in time, I will learn that such who enter the Earth Mother at the close of the cycle, is born again in three days at the birth of the new life of the Son of the Earth Mother, and universal Creator.

The fire is lit and I am supplied with food and warmth. Little attention by physical presence is shown by Blue Circle, but her aspect is all around me. They place me to sleep between the two who appear youngest amongst them. I am surprised to find I sleep soundly and wake fresh. In time, I will learn that one can be fed liquid or food that brings calm or deep sleep. In fact, they will teach me the knowledge of plants that can create illusions of happiness and sadness. A new world of great mystery will slowly be revealed to me, but in the years to come it is domestic duties that are foremost in this young life.

A full season passes and I am included in few of the ceremonies. At times I am not even a spectator amongst the clans, for the young amongst us remain often in one of their many locations.

Blue Circle becomes the centre of my life in a manner that is attentive to me without seemingly paying special attention to me. Regardless, I know that I am chosen, if that is the word, perhaps five winters before the time young girls entering the blood of their first moon are normally chosen. I am aware that it is a connection of great depth that conveys meaning without words between Blue Circle and myself. For this, I have been taken from my hearth before my time.

My blood flows on the third moon of the change of the thirteen seasons. With this, change comes, and in my developing body new sensations become increasingly more demanding. The young bodies that sleep in my furs become more than warmth as the winter intensifies. We move south, travelling the winter courses as the ice slowly invades water that has slowed as the wet times departed for the Son's high journey. Then we turn towards the mountains once again. Three new girls have joined our ranks, all about my age of thirteen seasons. I am happy with these women, and unaware that the presence of men may be unsettling to our young bodies.

Now our studies are of the world we dwell amongst, and the one above, of the Creator of life where those who have departed and those who are yet to be born have fires to keep them warm in the night sky, the home of the Son of creator and Mother Earth who brings us warmth and life at night. I learn to pick out the creatures that are represented in the homes of the departed in the vast panorama above. Long hours are spent awake in the moonlight and asleep by day. Slowly I begin to understand the images that cover the insides of deer hides and woven mats made fine to preserve knowledge, much of it very old, passed on from lifetime to lifetime with only occasional changes with the slow march of time across these lifetimes.

We feel great honour when we are given the task of copying scrolls that are close to perishing. My skill develops and I realise that I am well suited to the depiction of many creatures found on Earth and amongst star fires.

One day Blue Circle looks upon my work and I see a tear slide down her face. She turns to me and calls me by another name that seems strangely familiar and hugs me and kisses me on the cheeks, then to my amazement upon the mouth.

I have never seen her touch another or kiss me or express emotion by word of mouth since that day many years ago when she found me. Strange emotions and warmth spread through my body and mind. She gathers herself and continues to teach the other girls who I am relieved to see were absorbed in their own work. This part, although brief, is something that does not seem to belong in the comfort of our furs in the time before sleep comes. I now know the passage of the Son and its effect upon the cycle of life.

As the cold deepens, we arrive at a site with many round houses and a cave system that we are told is to be important at the time of the rebirth of the Son of the Creator. I learn that all that we are and all creatures, plants and even rivers are believed to be the result of the union between the Creator that dwells in all above and the Earth Mother that dwells in the world that we dwell upon and on occasion within.

My innocent mind learns (not without effect) for the first time that this union is that which brings forth life from the body of woman. So it is that the female form is seen as the image of Earth Mother in human form. Thus the reverence I hold for that group to whom I have been privileged to be chosen.

I learn that the Son of this union and the moon of the same union as daughter are first and second amongst the importance of all born of such union.

I learn that the coming shortest day (a time when all life in such cold world seems likely to come to an end) is our most important ceremony.

I learn that when the sun enters the Earth Mother on the coldest day we pray that it will be given rebirth and on the third day will rise again and descend into the realm of the Creator. We pray that it will bring warmth and the new life that sustains our bodies, the home of eternal life that is a part of the Creator and Earth Mother, our Profound Gift.

I have already learned to pick out those creatures at their campfire in the home of the Creator.

Finally, at the time of the initiation of my first blood with the rising of the full moon, I enter the domain reserved for this union. In the light of many lamps I stare in wonder at a great gallery of star creatures that are the image of those scrolls I have so often copied, a map of the night sky in all its glory. They await the coming of the Son of Creation to once more gain earthly birth and bring food and covering for the body both day and night.

Thus, the existence that is me at this time begins to make sense. I am happy in soul, full of wonder at all that for me, for some reason, seems to centre in the one who brought me to this knowledge, my Blue Circle.

The shortest day arrives and I now know how they count down the days as we arrive at this time. People arrive from many tribes to form the central clan. There is much pleasure in shared company. Cold at this time keeps people close to dwellings and shared central fires. It is not yet the time that sends young lovers into woods, for snow and ice cover the world in a beauty that will only part company with the Earth if the Mother gives new life to the Son and it once again ascends into the heavens, driving the ice from the river and snow from the mountains.

I take my place in the company of the young, but as a part of the revered Mothers. This is a strange name in part, for those with children at breast part to let our procession pass towards the entrance to the artwork that is the gallery of the life in the heavens above with the Creator to be given life through the Mother with the Son's warmth upon this Earth.

As morning approaches we are all placed in the cave and at the sound of distant horn music all lamps are extinguished. Quiet descends. I know not how to express my feelings for this is of profound importance to the beliefs of the life of the tribes. I am humbled to be a small part of those who serve.

At first, small changes come towards the entrance to the Mother Earth. Slowly, with gathering light, I see the rays of the Son, then the orange curve rises mysteriously above the entrance floor of the cave. It finally brings a remarkable and profound transformation to the hidden world. The Son's light floods down the womb of the Mother. Her creatures, so important to our survival, emerge around me in a splendour not before seen. The head priestess begins to call upon this force to bring hope, opportunity, good health and happiness to the clan for the cycle of life so dependent upon the rebirth and following assertion of warmth into our existence. Finally, the golden globe passes above the womb and darkness returns. We join the clan and great feasts take place.

The next two mornings are the same with the third arrival being the actual rebirth. Offerings are brought and I see that we have goods to live upon and trade into the coming warmth. It is good to be a part of this woman's life. It is good to be who I am.

I am aware that with the coming of my blood time and the changing of my body new feelings have begun to cloud my thoughts. My Blue Circle is no longer the only centre of this young person's life. The clan divides and we are left to our simple lives. For some two moons we remain in the presence of this reverent site. Some work is done on the walls of the cave. We gather and prepare pigments to give colour but only the highest initiates take part in the placing of the platforms then creating wondrous designs now so familiar to me.

Most of the work is done in cavities further back. The animals seem endless in the dark twists and turns. The flickering lamp seems to give movement to creatures suspended upon stone and I would not venture into the depth of these tunnels without the company of those who have played a part for many years of visits to these walls.

I learn that this is a central base for Blue Circle's people. She is probably the next in line to become the one who speaks directly to the Earth Mother and Creator.

It is five full seasons before we return to the land of my people and I find my mother and siblings greatly changed, but still full of love. Less than a quarter of a moon is spent amongst them. When we move on fewer tears are spent this time for the gap is filled by others in all lives. Riana and Bluebird are somehow distant. Men are their growing interest and soon they will be initiated into the ways of courtship. I find that the love I share with young bodies on cold nights is not common amongst the clan so our ways are not spoken of. Questions are not asked of us, for it is understood that those who deal with the Earth Mother should be surrounded in mystery.

Two more seasons passed before what I come to think of as my awakening occurs. The other young initiates have travelled to the transformation of boys into men and several now are with child. Children grow amongst us but are fostered out to clans at a young age. I discover Blue Circle has kept me from a part of life that should have been normal to me, yet only a love of the mind ever crosses between us.

Her thoughts increasingly seem to be mine, but her body is not the one that would be the warmth of my blood.

As I enter the camps, she now knows it is the hunters that turn my head.

So it is that in my fifteenth year I leave the camp towards dusk with several other young women with whom I have shared much, for an experience that has turned my mind to wonder, but my stomach to a sense of great unease. I can tell the other girls are excited and eager as their aura begins to carry the moment. Answers come to my simple questions, so I soon understand what is expected of me.

There are multiple entrances to the cliffs covering this valley, and a base is set up for those who guide us and will stay close through the night. Dark is coming and warm fires are lit in a well-used recess.

Our bodies are bathed and fine hides of deer and antelope are donned over decorations that cover face, arms and breasts. The other two have eyes that are alight, and voices that laugh like butterflies in a burst of sunlight. I am just nervous and wonder if I can achieve this.

One speaks quietly in my ear. "Teach him the ways of our play in hides after meal before the time of sleep. The rest will come to him naturally. Do not hurry him. Stay as long as you wish and then return to the Mothers here; they will be close by."

Darkness arrives and with torches held high, they are led away one by one until only one Mother remains with me. She can see my fear so more advice arrives and I begin to relax. Since the age of seven cycles of the seasons, I have not dwelt amongst men.

The time arrives and they leave me with a torch to continue into the depth of an unknown cave. Light of fire soon appears, and then he rises from behind the flames. I see he is younger than I, hardly more than a boy, with sparse hair on a face that may become the beard of man in time to come.

I place the torch in the central space beside the hides that are laid in preparation. His youth gives me courage and I can see he is afraid, perhaps overawed by the presence of a representative of the goddess in a site that is a part of her initiation into the transformation of one on the journey to hearth companion and keeper of a family.

This event will see two bodies unite in the womb of the Mother Earth and bring blessing upon the children that become the future of his tribe, then the clan itself. No words are spoken and I remove my robes. The fire holds warm for a time but cold will give extra reason to seek the furs. As I move to him, I can smell fresh herbs, and am pleased he is clean. He reaches for me but I still his hands and smile gently upon him. Now it is my turn and his robes come away revealing a young beauty that makes my breath catch in my throat. Now the words of my advisers click in and what follows is brief but a delight to I think more than I hope to the Earth Mother. He looks pleased, but I think it was too swift and the pleasure young hands and mouth have given me before the sleep time did not arrive. After a brief time I raise him again upon his knees and begin to guide him in the ways of pleasing me, eventually bringing his face down and guiding his probing tong to the centre of sensation that soon sees me also content in the ways of those who have created all. As he raises back it is obvious he is ready again and this time all is slower and the fire becomes low before I reluctantly take my leave of him.

There has been a new awakening in this young body and when I finally arrive back at our dwellings in this region sleep is troubled and slow to arrive. As the days then weeks pass, I find I envy those who dwell at hearth and celebrate the joy of the pole festival at the spring equinox when all life's fertility is celebrated in the freedom of open choice of partner amongst often many tribes together.

Blue Circle knows, as do others, that I have become silent of mood. I still work diligently but when asked to attend the initiation of the young into manhood from time to time, I plead illness.

Eventually she comes to me and asks. I speak openly to her and after a time I feel her arms for only the second time come around me. Then to my amazement, I feel tears against my cheek (hers), and feel her body tremble with a strange silent grief. She kisses me on the mouth, not quickly but long and deep, then releases me and, calling me a name that seems familiar to me (*Goroak*, my wolf love), she releases me with the words, "When the time arrives, you will be returned to your family's camp unless you find the presence of those that you wish to dwell amongst before that time arrives."

My body has been aroused by her presence and when she departs, I seek privacy and am quick to release the sweet tension of the Mother.

Four moons pass and the country becomes familiar as we move back towards the cave that is first amongst the constellation of the sky. My river is recognized and we follow its course until upon a hilltop I recognize the place where it all started. I can feel the tension and all have stopped singing. Without words passing all are aware that a decision has been reached. All are aware without words that for some unspoken reason this parting will bring grief to the one first amongst us. Just how much it will tear me apart I am still to find. My destiny seems to be in two worlds. Even, at times, it feels as if my destiny is in worlds that have effect, that have passed by or are yet to come; or worlds that unseen are only a step away yet full of the presence of a love that is also in this world.

A young mother is leading several children back toward the home of my people. They all stop to allow us to pass by. As I draw near, I recognize a familiar face. Then I stop and tilt her head to meet my gaze. Riana smiles at first, then gasps as her hand clasps her mouth to stop her call of surprise. I kiss her as once happened to me but with only the affection of hearth children, and still a lump rises in my throat at a memory soon to be placed in another time.

The back of the one who leads us remains strong but I feel her as if she is my own self and know she has seen this final decision that has been brought to me in the manner of events from time past.

BLUE CIRCLE

Human Journey is the way I think of the one who will soon dwell once more with the clans. When I don't look directly upon her lovely being, it is a multitude of faces that all belong to the one consciousness stretching back through many, many lifetimes that have touched my own in many forms, but always with overwhelming love.

Without turning I am aware that a young woman remains still as we approach a place still clear in my mind. It is one of the two who, then child hearth mate of Wildflower, is now a young woman of childbearing age. In a life eight seasons past, she stood beside a gift to my life. Now the empty space beside her will once again be filled with a gift, finding a life of children's laughter that my heart was denied as I waited for a shadow to return. That one arrived this time as often before in the body of a child when I was already an adult, arriving in the body of a child of my own femininity. How I wish she had come as so often before as young hunter of both beast and the warmth of my hours that have in this lifetime become too often lonely in the service of the Mother. Those two children born to my young body during its time of initiation have returned to give joy to others who already have fulfilment of new life in the fullness of evening fires.

When food has arrived in the hearth of Wildflower's people, I eat a little and watch as she quietly begins to assimilate with the one called Riana and others of her childhood. Children laugh and are quick to join her. Food and drink are brought to all. As always, they are reserved in the presence of the priestess who leads in the ways the Mother. This time it hurts so, without looking, I take warm furs and quietly move back towards the dark shapes that tell me valleys of privacy can be found. Water flows and there is comfort in this sound, with breezes amongst the moving plants, my Earth Mother, and the conscious world, which gives all life.

The moon comes clear of clouds, giving beauty to flowing water as it dances off rocks cascading down the ravine that is now clear to traverse. Before long, I reach the headwaters where it comes from the womb of the Earth itself and find a small cavern to shelter in. There is no light and perhaps it is home to a beast that may steal life from my seemingly barren form.

I sit with furs held close as cold is already upon this world at this time when the son sinks closer to the time of its death and rebirth. The moon, daughter of my goddess, comes out and gives light so any beast will have fine vision of the food that its keen sense of smell has perhaps guided it to as this easy meal. For I have only my staff which, although a spear, is in reality a symbol of my devotion at all times, but most especially in the ceremonies of the may pole, birth of new beginnings and summer but most of all mid-winter. This is the birth of Son of God, who once again rises from the Southern Cross.

I sit in a formal position so energy travels its course within and without my body, the consciousness of all that exists. I direct the old and negative energy to flow from my lower limbs and higher limbs. Then it flows up through my chest into my neck to emerge from the top of my head. Now as air enters I feel the presence of new energy that will shortly with the removal of all thoughts in my mind make way for knowledge as it emerges from the infinitely small worlds that exist, to enter my form. Pain ageing limbs becomes clear. Bliss enters, in time unknown to me new clarity begins to emerge and the coming of emptiness as all awareness of physical existence disappears. Only the silver blue circle of sparkling energy is a world of information and contentment.

Once again I have found that which is in essence the existence of all life, all wisdom, all designs; the home of the universe, the birthplace of design that gives the journey of all creatures including evolution.

I have no need to ask of pain of loss within for both Wildflower and Blue Circle are as one with this place of the origin of thought. It is only the observation of matter that brings into being the separate conscious state.

As thoughts come and go, I am shown how it is within my physical plane. I see the water leave as it seems to flow from the Mother Earth through my body and all merge to travel with mountain stream to river then to the great ocean, where I see vast swarms of fish. There is life in huge variety over the vast area of the surface of my home. Blue Circle of the Mother, I hear not sound but a symphony of minds that move in unison and with direction both to feed and to find the origins of conception, sometimes over entire oceans to enter stream and return to conceive or give birth at the origins of unknown parents.

I see numbers of fish beyond counting, as many as the eye sees, sons in the night sky. All change direction with one mind. On shore, I see multiple-legged crabs emerge from holes in sand as ocean recedes. These are also in numbers too great to comprehend if I was of single mind. Not so, for now I hear a total awareness as new life hunts, so all fade into sand to re-emerge as hunter departs to become hunted in return, with one mind but individual endeavour.

In the sky, butterflies find the place of their birth after several generations with one mind. Huge flocks of birds from small black starlings to sea wings with variety that almost is without number, fly as the creature of the ocean. They have one direction, one mind but still to emerge as an undivided thought.

Thought that becomes all creatures - mother and father and Wildflower.

With this new knowledge I see her life and mine both connected to all conscious existence and external. Immortal, to both be lost to the infinite communion, then if desired to rise and give joy and sometimes pain in the design of such Profound Gift, the Profound Gift to all life and connected existence. I am shown how this will come and go as knowledge without end.

Love will be parted by the complexity of existence but its beauty by the simple joy it contains for the origin of life (consciousness) will, if worthy, find such connection again.

From deep in trance, awareness emerges as if from great depth.

I am not alone. It is dangerous.

The door opens and the physical cold cave with now full moonlight is instantly alert.

My eyes open to see several dark forms. Low growls emerge and moonlight flashes off rows of angry teeth.

I hear movement behind and for the first time I smell the den of the wolf. I hear the noise of the pups. My body sits transfixed. I cannot pass them. Life seems to stand still. Then comes acceptance, that this is the end. With this thought, I close my mind and images of this life and others seem to flash before my closed eyelids.

Then I feel a most extraordinary sense of belonging to the wolf as images of a great silver beast move in and envelope my presence, then seem to stand before my presence.

HUMAN JOURNEY

This is Silver the wolf of Arrose and Garoak in From the Time of the Writing, the previous book.

BLUE CIRCLE

I am aware of great love between this creature and myself. Dark shadows pass by me in the cave and I hear the sounds of feeding pups. My eyes remain closed and the silver beast remains in my frozen presence. I will not register that this is the end. It should have already passed. My flesh should now be for wild things. Life should have gone past trance and my body should have returned to nature's creatures, new life to walk with the Mother.

WILDFLOWER

In the excited chatter of childhood friends and hearth parents it is long before I move to return for perhaps the last time to sleep with my sisters. There is a serious tension in the fire light and lamp on ledges above.

Blue Circle is gone and has been long part of the night. She took no food, just passed into the night.

Now my mind fills with her and I am full of a sense of pending loss. I lift a spear from a crevice and call for help as I pass back through the central fires. Hunters quickly emerge and knowledge is passed. She was seen to move into the valley of the headwaters of the side tributary to the main river.

We move out swiftly. She will probably follow the watercourse. I am afraid for I sense that she is not as one with all things. I hear quiet talk as we travel and the words come that no one uses the headwaters for they are the home of the wolf, the creature that is taboo amongst the hearths of my people. As we move higher up, the pace slows and I can tell conversation is becoming at first hesitant then heated. Eventually all stop. They will go no further. To enter the home of a family of wolves even in good moonlight is to give advantage to the beast.

I call her name. The only result is a look of dismay from those who are close enough to register expression.

The words are spoken; "the Mother has claimed her. She will not return if she has gone this way."

My heart sinks and I am last to turn for hearth. We move back with the plunging stream. I call again with only the sound of wind in treetops up on the ridge. Tears run down my cheek and I can hardly see. Two hunters drop back and another falls behind me. I feel strong arms around me, keeping me moving, and I think hoping to keep me quiet.

Then it happens.

The howl of a wolf comes and there, only a spear throw away from us, with moonlight shining off silver fur, stands the most magnificent wolf I have ever seen. Weapons are raised but instead of retreat, it bounds a great leap to the land no more than ten paces from us. Arrows fly and spears thrust. All pass seemingly through thin air and he stands calm before us.

It is a phantom and the hunters are retreating rapidly.

I am not sure what has happened and I am stuck dumb with fear. My eyes do not leave the creature. All of a sudden, he moves towards me and I feel great love and no fear. Upon reaching me both front feet go up to reach for my shoulders and tongue reaches to lick me, but this silver creature that to me is sheer beauty passes through my body and moves upstream. I turn to see nothing. Then again, it appears and it is showing me I am to follow. I think; is this creature leading me to certain death? I am unable to resist. Something deep within me tells me that this creature has a long-time bond between me and the one who is thought lost.

I follow rapidly up and the stream becomes louder as the ground rises. Then fear returns with a jolt for the silver wolf passes through at least five large members of very real and very dangerous wolves with hackles raised. They do not look pleased to see me.

I turn to flee and hear a quiet voice say, "My beloved Wildflower, you are safe amongst those that are ruled by he who has been first amongst creatures in lives past. It is you who have tamed and loved this phantom creature, leader of wolves through the ages."

Her hand passes through the silver wolf but then to my astonishment rests on a huge black beast. She kneels and it licks her face. Other creatures surround her and as she reaches me, I feel her arms around me and warm tongues and fur enclose us both.

As we travel, new escorts move with us. Dark forms recede as light from many fires appear. There is no sign of Silver and with this I feel only awe with great warmth. There is no feeling of loss of something once again found then lost. There is immense joy and gratitude for something wild rediscovered, the return of she who, regardless of the call of hearth mate and voices of children, is closest to my physical being, closer I suspect to any being that I may be when I am not of this body.

Tears flow but with happy acceptance as the Mothers pass out of camp and disappear with singing. I start to walk away with the one who leads, but with gentle words, she tells me farewell.

We both smile at the sounds of four-legged creatures in the distance. A huge creature appears on a ledge well upriver and she turns to say, "We have a new companion for safe passage."

In the spring gathering of new life to come, I find joy in a new hearth mate. Children follow and their busy bodies require all my care. A new leader is with the Mothers at the next gatherings, but I am told Blue Circle is in retreat. At times, it feels as though I have two souls not quite at peace that reside in my one body. Then my children gather to argue and seek help with new wounds or fresh tears, and I am required to help many people and become Earth Mother of hearth. I have no regrets, only deeper understanding of the mysteries of all creation.

Others sometimes turn to me for stories of the star creatures that appear in the caves. Even brave hunters who have entertained cold nights by evening fires became quiet as I talk, then turn to their own hearths later than usual. Much that has come to me from the one and those with her remain the responsibility of those who serve.

When my youngest child has reached eight seasons, we turn to the cave of the new birth of the Son of the Creator. As always, clans cover the plains in numbers too great to count. On the second day, I turn to see the most serene of the Mothers and even before they speak, a great pain settles upon my chest. They lead me to a place separate from the people and as I enter the sacred galleries, tears flow and I collapse to the floor.

Time passes without knowledge and sadness becomes the only feeling. Hunger with other body needs brings me to my feet. They come for me again and guide, bathe and feed me.

I hear quiet words say, "For the short time of healing allowed to a hearth mother of the tribes, you are once again as one with Blue Circle's priestesses."

Then I am once more by my hearth with children asleep and hearth partner placing furs around my shoulders. My forehead is tender so my hand reaches to rub the skin.

He smiles quietly and says with a quiver to his voice, "Does this round tattoo upon my hearth mate mean that you are to be lost to me and those of my hearth who are a part of you?"

With new light, I rise and prepare food for those who are of this world. With food in his belly and the quiet comfort of the inner parts of my body from early morn I turn him to the hunt. Others gather around and I know that new stories will return with food for my children even in this the coldest part of the cycle of life.

The white disease takes him in the nineteenth year of my return to hearth. New pain enters my heart and I seek solace at the higher parts of our territory. A silver creature moves close in shining form, lit up by a three-quarter moon. Dark forms surround me and I feel no fear. With the coming of those creatures acceptance of life's pain is easier.

My two friends are old now and if I look too long into still waters, I see a face not unlike Riana's and Bluebird's. We move upriver to collect berries, seeds and other gifts. At times, chatter of children is heard but stillness of all is obtained as we realise that even the birds are quiet.

The Mothers appear over a hill as almost a lifetime back they came. We remain with heads bowed. When they draw level, I see the small feet of one of about ten seasons stop before me. A tiny hand traces the outline of the circle on my forehead. A gentle kiss follows warm breath. A soft voice says, "I have found you, my love."

At the end of the gathering of local clans that have come to the Mothers, I once more depart. Old life becomes new warmth.

My children now return to the happy laughter of their own children. Their spirits, like mine, will find continuity within the mind of the Creator, the profound gift.

Sixteen

Return of the Spacers (ALPHA)

As I look upon this world with the large moon and expanses of water, I do not need the impact of life that we have assessed to tell me life is in abundance. This is a world of designs beyond chance. This is the evidence of the mind of the living universe. All that is needed for conscious existence is in place.

Betrana stands beside me with the young that look to her knowledge now. The memory banks we explored tell us that we were young, new with re-established existence and Betrana and Alpha guided us into awareness when last we circled this blue circle.

I was Yargrey, but now I am Alpha. Betrana was then Zeeta. Yargrey and Zeeta now stand quietly with two others who combine with single thought to absorb what it is that comes before them.

Cataclysm has occurred upon this world. As we approached, we heard fine minds of a race, far older than the majority living on the largest of the landmasses. Then we saw the reason we have returned, celestial bodies on collision course for this lonely world. Three of them are in space distance close together and now there is only short time until impact.

We watch in awe as the atmosphere is rendered and ocean floors roll back exposing seabeds already ancient at our last visit. Great walls of water roll across ocean and land. One-by-one great areas of consciousness cease. The lights of humanity are extinguished over vast coastal regions and far into interiors. We can only watch, for whatever it is that has caused this journey is to repair. The great iron ore walls roll back and we withdraw. It will be some time before we become aware of our purpose in this journey.

My great hall of Galactic world can expand at time of deep space. The region included in this interior will change to include this blue planet's teaming life in the period to come. The star's rotations, and days and night, will nurture some of the survivors that we will gather in their days to come.

My mind returns to the patterns of this arm of the Galaxy and the hall becomes a vast hologram of light. Spacers move to high position and minds centre upon this tiny world positioned south of the spiral arm but in space-time rapidly moving into the centre of the plane of the Galaxy. Equations adjust to the rotations of this world around its star and a time emerges for its journey into the north of the Galaxy. In 60 million of this world's years this is one of several most important periods of change. The slight adjustments we make to the planes within the Profound Gift are relevant to this. Fourteen thousand and twelve years will pass before the end of the era of this rotation of half 60 million Earth-years. This time we are here to build. This time we are here to stay for whatever time is required to prepare for changes to come.

As the oceans settle and life emerges across this world and its changed state, fifteen of our tetrahedron vessels leave Galactica and re-enter planet Earth. A new era of knowledge is to take place. New Sun Gods if need be may replace the old one until our task is complete.

Clouds part, and ocean and land pass beneath us. Only one craft circles now; the others are stationary, over the great southern continent. Many days pass as we slowly observe information until finally a picture emerges as to the most stable and suitable areas we require according to the laws of Geographical influences and the fundamental Geometric pattern of creation, fractional division of space within the boundary of the planet.

The climate has changed with the advent of the impacts. The climate will warm for thousands of years to come as the world is now leaving the isolation of space and entering the radiant heat of the entire Galactic plane. The great walls of ice covering vast land masses will melt and oceans will rise, creating islands out of part of the continents.

Those known as Poseidon's people are those we had nurtured to give wisdom for the new era of development and expansion that will come with the vast areas of fertile land and warm rains that will now emerge.

These people are gone. Their beautiful centre on island lands with connections and centre upon one large land were obliterated. Small numbers of ocean vessels remain. In this time, we perhaps will find these survivors to give birth to new eras.

In the first time on this world, our presence settles on a great mass of stability in the centre of all this planet's landmasses. Here we leave our mark and in other places upon this world. In time if the universe smiles upon this emerging intelligence an understanding of the pattern and vast energy of this Galaxy will arise in time for those that dwell to know of other worlds that exist within reach before the time of pole change arrives.

Technology not seen arrives with the other vessel and stone begins to take shape as an elegant structure in pink granite on the banks of an extensive river system coming from deep within this beautiful continent. True polar direction and many other messages will be included.

Time passes and three large pyramids arise, a signpost to the three stars that harbour life-giving planets beyond the brightest of all stars that shines in the eastern sky, the star of the east leading to the three kings.

In time, we teach these people stories that can be laid down in legend for time to come for we will be long gone when the descendants of the altered ones we leave behind emerge.

In time, those with some of our own features take their place as caretakers of the stories and knowledge we have left behind.

As our vessel rises, the great lion stands guard over three glittering white structures of a beauty and symbolism that would be equal of any world of physical creatures within the vast memory encrypted into the psyche of ones such as me.

In the heart of the greatest of the three lies the source of energy and knowledge of the entire universe and the power to use this structure and the sun's power that transfers physical form across vast time and space. If understood, the source of survival of this world's species when temperate climate and beginnings of the knowledge left behind rise to show them the doorway to the world awaiting.

HUMAN JOURNEY

Time and lives pass. From the eyes of my living hosts, I listen and view the transfer of the mysteries of those who raised great structures upon this world.

Eventually myth becomes those who come from the direction of the eastern star, the home of the three kings, to find the Son of God. The story is that the power of the Creators lies deep within the glistering edifice left behind. Now other stories of son-gods mix with the blood of the protectors left behind. Awe and fear mix with the great reverence for those who dwell around the polished pink marble centre on the banks of this continuous great river.

From this world of the spirit, knowledge guides me but the waking conscious mind of many lives can grasp little of the extraordinary gift that is in reality created from an entire and unified living conscious universe.

AUTHOR'S NOTE

To give a sense of reality to spiritual fantasy and create speculation biblical people and Egyptian data emerge.

Before Tutankhamen, the tomb of Tuya and Yuya was the most elaborate recovered. The Egyptian name Yuya they say in Hebrew means JOSEPH.

DRAWING OF TUYA AND YUYA IN FRONT OF MANY COLOURED SHANTI BOXES IN TOMB.

SEVENTEEN

TIME OF JOSEPH—COAT OF MANY COLOURS

(YUYA AND TUYA)

TUYA

T he worlds of our gods must be angry indeed, for the rains
have failed and the river of life has, for the second time in
the changing of two seasons, produced no flood. Great crowds
are drawn to the home of our beliefs. I have nothing left to offer
and feel shame in the presence of that which is really beyond my
knowledge.

I am here this morning as light appears in a thin strip and the
sky slowly glows. The great monuments of the sky gods boldly
raise their heads in the gathering light. The sun god comes to
the home of those who brought great wisdom in some, to me,
forgotten time.

I am *Tuya*, daughter of a grain grower and labourer of any
task that may bring bread to our table. No grain has grown

without annual floods and the river is too low to draw water for the fields.

My mother is the daughter of higher people from the land of Canaan. Her beauty was a fine gift but her fall from grace, which is a mystery not spoken of, caused her arrival by camel train to this land. My older sister was born soon after and her body was her only method of survival until Father, taken by my mother's fading graces, rescued her.

My only gift of this beginning is her beauty and I suspect the legacy of a soldier of the kingdom, for I resemble not at all the plain appearance of my father. Fourteen seasons old and without means, my future is bleak and I fear I will be put to the entertainment of those who have means to pay in hard times.

I am frightened. I will pray hard and often, that a wealthy man may rescue me. Perhaps he will come from the land of Canaan and my mother's people. Crops may still dwell to put food on their tables in the land of Canaan, although it has been said that the news that travels from afar with exotic caravans is of drought in distant lands. This I know, for the rich soils that come from the annual floods come from far distant lands. So, rain has not fallen over vast distance.

The sound of trumpets and drums rolls out of the temples that separate us from the sky gods, like thunder of a gathering storm that never seems to arrive in this land. My stomach rumbles in gentle answer to remind me that my days may be numbered.

Slowly I become aware that there is a growing sense of change, a tension - not loud noise, but whispers travelling through the crowd from those privileged to be far to the front of our position.

Pharaoh, the earthly image of the Son of God that gives us light and delivers grain in good times, has emerged from the temples, and on this rare occasion is to speak through the mouths of those that serve.

Now I can see groups of white robed soldiers of the divine moving through the people. Word reaches us that they search for maidens and young boys. The reason is not clear.

As they near, to my mortification, my mother thrusts my body to the front and I fall at the feet of those that search. Not a dignified attempt to gain favour for I know not what. None reaches to lift me but glimpse shows me bare legs as soldiers pass over me. As the chance arrives, I rise to my feet to escape to my not-so-loving parents, but am horrified to come face to face with two elderly priests who are obviously the ones who search.

No words are spoken but grave expression passes between faces and my life changes to new directions as I glance to the rear. The faces of those I have known for fourteen years are already in my past. This I do not immediately register, but time will make this apparent.

Those they may love rarely see those that go to the service of the sky gods, or their priests, again. My heart is full of confusion, dread and perhaps excitement. My body is full of hunger, so it is close to my mind that there is little for me to lose.

If I am to be sacrificed to the gods, it may avoid a limited life of suffering. If I am to be of service, then surely I will be housed, fed and clothed. What duties that involves I can only imagine. The crowds part and I go where no farmer goes, into the temples and dwellings of those who receive too much of the labours of many people in the form of produce.

Now a new shame is upon me for this world is without the poverty of dirt. My clothes are now rags, but the best I possess. My hair and all else are flawed. How is it they have chosen one such as me? Yes I am said to be beauty amongst the poor, but here all people who are not priests seem refined and beyond the judgement of a peasant farmer. Part of me wishes to stare at all, while the other pushes my face down as one too ordinary to be seen. Much of the journey is vision of the beautiful polished marble beneath my feet. That must be an indication of all that rises in increasing splendour all around my very plain form.

In a short time, I reach a destination and am alone with four walls and silence; a silence of which we who dwell amongst so many, never become aware. I fear to move so sit with feet against my chest and hungry body against a wall of pink marble. The soft pad of sandaled feet comes and goes, and I wonder if I am left to starve to death. With no sun, the passing of time has no meaning. Lamps burn in the entrance only, so I am in semi darkness with a small window on wall high above.

My eyes become heavy and eventually these frightening, and no longer exiting events fade into a world of dreams, dreams that belong to fourteen-year-old farm girls.

My eyes open and the smell of food fills my senses. They have come and gone. There is also a large copper dish and soap to wash, and a tunic of white cloth that I can see has gold and silver trim. Now my heartbeat increases. On hands and knees, I move to the door and peer down a corridor. It is empty of people but full of artefacts that would take my breath away, if food were not all that is close to my consciousness.

With stomach full and a quick glance to see that I am still alone, my rags go to the corner and I hasten to clean myself, and then dress as I have never before done in cloth so beautiful that the body I now live in seems to be that of a stranger.

My stomach is full, my body clean, and my spirit nervous but I am filled with a feeling that is new to me. Hope!

People pass and few glance my way. The lamp burns down and the window begins to darken. A day has passed with great change, but no results.

I lie on the hard floor and my eyes close again; this strange lonely world departs.

They come for me before light, raising me from sleep, four young women dressed with the same cloth that now attires my form and with hair done and faces adorned with I know not what. They are beautiful. The few implements are left behind including my forgotten clothes, for I hope I never adorn my body with the like again.

No words are spoken. It strikes me I have not heard a human voice since entering this world of the gods. Do the gods not like the sound of laughter? Perhaps the divine has no need of human voice, for I left the crowd before the apparent appearance of the God King, whom they said would speak through the voices of those that serve.

How many other young people were taken into new beginnings? Or taken into perhaps a preparation for a rapid decline? This does not feel like decline to me, but perhaps I am being made lovelier in order to enter the world of the gods through sacrifice. I am not keen to leave this world quite yet.

All about me now is splendour - statues, tapestries and furniture, rugs on floors that are sometimes polished timber. Now I feel as a stranger in this form, but not ashamed to hold my head up with eyes that see more than my simple young mind can absorb. My eyes have both fear and a wary sense of joy and excitement, all feelings mixed up together.

Now there are many in a room of still greater wonder for water enters through the mouths of four great beasts, and cascades down rocks into a quadrangle of water, then disappears into a recess at the opposite end. Within the pool reside perhaps fifteen people, with some coming and going all the time, all woman, mostly young, but several with grey hair, but still strong in body. Without words or indication, my four companions disrobe and enter.

I follow and am delighted to swim in water other that the Mother Nile for the first time in my life. No questions are asked and they converge on me. Gentle hands bathe my skin. Apart from my mother, no human hands have touched me so. Camp boys from farms up and down the river have often stared and on occasion loose suggestions have come my way. Poverty has kept us working long hours in unproductive fields, with body too tired and often hungry, only fit for exhaustion at the end of day.

No part of my body is left untouched and the sensations are not those of exhaustion. Nor are they those of the senses that fill young women, as my older sister tells, at the sight of young men's bodies. Hands surround me and I become aware that I am gently being restrained. I feel only small fear as the swift hands become intrusive and the private part of my body is penetrated. Then all are withdrawn and with an easy charm and some quiet smiling, I am left alone as they seem to convey a message about me to each other. They look well pleased. I think my youth and unworldly experience is in some way what they have sought.

As they leave the water, robes go back on and I start to follow. A change occurs, not subtle. Facial expression is now almost serene as, almost as one, they turn towards latticework on the far side of the pool. There is shadowy movement behind the screen. It is a person, but not to be seen from this room. Those remaining in pool have left and now stand as one with all others, a naked wall of bodies, some twenty in number, motionless. Others enter and become still. The room is crowded. The shadow departs and my sense of wonder is increased. My education would be a long way behind, if words from these women were to be the source of knowledge. Who is the shadow that can bring a room full of women to serene silent stillness? Who are these women? This is a part of the world of the Son God.

All things inside these walls and the great monoliths that must tower above are in service of the Son Gods. If I am to be of service to the Son Gods, perhaps for the first time in fourteen years this place and the gifts will begin to make sense. No rain and the lack of annual floods is something that the dead and starving I think would like to understand.

The centrepieces, the pyramids, stand alone and even I know that they were created by the gods before the time of the land of the Pharaoh. No hieroglyphs or song tell of the building of such wonders.

The days pass into months and peace in the confines of this place is acceptable compared to hunger that I know is becoming desperate. Even here, there is talk, for in only certain rooms and at the same times each day, is silence the order of things.

In a short time a new world of femininity and sensuality opens up. Soft hands and warm tongues come to my place of rest at night. My body puts on weight to cover bones and skinny arms. A new beauty that can be seen in the polished mirror-like surfaces has emerged, and I see that it is me. Perhaps now

I see why I have been chosen from amongst the thousands of starving. Now with time on my hands my thoughts turn to the young bodies of fluid hands, or the hard bodies of soldiers of the pharaoh, a restlessness that the soft world cannot seem to totally fulfil.

The older women seem to be held with great respect and soothe any discontent that may arise amongst sometimes-jealous lovers.

I become aware that they serve another purpose, never spoken about, as I observe certain woman are absent from the sleeping quarters. Even and more noticeable this time, a favourite companion is absent for many nights in a row. When she returns there is a difference, and it is some nights before she comes to my bed. She is quiet and affectionate, so I am not unhappy, and another obliges. Then her stomach swells and she departs, not apparently to return.

As time passes I am able to work in the gardens, and friendship with one of the elders sees me eventually emerge into the outside world on trips to the river. I even go onto the great barges that transport between Memphis and other cities up and down the river. Always I am in the company of women and, and never permitted to speak more than a passing thank-you to men at gang plank or market place as we travel through.

Conditions are bad. Our bodies are well covered, but still I see the looks of envy from starving children who look our way as we pass. There are fewer people now and many stores in the market place are empty. I wonder if my sister and parents have survived, and perhaps moved away with large parts of the population.

It has been said that, if we return to Canaan, at best we will await servitude, at worst, slavery and starvation.

Many have gone upriver, but knowledge from the elders asks why travel to lands that have not supplied rains to bring the wealth of Egypt in the annual harvest. Some wonder what lies in the lands beyond, lands in fact that may not exist for they are beyond the known worlds. Even in here, there is some sadness, perhaps only to be forgotten in the late times when soft sounds of pleasure quietly close the end of a day, then bring sleep to my now sixteen-year-old body for the day of my birth has just passed.

I am aware that my hips are wide, waist small and breasts full. Each day I go to the cleansing pool, now a place that the shadowy form is on only on occasion behind the screen. Still the process of disrobing and cleansing takes place.

Only when the presence exists does the silent serenity of absolute stillness seem to take place. Twice I have made gentle enquiry; both times the elders have gently chided me, even the one that favours me to the outside world. However, I now know that it is the presence of, if not the Pharaoh, at least those of whatever inner circle or family exists - those who travel amongst the people on rare occasions. Mostly the people are kept remote from the causeway that supplies access to the river highway used by the divine barge, they say on numerous occasions, sometimes to bless the first day of the new son, other days of harvest and fertility festivals.

PHARAOH

Days are long for one who does not dwell amongst his own people, who are to bow down to me and my ancestors who stretch back to the beginning of this so-called civilized world.

In form, my body and those of my offspring still bear the mark of those who came from the stars, and are now only distant myth in all but my image, the one that I stare at in this reflective surface.

She is quiet, as indeed they all are when aware of my presence. This one is quiet when she is not aware of my presence, for I have many ways to view those chosen to bring my children's, children's, children into harmony with those in this world. This is harmony in body, not harmony in knowledge or mind, for the truth for all that passes on this planet is for those that hold absolute authority and forever in all lands.

I think these words with absolute certainty, for the power that stands behind me is within the greatest of all structures, the grand pyramid, centrepiece of what they now call the three kings, Orion's belt.

Nowhere else in the known world is the source of all knowledge of the universe, the engine that drives all the laws of creation. These are all the laws of the one true God, which brought about the existence of this tiny God King, Pharaoh Thutmoses lll, from the infinitely small pattern of creation to the extent of this universe and beyond.

All from the conscious mind of the living universe,
Who in the beginning, or if that is not, time accurate,
At the location of existence, there became awareness.

I am.

All that comes into being will be me.
All one of a universal consciousness

The pattern of existence in universal variety, infinite diversity of fractal division,
> In its simplest form of me,
> The six sided star.

Once again, I turn and view the silent features of the quiet one, small delicate face on a human frame, small head and large body. I glance in the reflection and see my image, a larger head and perhaps different limbs and torso.

Even without the central object of the great pyramid, it is the capacity of the mind that rules over these people, not the power of the arm that wields the sword. It is the power of the mind amongst nations that define boundaries according to the strength of armies and weapons of war.

My ancestors of myth, who came in peace and left artefacts of profound knowledge for a future world as it matured into higher culture, would be astonished at the warlike beings that now rule over the animal kingdom. They alone of all this created world's beings kill their own kind.

All these faces have become lovely to me but this one seems to possess a hidden depth. Will this one deliver me from my sense of aloneness? My sisters and brothers who possess in part the features of kings seem almost entirely self-possessed in their tiny community, complete within their own selves; single units of contentment that want for nothing in my now starving nation.

I have watched her lovely body go from exposed ribs and bony elbows and knees to well-rounded flesh. Flesh fit for any God King. Such flesh fills the room all about her. It is the wonder behind those lovely eyes that I hope hold the key to my mental happiness, the key to my heart.

Time has diminished the features that came so long ago. The alien is almost gone, but I suspect that now the alien from ancient kings from Orion, the three kings, has left the imprint of their features all across this nation, and those of the known world; perhaps beyond the Hittites and Nubians for the pyramid builders knew no boundaries.

The known world was known world, beyond even a God King's recorded knowledge, passed down through priests to those that argue amongst their gods and prostrate themselves before me for a share in the wealth of Egypt. My father, Thutmose ll, has arranged wives for me from amongst my own blood, those known as the Mosis. Their children now abide. They are without my love. I wish a child of love to rule over people who are of the same being, with only that of me that is given with joy.

I will know this woman, but now I will know my Generals, for I have learnt that my father's lands that once kept Egypt's boundaries strong have once again fallen to growing powers in the north and south. New armies stand close to the borders of our ancient land. Can a God King rule over an army when I have learnt that weapons of iron are now manufactured in factories that far exceed the capacity of my own wealthy cities? These cities squander perhaps too great a share on priests who invent gods that are built on the legends of my heritage, now so lost in the mists of time, even to me!

She is not forgotten but will wait. At least she is well fed and protected. In all places, I can observe those who wait on me. Now it is the time of the Generals, the commanders of a sixty-thousand strong army. Once the equal of any in the world, it is now equalled by the Hittites and they tell me rapidly approaching Syrian civilization who inhabit Babylon of old.

Satiah the queen moves to inhabit her place beside me, and the screen rises to reveal the backs of the six men who hold sway over all that stands between the extinction of the greatest gift this world will ever know.

They rise and I immediately see something no king should see in the faces of those who hold power; fear! Fear! My strongest men are afraid. They are afraid of me, of what I will learn of reprisal. Questions are asked of all the enemies of the lands around. All are secure.

I ask, what fear they?

There are no answers. They leave and I know that in this the second year of my reign all is not well. I know that how the kingdom runs is not working.

The pharaoh cannot know what is most important, only that which will please his young mind. My queen is well aware I am not pleased. Those who run the household and grounds are brought forward. No rumours are spoken of and again I see the fear. In all places, these people, or perhaps I, must be failing Egypt!

TUYA

This seems like a timeless place, so boredom has set in. Still I will hold tight for that is better by far than empty belly and dirty body, with stale alcohol of the legions that would have by now been the only chance of survival.

Once again, I have been trusted and Grey Hair has taken me forth into the markets. We move quietly and people part in fear. As the empty stalls open up, with many of the old smells, but less abundant, the figure of a ragged woman falls across my path.

The street is narrow and in her panic, she struggles to rise, catching my long robes, and bringing me down in the dirty gutter.

I hear outrage and strong arms descend upon the poor creature while others more gently begin to raise me. Suddenly I am staring into the starving face of a now haggard once-beauty that is my mother. With a rush of anguish, I realize that they have not left for Canaan and in my good fortune, I have not attempted to help them.

The veil that covers my face prevents recognition. Heavy hands begin to thrust her aside, but anguish from me bursts forth as I command, "Leave her," and I say my mother's name.

She gasps and reaches for me but recognises her error and falls to her knees with face bowed. None may touch those who dwell in the home of the God King.

Adel, my elder, steps between us and all becomes still.

"She is my mother," I say.

I had forgotten that such emotion still survives within this body, so self-absorbed had I become.

"What is it you wish? She is a part of your past."

"I want her fed and clothed. I want a roof over her head."

The veil goes back off the face of the elder, Adel, and I see a look of stunned amazement. She laughs and calls me incorrigible then, to my surprise, hugs me briefly. A first!

No more words are spoken to me, but a soldier is directed with brief instructions, and I am turned away. I do not turn back.

The days pass and I wonder what has occurred. The shadow does not appear at the wall of the washing. Quiet talk says that this is unusual and that perhaps the God King is away. I have learned that the previous king, Thutmose ll, was a great traveller of the river world and even the oceans far beyond. In times of war the king was known to be in such locations.

As we prepare for the place of dining, Adel comes. She does not speak but leads me to the flowing water. I am left with two of those who serve - not of my kind – who wash and perfume me with great care. My body goes through a process I have not before known; hair is removed from many parts and my body anointed with oils. None of my questions is answered and Adel returns with a little food and wine to relax my now tense form.

If before the rooms were splendid, now I move into a world that gleams with gold fabrics and wealth that I am sure must be most of all the great riches of the known world. Even with the wine, my limbs are shaking, and without the adrenaline pumping through my body, I am sure I would be too weak to walk.

Adel tells me quietly, "You are to be honoured above all women of low birth. I will stay with you to guide your obligations to the lord of all lands. You will give only simple answers to any questions that are likely to come your way."

In the next room, I can hear much laughter but my head is lowered to the floor where I kneel. I do not need to turn to know Adel is in the same position.

Time passes and music, incense and the smell of fine food reaches our senses. My body I am sure would cramp if it were not for all the oils they have poured over every inch of my form.

I hear movement and am aware that someone has lit a small flame close to my face. The fumes quickly surround me and are inhaled. Change comes over the room. Now, it is not only the surfaces that have a pure gold glow, but a quick glance shows me that the whole room has taken on great detail.

I realize that the 'me' that seems to exist always feels like a remote person, one who, although present, is not this 'me'. I am no longer afraid and feel only a tranquil serenity.

Firm hands raise me and Adel's voice, from a great distance but seemingly close to me, guides me. I think my body has moved, but it is only vague knowledge to me. In time without measure, hands are on my body and in my breath.

My lips move under another's and I am now not a part of the female world that has seemed to be me. Is this the hard body of a soldier of the king? It is seemingly of no importance for desire rises as if from the very blood that flows through my veins, and a heat in my loins brings only intense awareness to this part of my body.

He is calling me back. I am rising as if from a deep well of water that which comes from the headwaters of the God River Nile. Eyes come into focus and an overwhelming feeling of both desire and love are within me. The eyes are not those of ordinary man but of a size far larger and deeper. I can see no white, only deep black darkness in their depths.

My legs move to receive, and the woman I was is no more. The maiden has departed.

In the second year of my time as consort to the one I now know as Thutmoses lll, a girl child called Tiye has come into this privileged world. I think I love the God King, but I do not think I am in love with the God King. Still the evidence that he favours me is obvious by the time I have spent in the arms of a body strange to ordinary man. Even without the smell of incense that changes my perception of material existence, his power over me has been total. I hungered for his presence and felt more complete after each night than ever before.

As my body swelled, he moved me to a room close to his. I no longer heard my own cries of pleasure, but listened with some sadness and pain to those that now share his pleasure. Adel tends to me often and others are ever-present. Still, life became isolated to the outside world and for a reason I cannot understand I began to miss the people of my birth. The smells and sounds of the street now seem attractive to my fading memory.

It is three moons after the birth of my daughter that Adel eventually allows me to venture forth to the market place once more. The mass of somewhat dirty peasants is both repulsive and pleasant to me, something I would never have thought possible even six moons ago.

My request for knowledge of my mother's fate is ignored. I persist and in two moons, a tiny frail old lady is presented to me in my rooms, then the old world of my youth returns, but in story only. She has been housed and fed, as has my sister, who has now wed and borne a child.

The rains come again and all have given thanks to Amon. However, those of my people have in many cases turned back to Ra, whom many term, the Aten, for when this orange globe shone every day so fiercely, it was only within its power to make way for the waters to fall in distant lands of Nubia so floods would cover our fertile plains.

The flood was strong and land more available for those that survived. For they say that only about one out of three farmers that were before the famine exist now. My sister's husband is a farmer. The sounds of many of the children who no longer exist will never call in the evening twilight.

From my new privileged position of favoured consort, who only sometimes returns to the king's bed, I see great lords and kings from all Egypt's lands bring offerings and negotiations to the table of wisdom.

Egypt's borders have suffered from attack during the harsh seasons, now past.

Today a strange request has come, for the Pharaoh has had troubled dreams. All the prophets of all lands have been called to give an understanding of the meaning. None has been able to interpret the hidden message of troubles from the mind of a God King.

My mother has spoken with great reverence of a young Israelite sold by his own brothers into servitude while making both requests and offerings to the lords and gods of this land. Today he comes, an unheard of event, and a result of careless words between passions, from my lips.

The God King will hear from a slave of Israel. I sit quietly behind, to one side, as many come and go. Great wealth passes before me in offering, from those who rule for people. All bow down in this presence.

My body has delivered me to great heights of privilege. Now a small mouth that suckles upon my breast gives even greater security to my position. The room is being cleared now and the great hall stands empty. Few are made privy to the inner thoughts of Thutmoses lll. Those who repeat his thoughts will probably perish in manners that will persuade others to discretion.

From a side door, he enters. Not a great entrance for one as low as he, whose only offering may see him dead within the passing of this day.

They have bathed him and clothed him in a simple white robe. He is little more than a boy, one who has left his boyhood behind but who still stands several years from hardened muscle of fully developed manhood. With face downcast, he approaches.

I am aware that my words have brought him to this fate. If I could, I would beg leniency from my lord for this one of my mother's people. I am aware that he must feel alone and have great fear. He has been taught well and his forehead rests upon the floor.

Words bring him to his knees, then to his feet. His face remains lowered. I now wonder what it is that hidden eyes appear like. I feel movement in my body, a powerful attraction to this youthful form. Before now, these are feelings that only the God King has brought forth from my loins. This is different, for the warmth rises to my breast. He seems to have an unexplained presence.

I barely hear the words for they are soft, and for a lowly Israelite's ears only. Even the highest advisers are not present. Although soft, they reach my ears and these are the words.

"In my country, you are known as Yuya. You are the one known by your people as Joseph. A mother of your people has spoken well of you. Speak, Israelite, so that guidance may be present in the future path of a king. Speak, Israelite, so that your family will walk tall in the light of Amon and the people of this sacred river.

"Who are you in servitude to and where do you dwell?"

The eyes do not rise, but to my amazement when the voice comes forth, it has no quiver. His words are firm and clear. "I serve only the prison wardens; my home is the lowest in your land. I have only the one god whose symbol Aten shines forth every day to bring forth light to your world, but a world of darkness that covers my soul as I reside beneath the soil that grows grain."

"How is this so?"

"I served as master in the house of Potiphar, captain of your guard. I was accused of making sport against the wishes of the head wife, and lucky to escape with my life. While in prison, I told the meaning of dreams, and those released have carried their tales. Only the success of their good fortune is remembered. The prophet is small in their memories so I remained in prison."

Pharaoh speaks quietly. "If you speak the truth of my night visions, you will not be forgotten. The word of the wife of Potiphar will be verified on your behalf and your future will be judged anew."

I hear words spoken and I know Potiphar's very frightened wife will be shortly on her way to answer many questions. This man does not look like one who has to beg favour of the fairer sex, this I know with all the private parts of my body without even a glance at eyes still hidden from all.

Pharaoh speaks again. "Tell me of your beginning of prophesy. Tell of early success, if that is the right term, and the effect on yourself and those who may benefit from such gifts. Tell me how it is so that you have such gifts. Is it the word of the god, Amon Ra?"

He speaks clearly. "It is the word of the God of my father's people. All knowledge is the word of the one God, the Creator of all. This is not Amon or Ra, but perhaps Ra is the best face of the image of creation from a world beyond normal vision."

Pharaoh states, "But your vision is not normal, and lives will depend upon it."

To my amazement, Joseph shows no fear, but seems only to grow with a strange inner strength, as if he has a glow of energy that surrounds and protects him. My eyes turn to those of Tut and now my body begins to shudder, for the power of what seems about like two kings or perhaps divine energy flows through my body. I know, as I always know, that he enters not only my body, but also my very thoughts. His thoughts are gentle within my heart, full of love, if not gentle in the turmoil that flows through the parts that are mother of the blood *Mosis* in all royal children.

THUTMOSES LLL

For the first time the one who is favoured by me above all women has desired the strength of another's loins. For this fact alone, he should forfeit his life. What man is this that stands without fear in the presence of his death? What manner is his god, for I sense no drugs in his bearing or the clarity of his mind.

Although I reach into his presence, I can only sense alertness and good health, and perhaps holiness of this simple prison slave, lowliest of all who have stood before me. The food sent to sustain him in his subterranean world should have seen that health compromised.

These words follow from the prison slave.

"When I was seventeen seasons, I had a dream that was both a revelation and my downfall."

The first he describes as the result of harvest when all bowed down before him.

Then he stops for a time to test any king's patience, before continuing. "I dreamed that the sun was my father. The moon was my mother, and eleven stars were my brothers.

All bowed down to the twelfth star."

My heart sinks as he tells me the meaning of his dream and I hear a gasp from behind as one who has already expressed herself beyond requirement lets go of self-control again.

He says the sun is his father, the moon is his mother, and eleven stars his brothers. All bow down before him. His father gave his dream his blessing. His brothers were disgusted and considered his favoured position intolerable. They cast him into a well, then at the instigation of his brother Judah sold him to a passing caravan for twenty pieces of silver.

His dream interpretation I can see is right but it is the older ancient knowledge that goes unheard amongst his words that concerns me, and the obvious fact that Tuya has understood the ancient wisdom he has ignored.

For where his knowledge has risen into her young heart, I do not know. His heresy to all ancient gods is clear.

Those for all time, and still with Horus, have worshipped the sun. Here Amon Ra has worshipped the moon as the holder of all fertility and the feminine.

The twelve stars are the twelve signs of the zodiac that govern the full season and give rise to many of the ancient worships.

He has in fact interpreted his dream to mean that a large part of all that Egypt and all the world gone before holds sacred will, including the gods, bow down before this lowly slave. It is not anger that I feel, perhaps I would laugh aloud, but his purpose still lies before me. He still has a chance to see Amon Ra the Aton rise tomorrow morning. My quick glance to the rear is not necessary to sense Tuya's fear. This man has still not raised his face. He need not fear offending me by looking upon my form, for he has offended not only the God King, but nearly every other deity both present and past. Perhaps it is fortunate for him that I hold scant belief in any of them, but not very fortunate. Still, he is, I think, more interesting than all the kings who come laden with golden gifts.

JOSEPH (YUYA)

Pharaoh is talking again. I feel no fear for I have suffered enough. When they brought me forth from the cells, I presumed it was my final journey. I have lost my family, risen to a good position for one in servitude, then plunged again. If my god is calling me from this world, then I am resigned. I am now only vaguely aware that this pharaoh has become aware that I interpret dreams. To be more accurate my inner self seems to listen to the word of God.

His words carry to me for what seems too long for a dream. How can mere man, Pharaoh or not, remember such detail? It takes time for me to attach concentration to his words, so by then I will not even with divine help be able to explain his nocturnal journey to him. These may well be my final moments.

I can feel another's eyes upon me now. A feeling of ancient connection or familiarity, it seems to feel like almost shock. This brings my mind to focus. I hear his final words as only a part of an extensive dream.

He finally says, "Seven lean cows rose up out of the river and devoured seven fat cows.

Then came seven withered ears of grain, which devoured seven fat ears of grain."

I have nothing to lose and listen as quiet descends upon the three present.

All becomes still within, and as if in another's voice, and from a distant one that is almost not me, I hear myself say, "All that is spoken of before the lean cows is of no importance to the wellbeing of the people. It is the private world of God Kings and not for the voice of a lowly slave. God will only give voice for the wellbeing of many peoples, so it is spoken through Joseph who stands in favour of the Creator.

"Seven years of abundance will be followed by seven years of famine. All the crops of all lands must yield to Pharaoh a percentage of every crop to fill silos across all Egypt's middle kingdom."

THUTMOSES LLL

This man who speaks in voice has now abandoned all conversation and stands mute. No word is forthcoming on all that I have said before.

In one sentence, he seems to have brought all that did not bear explanation to irrelevance. With one sentence, if he is right; and I have only wealth perhaps greater than gold to gain by hearing his words. In one sentence, a man of poverty if nothing else, has delivered me wealth not only from foreign kings and princes, but almost every second citizen of all my lands.

In one sentence, if he is right about famine, he will have delivered me total control over all the people as both their total provider, their wisdom and their salvation over seven years. While my enemies starve, my vassals will build even greater frontiers for Egypt's future, for Egypt's God King.

Perhaps indeed my beloved Tuya's body had good reason to sing to the presence of this lowly slave.

He will dine well tonight and for the next fourteen years if his god knows how to moderate other parts of his wisdom. In time, I will decide his place for he may be more worthy than those that wait outside with jealous minds to cast him into chains for the executioner's good will.

TUYA

His voice is clear as if it is coming from within my very soul. Then there is more, for my body has already had more than its share of confusion. His words ring clear of the father sun and mother moon and the twelve stars. I feel a burning tingle upon my upper arms, and look upon the blue tattoos that circle both my arms in the manner of both my sister and my mother. Tattoos, my mother tells me, pass from generation to generation down through the ages of the females of our blood. His words bring images of worlds so ancient and images long gone but in voice that all seems to belong to the one but coming to me from some forgotten perhaps lifetime.

Then I feel another sensation upon my body and open my eyes, from what can only be called a trance, to the words of my lord as he guides me forward to stand before one with still bowed head. One who to my knowledge now stands mute and has still not looked upon a body since he entered our presence.

Tut's words come. "You will guide him to Adel, who will see he has good quarters and those that will keep him in safe-keeping until he is ready to do my bidding. For now, I have to find someone in all these lands who is suited to carry out his words."

FUNERAL MASK OF TUYA

JOSEPH

I am alive. I am out of jail. I will eat good food. All this should be
of such profound shock that nothing else could exist but my change

of fortune. The part of my mind that deals with such is only aware of exhaustion. All energy for such thoughts has left and a different energy is upon me, the energy of almost another entity.

There is absolute clarity of the one whose face I still have not looked upon. Her body glides before me. My eyes are locked upon the wonder of femininity, but it is not desire from this jail-fed body I feel - it is an emotion beyond any I have ever felt. I know that this form, which I sense belongs to the most power-ful being in all known lands, a God King's woman, is to be the centre of my existence. If sense would return, I would know that to love such as she would not see me return to chains. Torture and slow death is the only reward this folly can bring.

Before long, she stops, and slowly turns, and we gaze upon each other. Eyes lock. Not a glimmer of a smile appears, but I know that we are both equally aware that a centre of existence has arrived for both of us. I could no more love another woman than take my own life. For this one I feel sure I would lay down my own life. That is probably what I am doing in gazing upon her in such obvious devotion.

Her voice comes like the sound of doves in the evening time. She says, "You are gifted my young lord, for that is what you will surely become in this kingdom. You are wise and know that restriction must rule for the time to come, with a lady of Thutmoses himself."

I simply nod. No words can describe my state, but no words are needed. She has gazed at my soul. We proceed and I am left alone in a room from where I can hear the sounds of many fe-male voices.

They return and a woman of advanced years takes the place of the one who is retreating, to once again attend the God King.

I feel no jealousy. No jealousy can enter the level of connection that has come from some world I feel is beyond the only one I have so far known.

Time passes and a world opens up that is beyond the experience of the most noble from the land of Canaan, my Israelite people. The lady, Tuya, becomes a shadow. Only one woman and now an elderly man attend me. He is one of the bloodline, a relative of Thutmoses, with his elongated head and large eyes. The words are few and at times I do not think he needs to talk, as he answers my very thoughts before they have left my lips.

At the end of one moon, or so I am told, for I have lost track of time, I am once more back before the God King. His words come and I sense that he knows that I have wondered where the lady Tuya has gone.

"You have learned well, and now have a fine knowledge of where the harvests fall in many parts of the empire of my throne."

The old cousin is beside me, and as we discussed, maps are laid out of all the lands. Within days to come, it will be known where storage for the vast quantities of grain will be built, from the fourth cataract of the Nile, to the Hittites and beyond. In all the lands, a percentage of all grain will pass to Pharaoh, in all years of good season. I pray quietly that the seven seasons of my young mind do not come to a sudden drought.

A glance at Thutmoses tells me nothing but I know from a sudden thrust, almost of pain to my skull, that he believes I would be well served to give positive thought to the harvests' wellbeing of his kingdom and leave carnal thoughts alone.

That night, a young woman of great beauty attends me. Although aware she is to be all I require, I am unable to see her as the one. She remains on the pallet in my room and her company, if not of the flesh, is full of deep quality.

Moons pass and my staff become the fingers of both hands. Through them, I am able to communicate with representatives of all lands. In over fifty locations along the Nile, silos for grain are given priority even over the temples of the most prominent gods. I am learning quickly the ways of safe storage. More importantly, I am learning quickly the importance of communicating with those who will administer the taxes that have become in the minds of peasant landowners a gift to the gods as thanks to the good harvest to come.

As time passes rains fall in far lands, and floods arrive in others both near and far. The gods have rewarded the landowners and few complain for they see the gift as assurance of good years to come. My mind does not forget the one of whom I have only heard whispers, and in time I learn that she has a daughter called *Tiye*. Now she seems even further away from being the partner of my dreams.

My body reaches out in loneliness and young maidens pass through my bedchamber. My body is fulfilled but my heart remains aloof. My life is too busy.

In the second season, I travel and am amazed at the vast storage that is growing across all the lands, the great majority within Egyptian borders. Vast numbers of cats protect this golden harvest. If it is to waste with weevils and vermin, my future will waste with it.

Seven good seasons pass and now I have a new worry, for surely, if good seasons persist, all this grain will be of no avail. So while all look to the gods for the annual flood my warehouses are full, and I fear going to the God King to tell him that perhaps the people will not need to pay taxes in the future. Then the rains fail. The river waters slow, crops shrivel and fields turn to dust. From all over the known world, people turn to Pharaoh.

Pharaoh turns to me.

I have barely seen him over all the years. Now once more I am before the same god man, and without looking up, I hear quiet conversation, and am aware of the voice of the one whom I have looked upon only once seven floods past.

This body that gazes upon the marble floor is no longer skin and bone but comfortable with excess. Words of praise come my way and I am bidden to rise, and for the first time face Thutmoses, who holds all life in the palm of his hand.

His hand reaches out and one who still holds my heart steps into view with a young daughter of both the beauty of Tuya and the feature of the *Mosis*, meaning they who have the royal blood. No others in all the kingdoms to my knowledge have alien features, the mark of the kings, those who have ruled in this land since the time of the pyramids and before written history.

My legends of Horus, Isis and Osiris are out of the minds of vast time. Now I gaze upon all three, finally coming to rest upon Thutmoses.

"Your predictions and interpretations of my dreams seem to have come true. Many times, I have been told to sell grain, for wise men have told me it would spoil, and that your words are not in the best interests of my people. Now the river runs dry and already people gather at the silos around Egypt and beyond. Already they are weak.

"If seven years of drought follow, few people will survive without the Pharaoh's dreams, without my wise council. You have been more important to Egypt than the generals of my strongest armies. The armies of the Hittites and all else will grow weak without the grain that they must purchase from Egypt. My armies guard them well.

"Now I seek your wise council as to how to feed the peoples of the known world, how to gain favour and long wisdom so that many will survive to bow before wisdom, not might."

I simply say, "I have no family, no wife or children at hearth. It is beyond me to know how much is consumed by how many between floods."

My eyes go to Tuya and our eyes lock. My mouth goes dry and all words fade. There is nothing else in all the kingdom that matters. The thought comes to me that for whatever reason, without the love of this woman my life has no reason to exist. I know without doubt that she, by gazing upon me, feels the same, and risks life for no greater danger exists than the anger of Pharaoh. No greater risk could we take.

I know without doubt that the God King reads every thought and perhaps feels the despair and wonder that exists in both our hearts.

I kneel slowly and turn to Pharaoh. "My life now has no meaning for all that is of value can never be realized. My life belongs to you. It may end now for I cannot function without that which cannot be mine."

To my amazement I see no anger in the face of Thutmoses. Perhaps there is compassion there.

"For seven seasons," he says, "I have heard the gentle weeping of the one who has borne my favourite daughter. I have many wives and children beyond counting. If Tuya's heart belonged to me she would have walked perhaps first amongst my wives. She will come to your office, not your quarters, and guide you in the ways of hungry families, for it is from the Canaanites that she rose. The child Tiye will grow in the presence of the bloodline.

"I release the body of the Mother, whose heart has been warm and faithful but never mine to release. These things I have known. In the time of my choosing, if it is to be so, I will release her from the king's chambers to find her own home. Within time, if you remain in good faith, you shall both be honoured, second only to Pharaoh across all the lands.

"Continue to do your job well. Both of you bring love to my presence for I am able to absorb the feelings of all that are pure in the heart. This gift is rare in my presence."

His hand reaches out and the child quietly climbs into the lap of one who is beyond reach to children of all lands.

Tears flow quietly down the cheeks of the one, and in this time only I am perhaps close to the mind of the God King in feeling and reaching the mind and perhaps soul of another beyond one's own body.

The next morning I return to the chambers where all records are kept and many staff attend. To my surprise, for the first time in perhaps seven floods, they are empty. My heart leaps in my chest. Has the Pharaoh changed his mind? Is this the end, and am I to be replaced? Have I lost Tuya after waiting so long?

A door opens and Thutmoses's old relative, with the God King blood, enters, leaving the door open behind him. As he passes through the room I see his expression of humour and rare words as he speaks only what's required. "You of little faith. Remain true to your heart and all will be as it will be written into history far beyond you. For it is not the grain to save hungry people, but the system of taxation that has risen to create new financing for a world into far distant futures." The door closes behind him.

I turn to the wonder of existence far more important than all words. The arms of a woman enclose my heart. A body of a matron but I know it will be more beautiful to me than all Pharaoh's gifts of youthful beauty across the years. No people arrive in the chambers that day or the next. In that time the body and all else are bound together for what future remains to Tuya and Joseph, son of Jacob, the boy who was condemned by his eleven brothers and sold for twenty pieces of silver by Judah.

In the second year of the great dry, people come in such numbers that we now control a part of Pharaoh's army. They organise and help distribute. I say 'we' for Tuya has become a constant part of my life, and sometimes Tiye too, but she remains loyal to her God King father even beyond her mother.

A messenger arrives to report that a large contingent from Canaan has arrived and I wonder about my long-lost father, he who so favoured me with the distant memory of the coat of many colours that perhaps helped lead to my eventual destruction at the hands of my eleven brothers.

With Tuya as companion I take the rare decision to open the doors of the large hall where decisions are made daily as to who is worthy to eat. In other words, who will live or die in these disastrous times.

The word goes out that the visitors are from the tribe of Jacob and I wait anxiously. In no time, the crowd parts and soldiers escort five men, whom I barely recognise. They immediately drop to their knees, face to the floor, before the two in this Egypt who are second and third only to Thutmoses himself.

My words come quietly. "What are you to Jacob of Canaan?"

"The four eldest sons and Judah."

I ask how many sons and daughters Jacob had and if he still lived in the land of Canaan. "How do his crops fair and those of the village of the house of Jacob?"

They tell me, "He has eleven sons, two daughters and he is well. A second wife now lives in place of the mother who has now entered eternal sleep."

I call for a scribe who holds records of the houses of Canaan. After glancing at the list, too vast for me to even observe in such a short time, I look up and comment that the house of Jacob has twelve sons. "Do you seek to deceive me? Your request for grain is granted in only so much as is required to go home and return with twelve brothers and your father."

Judah cries out, "The youngest was lost to the desert tribes and has long been lost to the grief of his father."

I turn away and tears that have not flowed for any other than my love, flow.

Two moons pass and word comes that they have arrived in the capital of the entire world. I watch them come and I can see that regardless of hard times my father is still a powerful man in the land of Canaan. Still hunger is the one thing amongst all that makes all people equal in status. For a rich man in a land of no food is the same as a poor once all substance is gone. No families are given enough to sell to those with money to spare. Thieves die quickly if they attack the escorts that travel with the food of the God King. Yes, the rich like Jacob had grain in storage, enough to feed their clan and many of the local villagers, but by the second year that was gone. Even kings above the second cataract have sent representatives to Pharaoh's silos.

The night passes and once again the sons of Jacob are separated by guards from their own countrymen. I see fear in their faces. My father remains at the rear of his eleven sons. On his face, I see no expression. He is strong amongst his own people.

Tuya parts the curtain and, as told, asks, "Where are the twelve sons of Jacob? Only when you have answered the question to please the king's man will you be given the means to feed your people."

Once again Judah and the oldest brother speak over one another, "He was stolen by the outlaws of the desert caravans."

TUYA

I see them now. Fear on their faces and confusion for my love long sold into slavery by these eleven. As far as they believe, he was long ago worked to death or, as many slaves are, allowed to starve when food supplies diminished.

I say, "Bring forth the father."

He now stands before me. This one is without fear, but perhaps a guarded anger.

He speaks. "Why have I been summoned by the king's man when he does not appear? Why do you and he cause an old man pain, for I have grieved long all these thirteen passes of the seasons for the one who had the insight perhaps from the mind of God himself. For no greater loss has a father sustained. Now I stand to lose not only my other kin, but those who dwell in Canaan whose care comes before my own life."

I reply, "It is known that the twelfth son brought twenty pieces of silver. The price for your grain will be three times twenty plus the normal rate."

The father turns to the eldest son who starts to retrieve wealth not known by my own now dead parents of birth, also children of Israel. I stop him and say, "It was to Judah that the twenty pieces of silver passed, so it is from this hand so it shall pass."

Slow recognition of the meaning of my words dawns on the face of the old man, who is so close to the heart of my Yuya who stands one step away behind the screen. Now the expression collapses and I see age wither the features. Anger to desolation passes before my eyes.

The screen parts and Joseph steps down to take the slumping shoulders and raise him up. There are tears upon his cheeks and once again, expressions of both concerned sadness and some strange joy to be in the presence of one so often spoken of by his own tongue.

I hear his words. "Now your twelve sons stand before you, you old man, great man of Canaan, who would starve before those of his own people. As for you, my brothers, for that is who you are, what say ye now of the prophecy of one who you disdained, and would have slain if it was not for the misguided leniency of Judah, amongst you?"

I know that if Joseph were Thutmoses, all before him plus the families would perish - the old man out of pity for he would perish through grief.

Seven years pass and once again, the rains come. The great silos are now empty. The nations of Centre Earth have survived. Pharaoh seems to have gained a quiet, strong gentleness only allowed to one who rules with perhaps the greatest power of all the eighteenth dynasty rulers, a power that has seen my position as consort and mother now to the children of Joseph as well as Tiye. Tiye has grown to great beauty, with all the features of *Mosis*, or as some term it, Moses, the royal blood, in her beauty.

Joseph has the full control of the collecting of tax that now comes not only in the form of grain, but labour or produce of other goods, even gold and valuable products from far kingdoms. All remains at a low rate, for fat bellies through years of drought are soon forgotten if hardship is imposed upon all the tribes of the many kingdoms.

Amenhotep lll now grows to manhood and has taken his tiny sister of three years of age called Sitamun as his first wife. The ancient blood of the line of Horus must be kept as pure as possible. Amun Ra priests, those strongest in the holders of ancient mysteries, hold strong the blood of Moses. The eleven brothers of the tribe of Jacob are given security, and although rarely seen by Joseph, remain humble, I see with fear, for he now holds the power of life and death over them. I think he feels this is sufficient punishment. Men who live in fear have little quality of life.

Jacob the father comes often and Joseph often to him. We hold estates of our own in Canaan and often it is our principal residence. The father returns to strength needed by one who holds value for a large tribe.

Eventually, his life passes, and that of Thutmoses lll.

Now a new king, Amenhotep lll, with his young first wife, Sitamun, rule over all these lands and it is with great joy that I see the love of Amenhotep blossom for the first of my womb, Tiye, who is first amongst beauty and gentle wisdom of all who hold the blood of Moses. She, who perhaps is now forgotten in the passing of the years, holds the blood of my Israelite heritage, a mother of good blood, a father who perhaps I know, for the one who gave me birth had few choices as those who starve are forbidden choices.

Illness takes hold of my body during the third year of Tiye's marriage to Amenhotep, and I know with both sadness and joy of all that has been my life. I am soon to find out if any of the priests that inhabit these lands in such abundance are correct about my journey to come. I favour the Aten, one god who is first amongst my mother's people. I see great sadness in the one I love, and my children. I am surprised at the number of people who seem genuinely saddened by my time to come. Amenhotep and Tiye endeavour to bring us to Thebes but I feel drawn to the estate amongst the now dead Jacob's people. I will pass over amongst the spirits of my ancestors. Those that sold my Yuya so many years ago seemed to have drifted to distant lands. Perhaps there they can rest easy with the journey of their own future souls.

As my time comes closer pain seems to dull and the world around me blurs. No longer consort to the third most powerful man in the known world, death or passing over returns me to the simple hungry peasant who fell at the feet of the king's men. The love of the one who never leaves my side is the one noble claim left to me. Consciousness comes and goes and the world of dreams seems to take on a greater reality than the world I am leaving.

Now I see Joseph as a man of many faces. I am too weak to be confused, but all these many forms of the one I love seem to be him in bodies over vast time. Even in woman's form, I feel love for him. As death nears, I recognise that many of the men and occasional women are me in life after-life. So it is that I depart this world with absolute certainty that I will see my beloved again. I know that love, like life, does not cease as the physical form returns to the earth of my body's ancestors.

Now I know that it is not race or religion that matters, for my ancestors are not a straight line of physical blood. They are a straight line of spiritual consciousness that is home to all colours, races and religions.

As my consciousness departs for the last time this once lovely form, I feel great comfort and a sense that could be called elation.

A great consciousness becomes once again complete as I return to the one complete awareness, the conscious living universe, the source of all things physical and mental, to infinity.

End of Tuya, Consort of Joseph (Yuya), Mother of Tiye

Author's Note

Tiye is the mother of Akhenaten, who some believe could have been the source of the exodus Moses. In this fiction, he is one who leads the exodus with those he chooses to protect the Moses (which means, in Egyptian, the blood of the royal line).

THE NAME MOS(i)ES: In 18th dynasty Egypt - *CHILD OF* OR *LEGITIMATE, LEGAL.*

Five royal bloodlines had the name Thutmoses, sometimes read as Thutmose, or Thuthmes.
The first king was Amosis, his brother Hamose, plus other royal blood known were Ramosis, Ptahmosis, and Ahmose.

This story is fiction but to give it a sense of reality such things as the word Moses or the like having great relevance at the approximate time the Israelites may have left Egypt. Many legends and perhaps biblical, Christian and Moslem stories are no doubt based on historical occurrence, if not, perhaps, fact.

Eighteen

Akhenaten, Sephron and General Aye to

the Exodus

I n the time between lives, new life comes to high people. A beauty for all ages is born in the form of Sitamun's and Amenhotep lll's child, Nefertiti: to marry Akhenaton.

SEPHRON

I am born again and die in the year 1418 BC, 3412 years before *The Time of the Writing*. I am born to simple parents without access to a doctor; life is cheap and often short for many in the days of the Pharaohs.

In a time Earth measures as three years my consciousness emerges again in the year 1416 BC, this time to parents of means, a father with land and ancient trade.

It is the only fortune that seems to arrive with this life, for when my eyes open no light appears. I shall travel this journey with all my senses directed to touch and hearing of all that exists in a blind person's universe. The touch of the wind, but above all the sound of the wind, and all that I can hear, must become my eyes. People are not always kind; patience for those who cannot help themselves is not in abundance.

All those people that see all that I touch and hear; these I can only imagine the shape of. Even the dog that has become my companion is beautiful, for beauty is to me not of the eyes, but of kindness and warmth. Affection comes to me from four legs without question and from two legs only at whatever time they care to please.

I help where I can, but those that serve in a house of wealth such as ours are expected to clean and wash, and all such jobs as may be possible for such as me. With age, I have learned to gather my clothes and wash body after toilet. My days are long, and when all falls silent, I know that what brings warmth but not light to my life has entered the under-world. This is what they call the night. I have learned that in this world the eyes of all are at times of low moon, my world of darkness.

So it is that the night has become my special time and if good fortune smiles upon me I can take my dog and move into the street. This I do when all the household sleeps, for my parents have, for my own sake, created a prison for me. This to one who has never known the world's differences is worse than the prison of the eyes that they say shine with a light that has beauty I will never behold. For I am told that in this year (1377 BC) of my twentieth birthday, that although I have never know the love of a man, and have no offer of a husband, I am pleasing to the eye. Few men want a woman for consort who can give no direction to household or finance. My parents are kind enough to inform me that the burden that I am to them would be the same for all men of this Amenhotep lll's kingdom.

I have learned that the world of the night is a dangerous and sometimes violent place. It is a world of strong drink and often mind-destroying drugs, a world where, I have heard the servants say, women who use their bodies for the pleasure of men, for money and other gain, are in abundance. These things I learn from whispers that the household staff utter in voices that no ordinary passer-by can hear. My eyes are my ears and I hear all that few others can gauge.

In the darkness, I have become worldlier than those that dwell in the light and those that should love me can suspect. My home is amongst many of the wealthy, and enclosed by walls that separate the privileged from those who inhabit the violent world. That world is forbidden to me and for this reason also the world of my imagination. So, it is that I enter the streets and with my one true four-legged friend, count each step so I have the freedom to return. In this way, I have become familiar with my enclosed world and move with confidence to the walls for my dark eyes on the side of my head to observe the occasional noises of the dark. From all of this I learn of lust and greed. This is how I learn of the birth of the children of Pharaoh, and his many wives: firstborn Nefertiti, daughter to Sitamun; firstborn son, Thutmoses, to be known if he takes the throne of Egypt as the fourth Tut to bear the name Moses (the blood of the royal line) the legitimate heir to the God Kings.

There are two entrances to the compound and the guards that keep it secure have become aware of my silent presence. They bring food for my dog so it has become my practice to bring sweetmeats from our kitchen to them on their long nights of boredom. They are men and I think they take pleasure in my presence so, as time goes by, I stay longer and they answer some of my questions about the world outside and those voices that I hear pass in the dark - their darkness, my normal world.

So it is that in the year 1393, my twenty-first year, I learn of the murder of the son of Amenhotep and second wife Tiye. In the quietness of the night, one who should know little hears that the priests of Amon, the protectors of the God King's bloodline, are believed to be responsible. It is said that the mother of the first in line is not of pure blood, but from those of Israel, child of the favourite of Thutmoses lll, Tuya of pure Canaan blood.

Tiye, the first love of Amenhotep, held all the beauty of her mother and much appearance of the God Kings. She was not to the beliefs of those who follow the ancient laws of the lawgivers, Horus's bloodline, with the knowledge of pyramid builders and star dwellers. This, like most of the world, is mystery to me but fills my lonely world and helps hold sadness at bay.

Then my father dies and my mother takes a new man and moves into a new household. The arrangements made for me are not meant for me to know, like all things, but I do know. I am to be given to the cult of Isis, to enter the world of priestesses who serves those who honour this goddess of the Nile. My little dog is old now but one of the few possessions to go with me.

I shed few tears as my mother says goodbye. I hear no sadness in her voice, but as she departs I hear her say, "She is a beauty that no man has known. Perhaps the goddess will be well pleased."

So, I am given training for the first time. This time the service of the goddess is repetitive and even in the darkness I am able to perform the rituals required of me. For the first time in my life, I sleep in the presence of other bodies. Company becomes a new and to my surprise a pleasurable experience. In their dark time, female hands seek me out and cover my mouth when my body stirs to sensations I did not know existed. I know that this training in their dark time is not in the service of Isis but whispers tell me it is a secret, one that will please the goddess. I take joy in the soft contours of female form and can only wonder what difference it may be to have a husband, and perhaps a child of my own, born to a normal life.

My little dog dies and I know my first experience of grief. The pain seems to enter me as I wake and lasts long. I try to sleep but the servants of Isis seek my body and sleep is less regular now.

In the year 1394, I am twenty-two and to my astonishment, I learn that no person in this place knows my name. Then I realise that few people have ever uttered my name. In a world that revolves around sound, I now feel that I have the freedom to choose the sound I like most as my own to cherish. I become *Sephron* and tell those in the quiet time that this is who I am. They continue to give favour to my form and words remain few. It seems that many think the blind have little reason to hear or talk.

My life changes early in the year 1394. I hear the sound of a baby crying. Soft urgent voices are close by as I perform my duties. Someone turns her voice in my direction and warns caution. The response is that I am blind and can pose no threat. They are to convey a royal infant by river in the celebration of Isis, this day to come. The child is in peril as Thutmoses the firstborn was killed, so this child is in grave danger. The palace of the consort Tiye can be reached and the brother General Aye will arrange safe harbour. The destination is to be unknown, and those that escort the child are to be silenced forever.

I hear the words, "Tuya's family outside the walls of Zahn in the land of Goshen." Then the words come to me, "Her ears are not blind, and she has knowledge to be silenced."

A child arrives in our presence and I am summoned to attend. I am mortally afraid, for this journey will be the death of those who have too much knowledge.

I say quickly, "I am good with babies," and for the first time in my life feel a soft bundle enter my arms. For the first time the crying ceases. All voices are silent, and I am, as always, aware that I am being observed.

"She will go with the child. The normal number of priestesses shall travel but none shall return. There will be a small contingent of guards. No suspicion must be aroused."

I do not return to my quarters, and the child's care becomes my duty. Another enters and I realize she is with milk so we become three. Each time the child leaves our company it expresses its anger or distress. It is only quiet in our company. I cannot flee. Fear is less in the care of the child. The child of Amenhotep lll and Queen Tiye is only a child when in my arms, but for some reason his tiny fingers seem to bring a gentling to my alarm. This tiny God King takes on a meaning that is perhaps close to every Egyptian who lives; those that see and those that only hear.

It is dark when the three of us feel the movement of what I can only guess is the sacred river below the enclosure that must be the Isis temple barge. The sun warms and new voices arrive. There is constant music and the child settles. Still, even his cries may go unheard in all that is occurring above us. We are in a confined space, I think as far from all others as can be arranged.

Time passes and we arrive at what I know is another temple at Karnak. Voices and music depart. We are moved to another vessel; by the movement of water, I can tell it is much smaller, but still we are under the deck. Men take to oars and I hear the wind in the sail above. Many hours pass and the sun returns to my dark world twice before the boat stops. Now there are new voices in authority and I hear General Aye's name.

The child is lifted from my arms and I am turned back towards the boat. There is great distress. The wet nurse cannot calm the god infant. Her words become my salvation for I hear death in the direction of the departing vessel. The child will settle only with the two of us present. She has become part of his world for this moment of transition. The blood of Moses is, for the time being, best in the care of a blind woman. She knows not where she goes. Her death will be wasted and her life is of use by he who counts at this time.

I who have never felt the touch of a man in consort now become a mother in all but the delivery of food from my breast. The wet nurse is no more to the child. When he has fed, he cries for me. For the second time in my life, I feel needed. The love of my little dog is replaced by this tiny bundle, who seems able to convey his feelings almost as thoughts that become my thoughts. He is inside my head, even closer than the soft touch of hands that entered my body in recent times.

These times do not return, for very few people visit this child and when they do, I try to withdraw. This, the child seems to understand. He no longer cries and I get the feeling he has claimed me and I am, in his infant, but not-so-young mind, not to be shared. His thoughts seem to be clear to me and I am sure, are far in advance of whatever thoughts may have briefly visited me at life's beginning.

A voice becomes familiar to me and accepted by the child. Both of us know that he is our main protector. For a time he has taken the provider's job from the infant's father and mother, Tiye, whose palace I now know is my new home. Although I am now virtually a prisoner, for in what must be a huge building amongst lavish gardens, I am free to move in only four rooms. One of these is for ablutions, and I gather another looks out upon open space for I feel the sun directly upon my face. Perhaps it is private grounds (perhaps a small courtyard garden), only occupied to tend the plants. Even to my ears, all move quietly. The child of my care is to remain hidden from almost all eyes for the term of his early years. His connection to me is probably the only thing that keeps me alive for those that can move freely in public to talk at will, would not live long if in attendance upon the God King infant. For the first time in my life, I see virtue in darkness and am aware that my blindness has given me this confusing and dangerous privilege.

One day as Aye enters too swiftly even for my ears, I am unable to withdraw in time. My body is in the process of being dried, for the child and I bath together, eat together, and even at times sleep together. I raise the towel while trying to attend Amenhotep. I am stuck. I cannot dress. I cannot leave. I cannot ask he who rules over vast armies of the king, and he who rules over me, to withdraw.

He commands and I obey. "Dry the child."

The towel is taken from me. Another reaches my trembling hands. I go to the child aware of my nakedness in front of a man, I think for the first time in my life. There is absolute silence. Child King's thoughts are silent. Even he waits to see what might happen!

The silence remains. Darkness has taught me that silence means one such as this is still because something has his full attention. I am deeply distressed to think that that something is I.

I wrap the child and place him in safe bedding. Even he remains uncharacteristically silent. Now I seek my own clothing, but a hand touches the side of my face, lifting my hair. "Be still!"

I freeze and stand with my hands over my breasts and other private parts. My hands are parted, then raised and in time I feel the loose garment I wear descend to cover my now grateful body. No words are spoken, but I feel the brush of his hand upon my cheek, and am surprised to feel warmth pass through my body. I am no longer afraid. New sensation has replaced fear. Then he has gone. He moves quietly so I know he has a body that is lean and athletic. He is a warrior, not a soft clerk or fat cook as men of households often are.

As the days pass, I find myself listening for the sound of his voice. The infant king is in my mind as only God Kings can share the thoughts of men or in this case the thoughts of women. One who has only just started to have vague thoughts that she is a woman? I feel acceptance of my strange feelings. Where Aye is concerned, the child seems to have a mind already aware of its own best interests, far in advance of its still tiny body, a body that is totally reliant upon me. She who produced milk has departed, and has been replaced by another, not long a wet nurse. No child comes with the wet nurse and she does not return to feed her own infant.

I think my saviour and sister is no longer in the world of the living. She now walks in the underworld. As one who served the God King, I think she will be well in death, probably more so than life in a sometimes-harsh Egypt - harsh for those who serve from a lowly position. I have had no communication from my mother or old household so I have a future, as long as it lasts, in the hands of a general and those in absolute power over all Egypt, Amenhotep lll and his wife Tiye.

I hear few rumours in this place as contact is with only those who remain silent, or of few words, those needed to explain the needs of my infant obligation.

I lose track of the passing days so now fear I will not know when another year of my life has passed.

Aye steps into my life,
Aye comes into my body,
New life comes into my body,
That much time has passed.
The God King child is aware in his beyond body mind.
I hear from both, you will produce milk for the child!

Time passes and I am tended in birth. There is much pain, but I survive. Aye is gentle with me and tells me the child of my body will live and be given a good home. The God King is now much larger and, as always, he enters my mind. He seems able to control my emotions, easing stress and removing emotional pain. This mind gift is, I know, amongst most of those who hold the Moses blood for when the parents come, as they do on occasion, they direct their thoughts to me without words. They bring another gift of the mind for one such as me for pictures enter me and for the first time I know what images of the world around me look like. Before only my hands gave shape to my world. I know the God Kings look both human in face and elongated in skull; perhaps this is where the gifts that separate them from common humans reside.

The child comes to my breast and I understand that they are well pleased with this. I wonder if another wet nurse has gone to the underworld. This thought is left in my mind. All is not kindness, for in my care and great responsibility, that I have not sought, I am a prisoner.

My body returns to its former shape with care and exercise. Aye returns to my body. He seems to care for me and is both demanding and tender. I develop a need for him and am glad when my body does not swell with a new child, for he did not require me when I was large with child. I enquire about my baby and am told to give all my love to the one in my care.

"Your birth child is no longer your concern, but it has a good future."

I think they tell the truth, for it is Aye's child too. That perhaps leads him to give me some small protection. My eyes must remain silent and my words must be directed with care.

In the fourth year of the God King child's life our doors are opened and our rooms expand to large gardens. Then, to my pleasure, a vessel is placed upon the river and we travel. He moves too fast for me to care for him now and others protect him. He swims like a fish and tries to teach me. He is taught to use weapons suited to a child. His life in a secluded world is opening up. I know that he is still being protected from the priests of Amun who seek only those of the purest Moses (blood of the ancient three kings, Horus' blood).

Tiye, the child to be king's mother, is half the blood of Moses, daughter of Yuya from the land of Goshem. Pharaohs rule Egypt's armies and their generals are a power to be feared. The silent army of priests of many gods are an army of a different power. Not the sword, but the control of the minds of the multitude, that on many occasions feeds the arm that feeds the sword. Others of course feed the spirit and arm of those that carry the armour of pharaoh.

The years pass and I am trusted more as time goes by. Now I hear my name spoken with respect, and move freely amongst the grounds and countless rooms of the palace. The young child who never had the mind of a baby has remained a close contact. So too has Aye, although only rarely now my lover, and the only one I have ever known. He remains close to me and has opened my mind in trust to many of the affairs of Egypt.

Sixteen years have passed since I left my mother. Not a word have I heard. I presume they think I am long dead, or old and barren in the service of Isis. Although I have learned much of the gods and goddesses that hold power with my king, none seem as real to me as the youth, once the child, with whom I have spent what seems like forever. I have been blessed, but it remains in my mind, and that of us all in the inner circle of this palace, that those who would remove any possibility of Amenhotep 1V becoming king, are still as powerful as ever. I know this because I share too often the thoughts of the young king in waiting. He has grown with this knowledge and has developed a fierce desire to destroy those that threaten him and those of us who reside in his shadow take caution in our daily thoughts and actions. As far as I know, they know nothing of his existence. If they do, they cannot reach into this world, but all his food and drink is tasted first by those who bring it to him.

He has given me a gift that I know has brought him plea-sure, and bound us closer in life. Through sharing his thoughts with me, a gift that his father has, and to a lesser degree, Queen Tiye, I have been given a picture of the palace the gardens and stretches of the river. When he is with me, I can walk with a view not available to the blind.

At times, those new to the palace are surprised to learn that I am one who resides in what would, without the God King, be a world without light, a world without the sun Amon, the one the young God King and I now call the Aten. He is the light of the world that I would give the life of anyone other than Aye and Amenhotep1V to see. So it is this that Aten has become to me, and Moses, perhaps in tiny part because of me what he calls the one true god. But in mind I hear him refer to the Aten as the Son of God, implying that there is a greater gift of life that is ancient knowledge to him and those of Moses bloodline.

SCULPTED HEAD OF QUEEN NEFERTITI:::

Nineteen

1378 BC Amenhotep1V (Akhenaten)

**3390 years before *The Time of the Writing*, 2012.AD
Sixteen years old**

SEPHRON

There is upheaval in the palace and the young God King is
both excited and concerned. Aye has gathered a large part
of the army in Goshen around Tiye's summer palace. We know
his father and many others of the Moses blood are present. He is
a man now and I attend him only as friend. My life has become
quiet and sedate. Still trusted, I have a lot of freedom. His mind,
not his words, tells me the laws I must obey. I am guarded always, for perhaps there are those who would torture or kill one
such as me for the knowledge in part that I possess.

He is to meet his siblings, those closest to him, children of
Amenhotep's Tiye and other chief wives. He is to meet the one
most talked about, his elder sister, Nefertiti. He has asked that I

be present. Strange that I, who cannot see, should be the eyes to access new images, images that I will see through the eyes of this boy man, who has been the focus for most of my life.

There is an unusual degree of silence, and there are few people. Aye is present and I feel the touch of the back of his hand. He is as always, strong and gentle. I move back and hear a curtain close. It makes no difference to this one, so I am the unseen observer. His parents speak. It is said that all who are important know him up and down the sacred River Nile. He is to return to the capital and take his rightful place as part of his future. I feel love in these rulers over all Egypt that would be so strange to all who have not lived as I have. I feel fear that I will not be needed and perhaps my life will end. He touches my mind, and then a new mind is here. Pure intelligence and love without direction is what I feel.

His eyes open to me and I see the image of the one that will be above all in beauty. I feel them bind together almost as one entity before all fades and darkness returns to my world. Peace and calm are left within me. They have removed doubt and fear but I wonder what doubt and fear will emerge as this young Amenhotep 1V, almost my child (but not), returns to a sometimes violent and dangerous civilization that has many representatives of the spiritual laws, but who fight to take power of those who have brought greatness and order to this world. I have no doubt that when this new part of the young king to be is present he will exclude others from their private journey.

My heart bleeds for I wish for the first time in a long period that I could gaze upon this great beauty that I somehow feel will endure far into the future when all those who live have entered the afterlife.

I see less of him in the coming moon, but am included when we move back to the capital. My eyes are once more my ears alone for his eyes are now only for Nefertiti and, perhaps, also for his new role as son of Pharaoh. Now I hear much talk of all the great complexes of Karnak, Luxor and Memphis.

I hear this amongst the servants, for I am looked after with freedom to move about certain gardens and rooms assigned to me. It is lonely for I have never known people who are my equal for many years, only those who serve and those I serve. In my life, that was Aye and God King to be. Now many are my superiors, but seem hardly aware of my existence. My importance will, I know, fade into the past.

Nefertiti is his wife and children numbering two have arrived. Five years have passed when news reaches me that he is declared co-regent with the great Amenhotep lll. This, I am aware, is to the great pleasure of the Queen Tiye whose roots lie deep in the land of Goshen with the Israelite peoples.

It comes as no surprise to me that he has created upheaval amongst the temples of Amen, Isis and others. He has taken a new name to distinguish himself from the older co-regent. He is now Akhenaten (word to his god, meaning, worshipping the son (sun).) New temples rise in all three of the greatest cities, to his god Aten.

Freedom grows for me and I move around the streets under the ever-watchful eye of my carers. The smells and sounds open up a world I have rarely known. My ears begin to learn the mood of the people. The seasons have been good and they have little care for the doings of the Pharaohs while their bellies are full and a roof covers whatever value they have.

Some of them utter the name of the god Aten, but in praise it is the river goddess and the Amun that are foremost in the minds of the people. I am not surprised that anger exists over the building of great wealth to Aten, from those that serve other gods. Concern is within me that I hear it said that Nefertiti is the rightful co-reagent and heir to the king, also that her children should have the pure blood of Moses of God Kings. There are many emotions and over time, I sense that tensions are rising.

So it comes to pass that, to my slight dismay, I am given perhaps my second real duty in a somewhat fortunate life for one who has never seen the light of Aten. I am returned to the temple of Isis as a lowly priestess, one who must serve. My not so youthful but still lovely body receives some attention in their dark times, though not as it did in my youth. I encourage attention for it is in intimacy that secrets can pass to one such as me. I think they know not of my high connections. It was a well-kept secret as was the life of Akhenaten for so long.

Now the aggression is spoken freely to me about the young king; it is said that he will not be long for life in the capitals. All that I hear is passed on and I know that because of the information I give lives will cease to exist and other tongues will not talk or plot. Regardless of this, or perhaps because of this, in part, the anger only grows. I learn that now plans have been devised to divide the regents. I am moved from the temple and once more reside in the palace. I think my life may have become at risk.

A new city not known to me was built in the fourth year of his regency, and named Amarna. Much of Aye's army is involved in this region. Akhenaten and Nefertiti are often for moons on end absent from the palace. I know from one of my talks with Tiye that she wishes them to move to Amarna. She is a power in Egypt of great influence over the Pharaohs.

We move in year six, (1372BC, 3384 years before the Time of the Writing).

I am given the great honour of being just behind the great pair as they enter in huge possession the grand avenue that leads to the new palace and temple of Aten. For the first time in years, I feel his mind leave Nefertiti and enter mine. Images of Amarna emerge and I once again see through his eyes and feel great love, and compassion from this complex, perhaps part alien, being.

Tears flow from my eyes and both joy and sadness are a part of my soul.

Then he tells me strange words that will never leave my memory.

"Your eyes are blind, but know this; the eyes of all that live, animal and man, are blind. It is only the mind of God, who creates all, that is seen by those that live on this world. Each individual being, whether large or small, is the centre of its own world and a part of the mind of all existence. So it is that they are a part of the mind of God, and can see and create what it is that is the will of creation.

"The Aten is an image of the mind of God that enables us to exist. So it is that it is the most important physical image that I can give to the known world to bring them closer to their true being."

Much of this is lost to me!

In 1370 BC, year eight of his reign as co-regent, Amarna is virtually finished.

In year twelve of his reign Amenhotep lll dies.

In year twelve of his reign, he bans all other gods and expels the priests from the temple of Amen. Armies go out and the names of other gods are removed.

He has, in theory, ultimate power.

He has in reality created vast enemies, not just amongst those who serve, but in the armies of all other generals, (perhaps even Aye's!), plus the people of all trades and agriculture. Tiye is old now, but gathers many of her people of Israelite origins about the Pharaoh.

AKHENATEN

For many years as this boy king grew to be a man and co-regent to regent supreme, he was educated by Queen Tiye's elder brother in the ancient knowledge of the origins of the pyramids and all that followed.

The coming of the three kings via the star of the east (the brightest of the night sky and second closest to the solar system).

This is the origin of the story - now legend - of Horus, one of the kings perhaps. Horus dies on the cross from the south (the Southern Cross) on the twenty-second day of December. He spends three days in the underworld, and is born again on the 25th day of the last moon, the day the sun rises one degree into the New Year. This is built into the worship of the Aten god for it is the Son of God. It reaches the lowest point of the evening sky on the twenty-second and starts to rise again on the twenty-fifth. The cross only appears in the night sky at this time and is perfectly aligned to the three kings, via the star of the east (Sirius via the Orion belt, bottom of the saucepan).

The worship of the son (sun) on these dates is ancient beyond knowledge. So too is the story of the three kings. Akhenaten tells me it goes back twelve thousand years to the time of the building of the Sphinx and the monuments that followed, the birth of all civilization but not necessarily the birth of knowledge, for it is believed that visitors from Orion and beyond have come to this world over time from before the coming of Horus.

These are the thoughts of the Moses bloodline, rare to many, even those who kneel before the many gods.

In 1366 BC, I am fifty years old. My child, a son, would have been twenty-six now. I have also become aware that in the mind of Akhenaten, the greatest power left on this known world, lies deep in the heart of the central pyramid on the plateau (Giza). It is not easy for me to comprehend his thoughts. For him it seems it is a similar form of the Aten but in miniature form. This is an energy force that is more powerful than many armies are. Only those of the highest initiated of Amun, now the Aten, can enter the ancient monument.

Now Akhenaten is the supreme leader and has power over all who attend the miniature Aten. He has trained with Anen, High Priest and brother of Tiye, from a young age and has beheld this profound sight with other initiates with his own eyes. The purpose of such Aten being left is far past and vague even to the Moses bloodline. Still it is of the greatest reverence, even before the coming of the worship of the Aten that brings life to our crops and our very being and life to all that supports us in order for all to live.

So it has been over many years, thirty of my fifty years of this life, that the head of the Aten has brought light to my dark world and from time to time allowed me to see. So it is that the head of the Aten has brought light to my mind to give wonders to all far beyond the knowledge of those of my humble birth. I think there are many in high places that are blinder than me although my eyes remain dark.

In the fiftieth year of my life a very unusual event occurs. Only those who serve are in attendance of my now spacious rooms and private garden. My life has many vacant days, but I dwell not upon loneliness, only upon the wonder of how I have been blessed.

I am told to prepare myself and servants arrive to bath and dress me. I can feel the finery of cloth and think, What a waste for one lady who is past the choice of handsome eyes. Then I hear the voice that has not been with me for a long time now, not with my body, but the only man I have known - Aye. He still feels strong and lean in my arms as he holds me briefly. I hear others, then feel the minds so familiar to me, God King and Queen Nefertiti.

I have felt the grief in God King's heart, for his mother has not long passed into the underworld. It crosses my mind what bond must exist between mother and son, and I think that I know this, for the one who leads is son to me. For this thought both regents touch my mind gently. My face must wear the happy smile that others see so often and take for granted.

My ears tell me two others are present. It is Tiye's older brother, Anen. He moves slowly. He is a very old man, the teacher of the early years of God King. He is thus known to me. The other is young. I can tell this because he moves like the young Aye that once filled both my body and heart with such joy.

Then a great stillness enters me, and something I can only register as perhaps shock. I have caught a glimpse of guarded thought. He is of my blood. Aye also filled my womb with one I gave birth to, one who never suckled at my breast, and one for whom I had no time to grieve.

From somewhere deep within a well of feeling rises. I am filled with emotions of such complexity that I am unable to move. A quiet voice says to me, "My father, the greatest general in all Egypt, has informed me that it is you that gave me life. It is you that I have wondered about for much of the last twenty-six years of my life."

I sense him kneel before me and although Akhenaten could give me sight to see this face, my eyes remain in their endless void. Strong hands take my own, and are guided to his face, and I take my first tentative exploration of the only thing I have, without knowing it, been grieving over for all these passing of the floods.

My face is wet and his hands, so strong, wipe the tears from my cheeks. Then we are alone and he tells me the first I have ever heard of his life.

So my life and my love become fuller.

It is one moon before he returns to his legions. He is a commander of many, the son of the great Aye, and grand-nephew of Tiye, important in this Egypt. Now, through him, I have learnt that all is not well in Akhenaten's Egypt. A great rising of both army and priests has made it almost impossible for Pharaoh to retain power without turning his back on the gift of one god he has brought to the known world. I have learnt from Aye, the father of the one who has brought me new joy, that my son leads the army that will have to stand before a superior force when it comes time to remove Akhenaten. My son so newly returned, for whom I now fear. Aye has advised the God King to abdicate to his young son, Tutankhaten, then withdraw to Amarna. This is possibly the only way to preserve the power of the Amarna eighteenth dynasty kings.

Nefertiti dies! He fears poison. His grief is complete. I hold him in my arms for a day and a night and for a time I fear he will die by the will power of his own lack of desire for life.

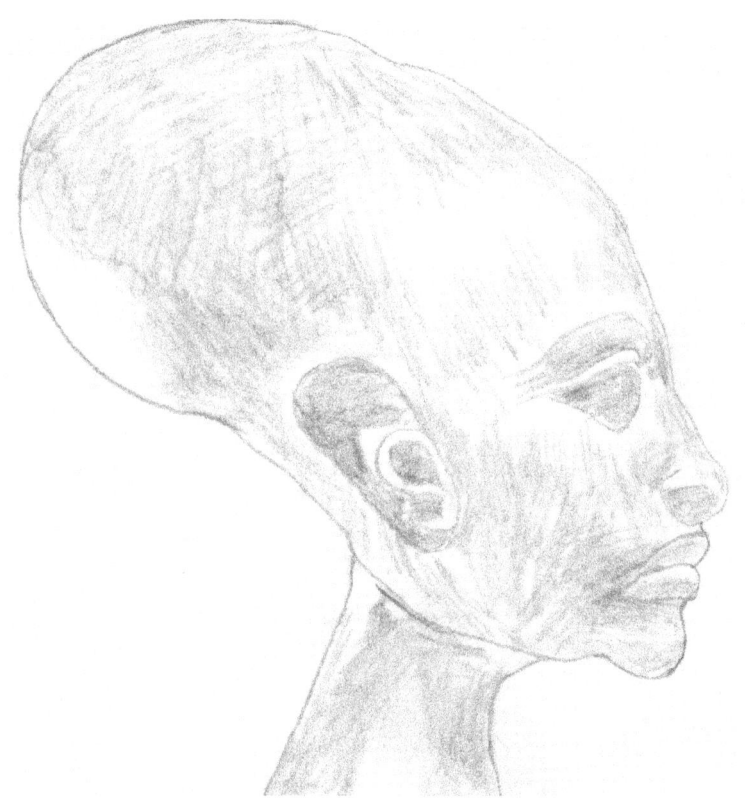

ACURATE DRAWING OF SCULPTED HEAD:::
DAUGHTER OF AKHENATEN AND NEFERTITI::: From
Tutankhamen's exhibition while in Melbourne.

TWENTY

THE TIME OF THE EXODUS

The family of Tiye has gathered many of the tribes of Israel. Many of those of the general army have left for the army of the priests of Memphis. Many of the population of Amarna are leaving. Houses stand deserted and the temple of the great Aten is empty. My ears tell me the palace is far too quiet. The voices I hear speak all too often in the language of the land of Goshen. We are leaving. No chariots will travel the delta west of the Nile towards the headwaters of the Red Sea. Word has come that if he departs the armies of the now ruling priests will not pursue.

A new fear is in my heart, for I have learnt that Akhenaten has decreed that the source of mystery from the heart of the great pyramid will go before us as the symbol of the one god, the Aten. I ride in front of a vast number of people. It is dark and although animals and people are a multitude, hardly a word is spoken. I sense great sadness. I sense fear. I feel the anguish of the one I helped raise. His name is not spoken now, and when I hear him referred to, it is as the blood of the Ammonite kings, the Moses. I feel he will go into obscurity, but he insists on the title of Moses in order to hold the claim of the rightful ruler of the known world.

The night is warm and passes without incident. My son speaks briefly to me and I feel the presence of people who are to increase the minders around me. There are three soldiers each side and behind me. We travel until the sun is high. We rest in the heat of the day. Night after night passes and eventually we enter the delta country. Now I am on horseback. All chariots and wagons are left behind. An army is forming behind us and it is said by my son and Aye that the tracks we pass along will be impossible for the army of the Amon priests to follow. It is hard and many horses founder. Eventually I am on foot.

Fighting breaks out on the third night in the delta, but although the losses are great the king's men have been made weak by the loss of chariot and army in the headwaters of the Nile. On the fourth day, we enter dry land. It is said that the power of the Aten from the ancient monument has parted the waters in many places, allowing the tribes of Canaan and Goshen to pass through, with the many supporters from the lands of Egypt. This has quietly increased the morale of the people and they are strong in support of Moses and his one true God.

With dry land we turn south, or so I am told, for my ears are my eyes. Still I feel the Aten sun (son) and know that the direction of our journey has changed. Now we move towards the Red Sea, so it will be a vastly different people now, perhaps armies that will blend with the Moses. With luck, the power of the Aten will hold persuasion over the tribes to be encountered as it rides before Israel.

Almost every night my son spends a period of time with me and my knowledge is perhaps as good as many who have eyes, but cannot see what one blind woman with the best contacts sees. Bedouin tribes become our companions as our tents dwell for several moons amongst them. It is said that they are greatly in favour of the Aten, so support Moses. I miss the comfort of palace life for I have never slept outside of a fine house, Temple of Isis or palace of Amarna blood.

There are others who also tire of desert sands blown by wind into eyes that grow red. There is much talk of the need for a new homeland. Word goes out that one will be found and we move on with the company of many tribes of the Bedouin. The army is now strong amongst the tribes of the increasingly foreign lands. It was weak compared to the armies of the Amon priests. Here it grows. Many herds are swallowed up as need for the great supply trains of food grows.

We move south with speed, looking for fertile land and battles are fought. My son is wounded, but assures me he will live.

For several days, I have more of his company as he recovers. I am growing tired; this body of mine has long achieved more than I could have ever thought possible. It is growing old. I will not see the Promised Land. My mind returns to the thoughts of Akhenaten. Rare now for he seems to have devoted himself to the Aten and become reclusive to those that he once held close. Still I feel his love. I feel his fear and doubts. I feel his great awe in the presence of this artefact from the heart of the great pyramid.

ALPHA BETA ZETA AND YARGREY (RETURN OF THE SPACERS)

Once again the eons (as they will view it on the worlds) have passed. It is a return. We have been here before, on many worlds, many times. It is a new awakening, my rebirth after time that is not measured over space and not understood on the worlds we visit. It is a return, to a blue planet with a large moon. A single moon about one quarter the size to stabilize the world of living life that is the result of the pattern of creation, all this the signature of the design of the living universe, one consciousness of all things.

Proof of our concept lies in the existence of the pattern of creation; Star of David, 64 tetrahedron grid, flower of the grid as on many ancients.)

Something has gone amiss. This time I am Yargrey, and this time it is Alpha who stands before me, waiting for the decision, one to be reached by me, a reborn individual elder, or one to be reached by the collective mind of those spacers who have emerged to assess the health of a lovely world in the habitable zone of the galactic plane.

All around the habitable zone of this galactic life, spacers, as some know us, have left the power of the beacons that guide and enable the travellers to reach this remote destination so far between the arms within this galaxy.

This is a privileged position for emerging life to view their heavens in order to ask questions that, with our guidance, will take those fortunate few into the collective wisdom of many ancient living worlds.

All will owe their existence to an orderly well-structured universe as it births and dies in all forms of the continual cycle of life. Galactica is stable now outside of the fifth planet from this kind star. We rise in unison to greet our other ancient elder colleges at the viewing station, and walls roll back. Hearts swell in a uniform emotion of wellbeing.

Communion, communion, communion, the most precious gift of each new birth, some to last a thousand years of this Earth planet's rotations.

Our minds centre on the distant point of light hardly brighter than the vast Milky Way that is the inner plane of life of this part of creation. Our minds centre upon Earth. It is beautiful.

The beacon is still there, but it is not enclosed in the ancient monuments we left behind to protect it. They were to guide emerging life to eventual knowledge, to the gift of wisdom we distribute to those who reach a developed state of readiness.

I enter the airlock and move into one of the vessels that will travel the final jump to the planet's orbit.

Time passes and we move into the area of greatest land stability, the longest point of land from east to west and the longest point of land from north to south. The pyramid is sealed. Those left in charge have removed and shut down the monument; the bloodline is broken.

Our minds zero in. The region is full of the blood of the spacers' genes we left behind. Their minds are in turmoil. Then the signal of the singularity that is the signal emerges. Much of the bloodline is with it, plus a multitude of others. They have moved southeast to the inlet of the southern sea, a slightly mountainous region.

There must be still knowledge for those who mind it are still alive. Under the cover of darkness, we descend. The leader is located.

They call him Akhenaten, the multitude call him Moses - it means *of the blood*, or *the rightful heir*; the blood we left behind, some eight thousand years of this planet's rotations ago. If wisdom is to come to these people, the key to the living universe, perhaps it is through him that wisdom must create a new dawn for this world once again. It has become a world of divided kingdoms of great aggression, all this centred on the beginnings at the laying of the beacon. This is not unheard of, but not as we would choose. These people have a long way to go before they expand into space to become a part of the universal wisdom.

AKHENATEN

My dreams have taken a turn into reality that has no explanation in modern Egypt. Perhaps the answer is hidden in the depths of the passed-down myths of my ancestors and the inner sanctum of the priests and priestesses. For some reason these events are calming, and the word that is coming to me that these strange beings in what I can only call Sky World are bringing me closer to the creation, the one true form of what we have called gods which I have believed are beyond the Aten, that encompasses all.

The first time, I awakened in the depth of the night. Without fear, I opened my eyes upon tall grey figures with slim arms and legs, large heads and huge eyes, tiny ears and mere slits for a nose.

Without voice, they spoke to me in the mind way of those of the purest Moses bloodline.

Without fear, we rose in a ray of pure light, that which shines from the Aten, but here rises seemingly without end into the stars above. The land and tents shrink and clouds pass beneath me until all is black. Then an opening appears, eventually revealing a huge black triangle sitting in the sky as a giant bird, but without movement.

My memories are vague now but I have a feeling that the walls of the interior almost seem alive. I was laid upon a raised area with beings or gods all around me, with instruments that to me had no meaning.

Then the first I was aware of is that I was awake and felt fresh and had new hope, and a sense that I was to find new direction to a world that had been full of doubts, even though the people believed in me.

More nights followed and the figures did not appear, but the sky light did and I felt myself lifted through the very walls of the dwelling. Wherever I arrived there was light as that of a burning bush, but one that continued to burn long after the bush had ceased to be. Each day I awake refreshed and feel greater knowledge than even that passed down through the ages.

YARGREY

We have assessed our ancient connection to the product of life on this world, the key to civilization, which has gone aggressively wrong. We have entered his mind, strengthened his body and opened wider his ability to influence his people. Most of what we have done will remain in his subconscious. Direction will now be available to these people. The beacon will remain as a source of protection without returning to its true home. That has been compromised and would no longer be safe with the diversity of beliefs that inhabit the central location we gave it.

Perhaps new complexes will be built to house such form in other locations upon this pretty planet, pyramids in the form of the three kings, or maybe what they will in the far off future call the Belt of Orion.

Those close to him will be influenced so the journey is clear for him, one called Aaron and a woman called Sephron, her love

Aye, and her son, plus some of the Moses blood that has travelled out of Egypt to seek a promised land.

AUTHOR'S NOTE:

The dimensions of the Ark of the Covenant, given in the bible, fit precisely into the sarcophagi in the King's chamber. In ancient times the Belt of Orion was called the Three Kings. Sirius the second closest star to the sun, was called the star of the east.

Belt of Orion, so be it. (The nine major pyramids on Earth. Three in each location).

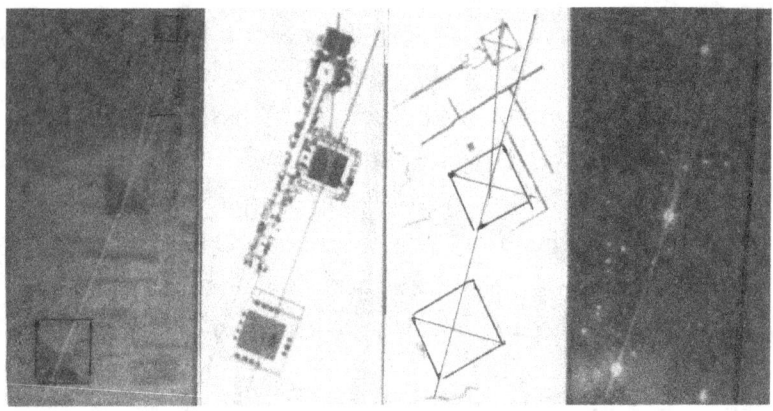

CHINA   MEXICO   EGYPT   GIZA   BELT OF ORION
TEOTIHUACAN

SEPHRON

Without fear, I felt myself rise into the air, and my world become small below me. I thought I must have died and wondered why I was not entering the underworld of Isis teachings.

Then I awoke in my bed to astonishment. I felt energy and youth were upon my body. I felt calm and great hope. I opened my eyes to eternal darkness, and I wept. Tears ran down my cheeks from eyes that I have not felt wet for many seasons. I did not see the world around me but I saw light. Behind the light was shadow. Now it pained my long dead eyes to view so I gathered cloth and wrapped it around my face. I called and they went to fetch the healers from amongst us.

The one I had suckled from childhood came, and others. I was confused. Aye came, and my son. I did not seek more than a healer.

They took me from my lodgings that are always close to those that rule, to the great tent of the Moses. In the light of day, even with the cloth, the new light hurts. I can hear many people gathering to see what has arisen.

Akhenaten is in my mind. There are others who can hear, including his kinsman, called Aaron. Then the cloth to my face is removed. My eyes open and without the aid of the God King's gift of his eyes, the light slowly adjusts and an image with a voice that I know as my son's emerges.

I weep!

Akhenaten softly says, "Give glory to the angels of the one true God."

The people take up the glory. My life that I considered gifted beyond all hope changes. Aye comes to me we are as if returned to youth. Life and love stretch before me.

YARGREY

Alpha stands beside me once again as we pass around this world absorbing the thoughts and health of people in almost all areas of all continents, many lands in places far into vast oceans. They are not altogether peaceful, but they are resourceful. Perhaps in the far distant future the words of the bloodline of Moses will filter to the far corners of the planet. Eventually we reach the centre of the landmasses and the capital resides below, with the symbol of our far origins in this journey.

A young king has just taken the throne of Egypt, a boy now called Tutankhamen. They have removed the part of his name that connected him to his father, Akhenaten! He is ruled by the priests of Amen. (Amen will filter down through history into prayer.) Tutankhamen will be the last king of the Amarna eighteenth dynasty. He will be the last king of the Moses bloodline in Egypt.

The Moses bloodline will not reign in Egypt, but it will hold the reins, and the ancient knowledge into the far distant future. For a time to come it will remain the custodian of what our beacon will come to be called - the Ark of the Covenant.

As we rise through the clouds, the elders upon this triangle view the stars that open before us and I see the vast area of space that the spacers of Galactica have traversed. There is a small clump of seven bright stars, like seven sisters, in the far left of another that appears on my right, the patterns of the monuments below. (Seven sisters are the Pleiades. Monuments are the Belt of Orion as will be in China and Mexico, all identical).

Our minds come together with the pattern of the stars, and this home star with this planet's moon. We project our thoughts into a field upon the surface of a continent far to the north west of Egypt. With a gentle swirling the grasses twist and turn to perfect patterns.

My last glimpse is of a tribe of hunter-gatherers bowed down before this beauty with the central seven sisters.

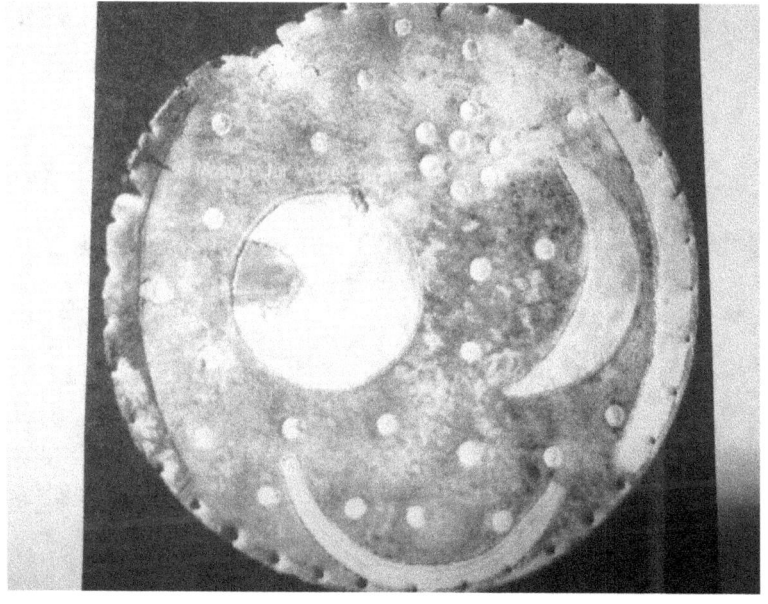

Picture of the Nebra disc, Germany 4000 year old depiction of the seven sisters, the Pleiades.

SEPHRON

We travel for many years through battles. Moses departs this planet, and one called Joshua follows. Even with the new body, I grow old, and one day the love of my eyes, ears and form departs. Aye.

Grandchildren are beside me when I close these eyes, a gift that I can only guess at. For the last time, I am at peace. Although this remarkable life is over, I feel knowledge that many will follow and that somehow I am a part of a total consciousness, the gift of all awareness. That wonderful vision laid open to me, the stars above, is perhaps a clue as to the pattern of creation itself.

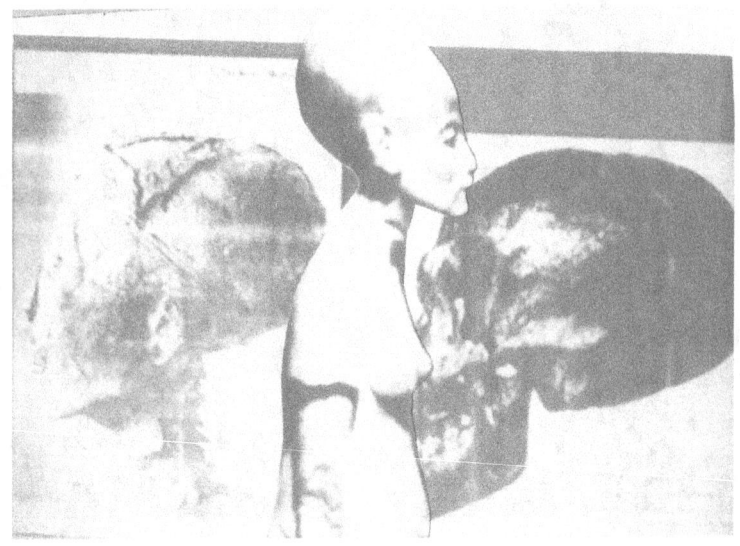

SKULL OF TUTANKHAMUN AND PERHAPS OTHER FAMILY MEMBER SHOWING ELONGATED HEAD::: ABOVE SCULPTED NEFERTITI..

TWENTY-ONE

MALCOLM REDOME FROM, THE TIME OF THE
WRITING, 2012

For the sake of the book, I tell stories of lives that are out of the ordinary, and connect with some continuity. Most of the lives I live over vast time - Samsuric, in Hindu belief, re-incarnation - are just ordinary, lived in happiness, sadness, struggle, mild success sometimes, euphoric, sickness and pain.

Sometimes I live to a great age, sometimes for a few minutes; sometimes on other worlds, in other beings altogether. Sometimes I am male, sometimes female. Karma has effect.

I have always been ordinary. I am still as I write, ordinary. These stories are for your mind to accept, or reject, with or without offence.

You have your own journey.

You have your own beliefs, (perhaps religion).

You have your own wisdom.

You are perhaps the centre of your own universe; you are definitely the centre of your own existence.

You affect, in sometimes-small ways, the world around you. **You have effect.**

Your potential is unlimited, but it is yours - good or bad.

The first law of physics; does it not state: For every action there is an equal and opposite reaction? Cause and effect. Karma

So it is that I will open my eyes to lives connected to the other great beliefs.

Separate to your way of viewing, perhaps the billions who gain comfort from those great teachers, Hinduism and its child, through Buddha, Buddhism.

So it is that I have opened my eyes to Egypt, with its beliefs and perhaps the child of this Akhenaten's land, to be the beliefs of the Israelites.

So it is that I have opened my eyes to Christianity, with its beliefs drawn from pagan, Celtic and Egyptian ideas, but mostly the child of Jewish beliefs.

Then comes the Muslim religion and its original beginnings and connection to what has gone before; a child of much of the same ancient beliefs that have gone before.

I am born again 2600 years before the Time of the Writing, (now October 2012), this time in the land that will eventually be North Western India, on the Indus river.

(From the human journey! Spirit of Malcolm Redome, on the basic beliefs of one billion Hindus.)

Dharma, path of righteousness - Codes of conduct from scripture

Samsara, Rebirth.

Karma, Right action, effects on rebirth.
Moksha, liberation from cycle of Samsara, (rebirth)

Simple poem passed on from Dalai Lama, as gift of Nagarjunas, about 400 AD.

> *Just as one comes to ruin*
> *Through wrong eating but obtains*
> *Long life, freedom from disease,*
> *Strength and pleasures through right eating.*
> *So one come to ruin*
> *Through wrong understanding*
> *But attains happiness and highest enlightenment*
> *Through right understanding.*

Twenty-Two

Three Births, Three Great Religions!

Gyatso Kelsang

I can see her over the river, the great river of life that is the centre of our existence, in this ancient land of my ancestors. For seventeen changings of the annual floods, I have lived on this land. For fifteen of the same, the one promised to me has dwelt in the village that almost reaches our own, apart from the sacred waters that separate us.

I stand with my father. Now he enters a conveyance and moves towards a figure coming towards us. Much discussion will take place if our two clans are to unite. Our union will perhaps heal old blood feuds and give strength to the walls that surround our villages that border the one water, giving us a common bond.

I am deeply aware of the responsibility of the union of the tiny distant female and myself, the middle son of the leader of our village. My emotions are mixed for in part my heart and my body have for several years spent many times in the arms and lovely body of a woman of grace, beauty and laughter from my kinsman's daughter.

The days have passed and agreement upon the result of my coming union has been decided. No one has asked me and I am aware that her permission will also not be sought. We are second to the wider needs of the greater community. We, I imagine, have both been raised from birth to accept this.

If the marriage is not good, I think I will seek time to visit the pleasures of my kinsman's hearth.

I am in her presence, but divided by a screen. At a glance, she is slim and moves with grace. Her face is veiled and will not be revealed to me until the communion takes place. The old sage sits and we bow our respects and remain silent. All his words I cannot remember to include here so in brief this is the essence of his wisdom.

- There is only one supreme absolute called Brahman.
- All other forms of deity represent the many aspects of THE ONE BRAHMAN.
- A trinity exists, Brahma the Creator, Vishnu the preserver, and Shiva the destroyer.
- All humans who seek enlightenment learn the four basic tenets.

Dharma-Ethics and duties

- That in your coming unity, that which helps you reach Brahma, is Dharma; that which hinders you is Adharma.
- The paths of Dharma are austerity; purity; compassion; and truthfulness.

- Adharmic or unrighteous life has three vices, pride, contact and intoxication.
- This is the teaching that suggests methods for the attainment of the highest ideal and eternal bliss. Here and now on Earth AND NOT SOMEWHERE IN HEAVEN.
- It endorses that it is your Dharma to marry, raise a family and provide for that family in whatever way is necessary.
- The practice of Dharma gives an experience of peace, joy, strength and tranquillity within oneself and makes life disciplined.

The couple-to-be remain silent.

My name is Gyatso Kelsang, and my bride to be is Avish Geshe.

We turn towards each other as the sage leaves. I am aware that she is studying me then I look into her eyes and am shocked to discover two blue circles are searching my features. No one I have ever known has had blue eyes. I become aware that I am staring and am struck silent. Then I see those same mysteries light up and display the impish smile that I know has taken place behind the veil. She turns and leaves. A hand upon my shoulder, that of my father, makes me aware that I have been standing still and time has passed. Now I wonder who it is to whom I am to be betrothed.

The day arrives and I am aware that I have thought of little else but those eyes and the slim graceful form under those robes. All thoughts of other pleasure have departed. Perhaps it will not be so hard to live up to some of the sage's ideals. This undesired union may turn out to be good Karma for this very earthy young man.

Time passes, the union passes. She is more than I could have hoped for. No day is the same as her laughter brings reality to my life. Then her love brings reality to children's lives. Then her loyalty brings acceptance to old age. Then her compassion brings understanding on the day that I know will be the last for this life on the Indus River that now flows through a unified community that grew prosperous in part because of the love that came from wisdom, wisdom that seemed eternal in the delights of those blue circles enclosed in the female form, my Rati on Earth.

I am born again several times after the great Buddha and witness the birth of Buddhism, the child of Hinduism Vedic scriptures and Sanskrit language.

I am to open my eyes again on southern Britannica, 352 AD (1660 years before this 2012 of Malcolm Redome).

We are few now who dwell on the banks of the Avon in Roman Britannica. The words of the prophet Jesus have swept this land. Few people enter the ancient temple of the Son (sun). Some of the great monoliths have departed. It is the twenty-second day of December and I will meet the one who holds my heart in this place of mystery for we are not disturbed where others fear to tread.

She is there just after sundown, and our young love finds the furs on this cold winter's night, the shortest of the year. Warm bodies blend and for a time the cold is forgotten. Our young love is of different tribes and is not sanctioned by those who control our lives but the blood that flows in our veins will have its way so we have met here every chance we have for several moons.

She will sleep in my arms and rise long before daybreak, to depart her way and me my way, with weapon at hand to claim the hunt, or protect from the dangers that are prevalent in our time.

Sound brings me to awareness and I cover her mouth. Light is on the horizon. We have slept too long and people are coming to this place that is never visited. I roll over and some fifty people in long white robes surround us.

We rise to our feet and a woman steps forward. She has lovely but mature features with a prominent blue circle on her forehead. As her hands rise I see the same on her staff, and bands around her arms and waist are all blue circles. Then I see others amongst them all the same in attire.

"You are here at a time of reverence that is as old as time, when the son (sun) of God enters this symbolic womb of the Mother Earth. Your young love must be blessed at this time in the old ways. People have turned to the Roman gods, and now the sign of the fish with the Nazarene teachings.

"To us of the old faith we still ask the son to rise again on the twenty fifth of December to bring life to Mother Nature. This is our ancient law. So you will if you wish, honour the laws of your ancestors, for it is in your features that you are not of Roman blood."

I can see that Arose is deeply affected by this so I stay my hand, and we fall into quiet witness as a ceremony to welcome the rising son (sun) takes place. The light enters the circle, now in disrepair. Strangely, it comes to life as I have never seen it before, and images flash through my mind of vast numbers of people reaching back through time.

They start to depart then she turns to me and says, "You will return if you wish on the sunrise of the twenty-fifth."

I wonder if this is possible for it is the day of the birth of the Prophet, and our absence will be deeply frowned upon. I can see that most of her attention is focused upon Arose, who no longer seems smitten with me, but is seemingly mesmerised by this graceful mystery, this leader I think, perhaps more than all the priestesses present.

She turns to me. "I have dreamed of these ladies of the blue circle. Images of the one have long been a part of my life; an image I thought was the world of dreams only."

I feel slightly isolated, but return on the night of the twenty-fourth. She does not come but I sleep and as the creatures of the night stir, I wake to find her sitting peacefully beside me. As I reach for her she stills my hand, this is not the time.

I wonder if I have lost her.

The others appear, then more, perhaps three times the number. The old ways of the Son of God are far from dead. I see the men carrying the cross of old, the Nazarene crucifix with the circle of the sun (son) imposed, ancient symbol of the sun dying on the Southern Cross as it makes its brief appearance in the northern skies only on the rebirth of the son on the 25th of December.

The singing and chanting is kept at a low pitch and I get the feeling that there is a desire for caution. As the light reaches above the horizon, the ceremony ends and people quickly begin to disperse.

Then they appear, Romans in four directions, many on horses. My freedom ends. Perhaps I am fortunate. The older ones, who are in the majority, perish on Roman swords.

I seek to help Arose but am in chains before I can reach her side. I do not see her again. I do not see the Avon again. My new home becomes Londonderry. In time, my fortunes change and I enter service as a house slave. Life will be a long journey, but Roman ways and comfort affect me, so eventually I almost forget the simple life of the Avon.

I do not forget Arose.

I grow old, the journey ends.

In this life, I witnessed what, in many ways, was the child of pagan beliefs, the birth of the era of the fish. Start of year one was end of the ram and beginning of Pisces, the fish, thus the Christian symbol. This was to be written as the words of Jesus - to bring together adverse peoples over vast areas for a long time to come as it will be the child of Judaism, who in turn was, in many ways, the child of Egypt.

I am born again in 670 AD, amongst the tribes of Arabia, at the trade centre of Mecca, home of about 360 deities, the chief amongst them being Allah, the moon god represented by the crescent moon. This is the symbol that will rise above almost all future mosques, and dominate flags of a huge uniting wisdom of belief.

This year will be my eightieth year. Most of my life has been lived in Mecca. I was born in the same year as the one who has taken my whole world and turned it upside down. It has been a life of great confusion. I have seen the tribes lay down weapons that had been raised against their neighbouring clans for hundreds of seasons. I have seen the old gods torn from their shrines. Now to my amazement the moon god Sin is no longer supreme amongst a vast number.

Allah stands alone as the one God, with no other. Mohammad is his one true prophet of my lifetime, who lived and died, who fought and conquered in my lifetime, who wed fourteen wives and kept two concubines in my city.

I have much confusion.

The kingdoms are united under the prophet's words. Even after his death, the words of one who could not write are spreading across my known world. The scriptures are full of the Israelite and even the Nazarene (Jesus) prophets. Their words of old have been re-interpreted by God's servant, Mohammed to the one true faith.

I do not know if I am to live to an old age in peace. I too will bow down to Allah. Still, like many of my age, and there are few, I am grateful that the crescent moon still represents this god of our future for I am sure it is here to stay.

I, like Mohammed, was of the Quraish tribe which primarily worshiped the Moon god, Sin the Allah. That is why the prophet's father (Abdullah, meaning servant of Allah or slave of Allah) and uncle both had the name *Allah* as part of their names. There are many names for the moon God; Sin, Hubal, Humquh and Al-ilah, (Al-ilah also meaning *The God*).

I am just grateful that I am still able to start our ancient fast of the now Ramadan at the start of the crescent moon to next crescent moon. I will die in peace with a part of my people's Pagan beliefs, a part of a unified world under the God (Al-ilah).

I don't doubt that Mohammed the prophet has above all men heard the word of a supreme consciousness.

TWENTY-THREE

HUMAN JOURNEY

Although greater unity of belief exists in all regions, now greater unity means vaster strength in armies. Wars are devastating. I fear it will be long before human kind obtains understanding.

The spirit of Malcolm Redome will live and die in many of these wars. Not as a hero; a soldier of necessity of the times, including eventually the Great War that will be termed the 1914 war. In this war was the greatest loss of human lives over differences of humanity, ever. There I died in Gallipoli in 1915.

Then in a tiny town in the South of an ancient continent now called Australia, I am born again into the time of the writing of *A Conscious Universe*, 1955 years after the time of Jesus.

I am moving now across distances well understood for longer than the rise and fall of billions of universes. The consciousness of our kind has penetrated to beyond the boundaries of human imagination. I pass the lights of great clusters at infinite

303

distance, until I see the light of the universe, which holds the spiral galaxy called the Milky Way. My speed must slow if my journey will take me back to the tiny yellow star called the Sun (son of old), with its pretty, blue planet called the Earth.

I am the spirit of the man who will be called Malcolm Redome.

I am, like all spirits of humanity and thousands of other spirits of species throughout this galaxy, connected to the laws of the most complex, evolved, intelligence known. This is the law of the Spirit, known by some on Earth as God, or by other names.

As humans struggle to civilization, they are beginning to look into distances and become aware of the probability of higher intelligences. They seek, through their greatest discoveries, for communication with other life. The spirit is within; it has journeyed with man for millions of years, and beyond death to understanding.

So it is at the point of conception I flash into this universe, galaxy, solar system and the womb of my mother, to depart from conscious knowledge of the spirit, and once again learn, or lose the lessons only the physical birth can give.

I am human without knowing my alien, spirit soul. I am also no different to any other person, as all are possessed with the life force. All people have this ancient, alien, subconscious identity.

I open my eyes to hear, touch, see and learn. My new journey has begun at a time when humanity has the capacity to learn the knowledge that will save their living, conscious planet for an enlightened future.

Today has been a good day, swimming and eating ice cream. We have a private bathhouse at the main beach at Portland for our annual holidays. Our house is high on the hill overlooking the fort that we have crept into, to explore. It frightens me. My brothers are older so fear not the dark.

I have been alive for five seasons. I only vaguely remember our other holidays by the sea. I am tired so go to bed earlier than the other children do. They are all older than I am.

My mother has put me in her room. Dad is still home running the farm. Maybe he will come soon. Mum says to sleep here for the other kids will wake me when they come to bed. I think they have gone down the hill to the carnival. I am too little. My eyes close and a happy day recedes.

Something has woken me and I feel a strange prickling of my skin. Fear! There is a soft light through the window and I can see all the walls. No one is in the room. What woke me? I feel sure something woke me, a person or a presence.

There is no one on my mother's bed. I wish I could get up and look, but when I try to rise, I cannot sit up. Now I am scared.

I try to call out but no sound comes. The house is quiet. There is no noise, not even the creaking of floorboards or the branches of the trees hitting the roof in the wind. This silence is unnatural. The silence is frightening. I know I am not alone. It is as if there is a voice in my head, but it is not a noise.

It is telling me to be not afraid. I begin to feel drowsy again. Something seems to be making me want to be calm. The last thing I remember as I enter the sleep world is my body sliding down the mattress.

When my eyes open, the sun is shining through the window. A vivid dream begins to recede, as dreams do in a small boy's waking moments. This one is strange though. Not my pony, but flying. I have never been in a plane. My older brother speaks of little but aeroplanes. Perhaps it is his thoughts in my head. Then I remember being awake and not alone in an empty room.

I do not sleep alone for the rest of the holidays. My mother wonders what has changed. For some years, I am afraid to go to sleep until others are present.

The years pass and memories fade. Fear fades. Older children go off to boarding school. There are only my parents and me now on the farm. School is busy and riding keeps my spare time full of many miles of adventure every weekend. I am twelve and next year I will go to Melbourne for school.

I have been asleep but my eyes are wide open now. The house is quiet. My parents must have turned off the radio, be reading or gone to bed. If so, why am I awake? I don't need to pee. There is no noise of the wood fire or hot water system in the roof above my bed. No wind, yet it is winter.

Then I realize the blankets are on the floor. Yet I feel no cold. This makes the skin prickly. I am not afraid but for some reason all the frightened times of the dark return to my mind. Then to my astonishment, my body begins to slide towards the foot of the bed. There is soft light from the window. There is no one in the room. I do not know why I feel only remote fear. It feels as if my body is lifting off the bed.

I am wide awake.

I resist and my body flicks back onto the mattress, only for a minute for it happens again. I feel myself rising further this time. I start to circle. The room seems to have grown higher. I'm moving faster now. Wow! Wow! I am through the wall, a solid wall. The house is below me and the night is a shining silver blue. My mind tells me there is no moon and clouds cover the stars. Clouds shimmer as if covered in silver.

The next thing I am aware of is that I am back on my mattress. My blankets are still on the floor. I am cold now and feel as if I am falling, like waking from a bad dream, like just before you are to be hurt in a dream.

This was no dream. Life returns to normal. This time I do not fear the dark.

Months pass and I enter the trauma of boarding school, and homesickness, sometimes excitement, and new friends and the cane on my bare arse.

This first journey, or perhaps a vague memory of a strange event by the sea, I will later learn is perhaps a kind of twilight world, halfway to the natural world of my inner spiritual self. Or is it? Why the feeling of a voice in my mind, the feeling of an unseen presence, of lost time? These seemingly out of body experiences, if that is what they are, come in groups as the years pass.

Most of my experiences are of flying. I am always alone. I see landscapes, often in silvery blues. Many times I try to visit people I know, but I am either unskilled or disobeying the laws of the spirit, as I will come to think of it. (In this eventual writing many years later I simply call it the profound gift, with reverence.)

The only fear I experience is when I attempt to land often from great heights. It feels as if gravity will smash me into the ground but it never does. I always land, I presume on my feet, without pain.

One memory that is very clear is when I travelled away from the Earth; it seemed to me over vast distances in only seconds. I could see flashes of light, which I presume were stars flashing past me in great numbers. These events are in groups during my early years, up to about the age of thirty, then they eventually ceased. I could perhaps help bring them on, but never had total control of when they would come. However I could stop them from occurring at any time, and I would instantly return to my place of rest, even from my journey into deepest space.

At the start of these events, a lump appeared on my forehead, just below the hairline. Cluster headaches came.

My parents console me, and partly convince me that there is nothing but my imagination. I obviously have a good one. Regardless of settling down, and at times being less aware and sometimes going for years for without thinking about it, the identity and very real presence stays with me all of my life. Eventually it becomes common and a source of knowledge to me. The combination is not always wisdom.

I, like all or many people, question my sanity, and as I grow older, I put the presence away in the dark. I wish to be normal, but I suspect it is not intended for this presence to remain in the dark. From the time of eleven or so I am afflicted with short periods of pain, which many years later will be called the cluster headaches, which will come and go from time to time for many years.

Thirty years old and the pain is extreme, but I feel I am not rare in the pain, as there must be many that have all of or much of my awareness.

The lump on my forehead was removed during my thirties and I have no more out of body experiences. Another grows on the back of my right shoulder. Other experiences come, unusual awareness. Sometimes over space, I see clearly events as they occur. In old age, I will question all these events. Then I will write.

YARGREY

Alpha is my partner this time. We have lost the one I would have spoken with over the continent that they now call America, in the year they call 1947, at Roswell. It was distressing to the combined mind of our type. We rarely lose the life force of a spacer, as the bodies are re-formed to accommodate individual consciousness at the times the conscious universe requires.

We are over the southern continent that our vast memory banks tell us was the empty land so long ago. We have found the spirit of one who was here in the beginning of human species to this land. He is a boy child now, near puberty. It is not the first time we have taken him in this body. He is not exceptional. His consciousness has been formed over vast time able to be directed to the requirements of this time.

We are slowly placing influence in the minds of many as this species reaches a stage of technology that is both dangerous and capable of opening windows to the wider knowledge of the universe. This species and their wars are not ready to enter such responsibilities. This humanity cannot find peace with its own kind. They are under observance.

This humanity cannot direct itself in the way that will give continuity to its beautiful planet.

This humanity is in the goldilocks time of its galactic journey. At no time in its future will it dwell again in the warmth of the line of stars that see it central to the most required position for 60,000,000 of its years. It will pass in this plane for 30,000 years; of which 15,000 have passed. Change can occur without the help of the conscious universe.

The probes have entered his forehead. All that he is in this lifetime has been read, all that he will be through weak and strong can be directed. Through difficulties, he will learn life. Eventually he will arrive at the required task of his journey. This imagination will grow in our service. He is not special, but he will serve a purpose. The lump remains on his hairline, a genetic protein of amino acids that holds the door to our requirements.

MALCOLM REDOME

I am disturbed today; I do not know why I should be. In 1986 when I was thirty-one years old, I had a fatty lump removed from my forehead as the hairline was receding. Now, not much more than a year later, I have found the same has appeared on the back of my right shoulder. The cluster headaches stopped at the time of the forehead lump removal. Strangely, so did the events that I have come to think of as astral travel.

Now there seems to be another strange change. It is as if I have company and images as clear as day appear behind my eyes while they are closed. These images are not like my imagination. The thoughts are as clear as if spoken by someone in my presence. It is not frightening. I have, amongst other things, been to a theosophical, spiritual group in Melbourne, as I wonder if it is a connection to another world, perhaps of the dead. The astral journeys that are drifting back into memory have made me aware of possibilities. Still I have always been, I think, one who likes to dwell in the physical world, perhaps too much so. Too much strong drink, too much pursuit of female delights, too much lust for the physical joys of living. One should have more respect and discipline in the journey of living. Still perhaps this hunger stops me from dwelling too much on messages that may be coming from a world that all mortals arrive at without choice.

It is 1979 and I have a flashback as I write. Someone has seen me in the street of my town. My dad has been ill. He has had a couple of strokes, and heart problems for some years now. I rush to the hospital. My aunt is with him. She looks pale and slightly shocked. Dad took a turn. Maybe his heart stopped. She says they jolted him back to life with shock treatment. He seems to be sleeping now. He looks at peace. I love my dad, a gentle man of higher moral values than his children. Perhaps that comes with age. My older brother and I are with him now. A day has passed since his attack. He never speaks of God or religion. He was a churchgoer in past years but I think that was community expectations.

His words come quietly to our ears. "I did not want to return, to come back. Where I was, it was wonderful."

My brother tells him of his experience when he heard a nurse tell his friends who were in the grounds outside the hospital at boarding school that they were not to call out at the ward window, because he was dying. My brother says he was leaving his body but these words somehow helped bring him back. His fever broke and he lived.

I remain silent. I have never spoken about the strange events of my life. Country people are down to earth and I have never sought to be a freak amongst them. This event makes me tune into my own subconscious mind or spiritual existence.

As I grow older, I learn that there is much that science, archaeology, physicists and evolutionists take for granted that seems questionable to my simple mind. In fact, there is much from the past that simply cannot be explained. The explanations given by wise, educated people for such existence are simply strange.

Reason and intelligence do not connect.

Life passes. I build a farm and fall on hard times. I marry and separate from a good woman. I have joy and hardship, develop an industry and eventually fail. Still I produce much food, clothing and timber for the people of my world. I seem to be the loser, but for whatever reason, regrets or anger, even depression during hard times, none seems to dominate my character. It always seems to me that there is a future purpose. As one door closes, I attempt to open another.

I am fifty-two and I have lost everything; I am broke now. I left my lovely old home with only an old car, an even older caravan and a little cash. I have given seventy per cent of whatever cash I could rescue to the woman who dwelt here for some years. I will move north to seek work, far away from hard memories.

For whatever reason, I have begun to write. Perhaps it will become a book, pure fiction, influenced by the events of my life. I do not pretend to be a learned man or to have a scientific mind. My book will be just entertainment.

I have begun to paint again, the first time in perhaps twenty-five years. I move into an old boat and the next two or three years are extremely poor. Perhaps I struggle with nightmares that visit me every night, but by day, I have a strong spirit, if that is fair description. I am reclusive now. I work at all jobs, from fruit picking, to driving, even working in laundries. Slowly a book takes shape. I call it, *From the Time of the Writing*. I become fit and strong for my age. I give up drinking alcohol and women have little interest in me during my difficult days.

By 2005, I am beginning to earn a better income. I have moved to desert country, where the pay is good. I now have enough money to self-publish the book. It is in rough self-edited form, the best I can do. Some interest occurs and help arrives; it is worked on by others.

YARGREY

He is making progress. He has a slow mind that observes information with the natural confusion of his humanity and his environment. He has reasonable imagination and warmth of emotion without the negative emotions that we have helped him avoid.

He has published with only mild success, but slowly prospered in his worldly work, become strong in willpower, although he is too much alone. Still, it works well for our purposes.

MALCOLM REDOME

I am fifty-eight and it is the year 2008. The job is not hard and it pays the first big money I have earned in many years. Still it is seven days of twelve-hour shifts in the largest open-cut iron-ore mine in the world. Then seven nights of twelve hour shifts. There is one day to fly back to Perth and five days to recover, another day to return.

It is hard for one my age. I am run-down and have the flu. I take prescription drugs to stay at work. I should take time off, but that is not my way.

I am in the dining room now. A woman opposite me is talking. Strange, I cannot feel my arms or legs and it is as if they have ceased to be a part of me. The world around me has ceased to be. I am in a silvery blue place of complete peace. Vast numbers of thoughts cross my mind. It is okay to be here. It seems that a long time passes.

Who? Who? Who! My eyes open. The woman looks shocked. My head rises from its slumped position. Sandy says, "What happened?"

"I don't know," I reply.

She walks me back to my room. I seem okay. I can feel my heart beating, very fast. I tell her I will be okay. It dawns on me that I have had a heart attack so I phone the local hospital. I phone the taxi. The nurse tells me I have the flu and to wait. She treats me with contempt. Ten minutes pass and another arrives, so I walk into the emergency room, get on the table and tell them I am having a heart attack.

With resentment they attach leads, then panic. A valve closed on my heart. By sheer luck, the blood bypassed somehow and I survived.

Some months later, flying back to work with two and a half hours to go before we reached the mine, bad storms hit. The plane can't fly around and it is extremely rough. There is lightning all around, but for many years now I have been adept at meditation. I do this often to make the flight pass quickly. Time passes without my knowing it. The people are all calm on the outside, but I can sense their fear.

This time, for reasons I don't know, I enter a deeper trance. The plane, my body and the world disappear. I know that if the plane crashes or burns I will not know or feel it. I can flick back into my body state, and back to this state of what I have heard the Dalai Lama call emptiness.

In this state, I realise that it is consciousness that is creating reality.

In this state, I realise that each person is the centre of his or her own existence, an infinitely small part of a total consciousness but central to an individual awareness.

Where I am is as it was when my heart stopped.

As the years pass, I learn in a simple layman's way of alternative explanations for ancient monuments. There are strange connections from the distant past to the present, connections that seem to be denied of some UFO sightings and dismissed with crop circles that in some cases seem to point to a pattern of creation.

I learn of seven thousand scientists at the largest scientific experiment in known history, (the Large Hadron Collider) looking for the Higgs boson (the god particle). I wonder indeed if they should be looking for an intelligently designed pattern of creation, based on fractural division, as has always been symbolised by religion and masons for the sign of God, the six-sided star. (I wish I was at liberty to acknowledge the great mind that supplies this information. Perhaps someday, he will grant it.))

Star of David   Division of Star.   64 tetrahedron grid?

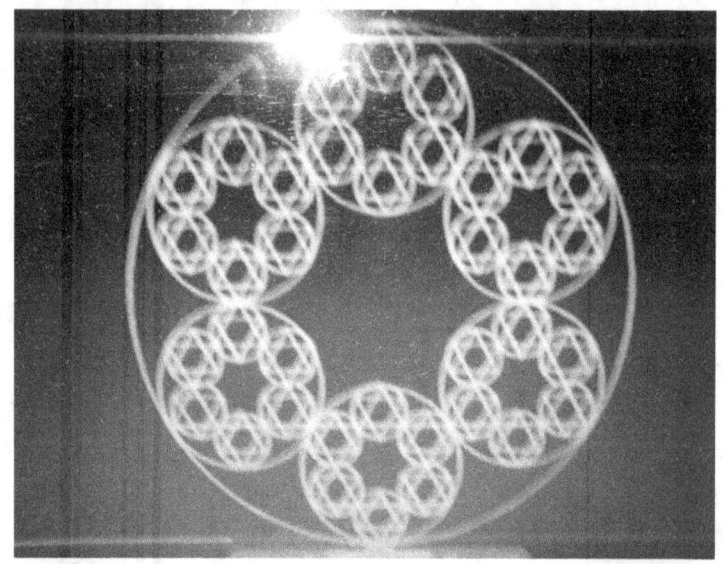

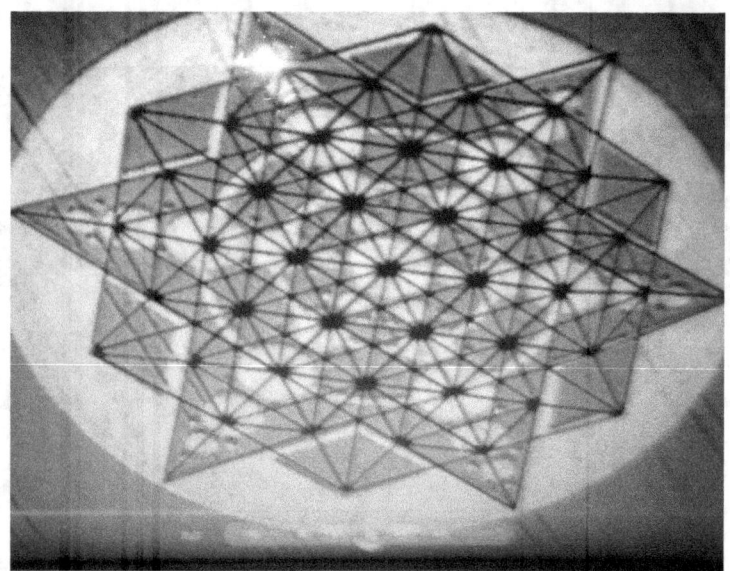

Star of David   Division of Star   64 tetrahedron grid?

My years pass and I disappear into obscurity. I remove the lump off my back and I find peace.

YARGREY

His consciousness grows old then ceases this earthly journey. His consciousness returns, to get the job of writing closer to our requirements.

A new book begins. This time his imagination will have greater awareness to a connection to a consciousness that is all creation, including Alpha, Zeta and Yargrey.

This time his imagination will give humans, perhaps, purposeful awareness of the caretakers of this part of the living universes, galactic plane.

REDOME

I am old now and my eyes have long grown dim.

My life as Malcolm Redome is fading fast. I wonder after all the stories I told and sold in connection with the books called *From the Time of the Writing* and *A Conscious Universe*, what answers lie before me. Regardless of the money that came late in life, it was a lonely journey.

As the light slowly fades, the pain begins to recede. I can feel the body becoming light as if it is becoming less of a part of me. A new clarity of mind is upon me that I feel may have occurred in another time both familiar and distant. I wonder after all I told am I to take my Karma to an eternity of darkness, or as most people hope will there be life after death?

The voices are growing dimmer and the long ago journey of my astral youth is re-emerging. I see my body and the activity that surrounds it. Then the walls and ceiling grow larger and in a flash, a journey has begun.

I am moving now across distances well understood for longer than the rise and fall of billions of universes. The consciousness of our kind has penetrated to beyond the boundaries of human imagination. The lights of great clusters pass at infinite distance until finally I am above the plane of the universe. Now there is an unbroken endless series of lights in a profoundly beautiful night sky.

It is changing now, as the dark of much of the empty space is growing brighter. In fact, light is sweeping towards me, or I towards light, and I can tell that from empty space I am to arrive at what feels like home and total fulfilment.

My mind is perhaps more aware than I have ever known.

All time and space seems to be communicating and the feeling of body is no longer relevant.

I feel profound warmth of mind with an intensity I have not felt with my heart or my earthly loins, but which seems to encompass all the senses.

Somehow, over all this, is a sense of harmony, humility, and wonder.

In this world that somehow seems to bring body and mass to empty space, the galaxies are spreading their spiral wings and the once beautiful arms are now central to great glowing arenas.

All space seems to be filling with a vast panorama of a consciousness.

Now I seem to become a part of as well as aware of a cosmic intelligence. This I cannot explain with the voice of an individual, but the knowledge of all, and coming to me in a way that even with heightened awareness is simple enough for me to understand.

I sense that I have been here before in a different life but one that is in space-time parallel. I can sense clearly that this same life is ending as before. I can sense clearly lives as an endless line stretching back, all with total comfort.

I feel the thought say to me: *You were the spirit of Malcolm Redome, the spirit we call the Human Journey. You are no different to the spirit of any other living creature. In the living flesh, you suffer the endless hungers and joys. You still have your share of sin and goodness.*

In short, you are an ordinary traveller, an infinitely small part of the life that makes up the conscious, living, universe, which again in turn is a part of endless other universes that once again are total cosmic intelligence.

All life of the spirit, infinitely small and infinitely large is a part of a whole, so Karma can exist as your deeds, whatever their merit, contribute to life.

I become aware that I am to journey to look upon something beyond what I have seen, then the light begins to clear, and into the far distance, I see endless plains with what at first glance appear to be galaxies. Then I realise they are universes stretching endlessly beyond vision. Then plain upon plain appears so that all is full of universes, and even this somehow is all a part of a total cosmic intelligence.

I wonder: How is this so?

The answer comes: *On your beloved Earth you wrote that awareness, perhaps, is reached after about four billion years and that those that you dwell amongst have only emerged into awareness. Countless millions of species have reached this stage and have gone on to survive for billions of years.*

The level of wonderment they achieve is beyond the difference of the start of life in your first writing and the last, three and a half million years later. These stretch back in time for all conscious capacity for such as you, perhaps all originating in a pattern of consciousness that is one.

"Who are you? Are you what I am to know as the profound gift, the Holy Spirit?"

No, we are just like you but far older. Still we are an infinitely small part of all you view. We are the collective mind of the spacers, and I, Yargrey, open your mind for your continued consciousness. Your spirit will continue its journey. Your physical reincarnations will, for long to come, remain the same humanity, with ordinary human qualities. You will often have too much desire and sometimes be too greedy for strong drink and the gift of the Mother Earth. Your spirit, the spirit of the Human Journey is not of high order.

Simply the susceptibility or perhaps lack of strength made Malcolm Redome (re do me) easy to direct.

HUMAN JOURNEY

He will be born again many times, until it is the year 2213.

The sun is about to rise on this Christmas Day 2213. I stand between my daughter and granddaughter, proud to be present at the opening of complete restoration of one of the greatest temples to this planet, the sun (son) and perhaps the moon and its connections to all creation. No one is sure exactly why it was built, or even when.

There is much speculation and varied wisdom has been cast towards it during its centuries of decay. As the beautiful violet horizon gives way to the orange orb of this, the first day after the shortest day of the year, the rays pass over the heel stone and enter the ancient pathway into the interior of perhaps this symbolic Mother Earth we can now see shining in all its glory. The Son of God, reflected in golden light in the great outer circle of leviathan stones, encloses the blue circle of perhaps Mother Earth stones, to the central moon shape of golden giants.

I hear the voice of my granddaughter. "What is it, Grandfather?"

"For you Woodlands, and you, Wildflower," I say. "These builders came when the alignment of stones told them it was the day of the least of the sun's warmth. These people were asking the Son (sun) of God to hear their hearts and witness their respect for the health of the Mother Earth, or Mother Nature. They asked that the great ice that had come so close to these temples in times of adjustment may remain in far places so flowers may bloom and monsoon rains fall to deliver the cycle of life."

"Grandfather, is this certain?"

"There is no certainty, but I am happy to choose a faith and abide by it. In this case, it offers the best I know, of a place for happiness for all who now live, and gives hope to the unborn to live their own future, beyond the promise of divine reward.

"There is happiness within our own resurrection, and this heaven on Earth."

HUMAN JOURNEY

During the start of the Twenty-first Century, those that have been guiding this planet's development since departure from Egypt and perhaps before began to restrict growth of world economies.

It was in the loins of woman that the future of humanity and this blue circle was to be entrusted, first in China by Government decree, then Brazil, and Russia populations stabilised. Western democracies followed, then Asia's rapidly developing nations. Initial hardship was followed by a greater quality of life.

The people of the world began to seek a harmony with Earth that would give their children's, children's children and beyond a place of reverence in this, *A Conscious Universe.*

THE END

EPILOGUE

For Judaism, Christianty, Moslem or

Fundamental Atheist

I say with acknowledgment of all religious beliefs this book is
not for those who are content within their faiths, of Judaism,
Christianity, Muslim, or those that are also content to be funda-
mentally Atheist:-

The fictional fantasy, and love stories that exist within these
pages have an underlying alternative history of the development
of beliefs on Earth.

It is written for those who have like the author grown up as
Christian, (or any other faith)

With the modern world questioned the accuracy, probability
or possibility of there being a God.

Eventually progressed to being perhaps an Atheist.

However, continued to question the extraordinary complexity of life and beauty and how such was necessary according to Darwin's survival of the fittest.

Eventually learned with a simple layman's mind, that at the smallest scale of existence, atomic through to amino acids, proteins.

The structure and extraordinary complexity of DNA. And the mini universe that is each of the trillions of cells within each individual life form.

All precisely organized for amongst other things this author to exist.

Eventually learnt that on a Galactic scale the factors that are needed for a higher life support planet to exist are complex, and these factors by evolution would mathematically create an equation that would mean one Earth like planet in every one thousandth of one trillion suns.

By evolution with time factor, 3 million years of humanity (out of say 4 billion years of Earth's life) evolution has an infinitely remote possibility of being the reason for the readers consciousness.

Eventually learned still with a layman's mind of Quantum physics (mechanics).
Experiments that Einstein found difficult to accept.

That at the atomic level, atoms while observed behave in an organized manner.

That while unobserved behave in waves of potential order.

Quantum physics seems to show that every living thing has a conscious affect upon the existence of their own reality.

Indicating to the author that the universe is aware.

Eventually learning from scientists such as Dr John Haggar and physicist Nassim Haramein, and others available to ordinary people such as all humanity, with a total connection of information today, of unified field theory that explains I hope, for a more harmonious future for this planet.

Some of the seemingly spiritual experiences of the fictional author in the closing chapters are to my knowledge my experiences.

Astral travel near death experiences etc.

The book is for a small portion of humanity's future who have travelled this journey.

It was hopefully written in a manner that would be entertaining to ordinary people such as the author.

It is pleasing to see the potential Nobel award winning scientist of Higgs boson fame question the views of the famous fundamental atheist, Richard Dawkins. (*The God Delusion*)

At the end of book one *From the Time of the Writing* the fantasy author Malcolm Redome and his perhaps spiritual companion or guide, wrote a letter intended as the prologue for the next book, *Conscious Universe*. Upon advice it has been moved to the end for any who may be interested.

LETTER FROM MALCOLM REDOME, WITH THE SPIRIT OF THE HUMAN JOURNEY

AT THE END OF THE LAST BOOK, WE WROTE:

Perhaps for readers who have made it this far it is necessary at this time to state a simple belief and use a little (we hope) correct science. We will simply say that in all that exists that is beyond human knowledge, we will underestimate to a vast degree the figures we put to you, and the conclusion reached here.

More galaxies than we can see make up the Universe. (The science I have read says they know there are more than 100 billion.) A vast number of these are suitable to develop stars that will have planetary systems that could support intellectually aware life, if you like, civilized. They tell me our galaxy has a least 100 billion stars. (Ten years ago, they thought four billion so perhaps it will be higher.) They tell me life is only likely to develop with second generation stars in the outer part of the galaxy.

They tell me that life of a sun-like star or perhaps binary star supporting life is maybe 12,000,000,000 years, that it has taken 4,600, 000, 000 years to develop our awareness, our knowledge. That means some part of 7,400,000,000 years remain for our species if we can find the answer for balance and protection within the galaxy.

They tell me that a large number of life supporting planets in our galaxy can have reached a life as aware as our own and beyond, for up to 7,400,000,000 years. They tell me that very few of these planets are likely to be at the primitive stage we are at, 5,000 years or so of developed thought after the 4.6 billion years of development stage. They say many planets will have been destroyed by the aggressive traits that are perhaps necessary to reach awareness. Sheer odds say many will not.

We believed the galaxy was full of aware species, which would have had super human development compared to us, Malcolm and Human included.

They say even with large numbers the average space between aware planets may be far greater than 500 light years - less than one star in every 500,000. So any way such civilizations have of communicating, covering such distances, or being aware of each other, would have been accomplished (if ever achieved) long ago and will have existed at a higher level of intelligence, responsibility and morality among the possibly many who can exist in our galaxy alone.

For an emerging species such as humanity to become a part of the consciously participating and communicating and perhaps travelling members of the galaxy/universe/Universe's, our scientists have to learn what our inner alien (spirit) has perhaps implanted upon our subconscious.

Messages at the speed of light are still in space distances, a communication similar to seeking a puff of smoke 20,000 kilometres away.

When a species survives to a level of scientific understanding of spiritual belief, we are able to take our part in the profoundly fulfilling universal completeness.

The door opens to a vast panorama of consciousness. The door opens. The means are within human capacity. The obstacles are immense; the rewards beyond our imagination. The alternative?

MALCOLM REDOME

(These thoughts are based upon the ideas of the great science fiction writer Isaac Asimov and the renowned intellect, Carl Sagan.)

I have since observed the information of SETI scientists and the information supplied by the authors of The Privileged Planet (intelligent design etc.) Whether such information is correct or not, I do not know, but some scientists have worked out an equation on the probability of another Earth based on the principles of evolution or chance. One in ten planets has every one of the twenty absolute requirements for developed life. When multiplied out mathematically, this results in one EARTH in every one- one thousandth of one trillion stars. (One hundred billion stars in the Milky Way, our galaxy.)

However if this is the end of the story to be conscious to write this, I have won a cosmic lottery of enormous proportions.

THIS WILL NOT BE SO.

The DNA in vast numbers in all life seems to be an artefact of intelligent design. If so, it is more likely that this design will be very much a part of an intentional and immense requirement for observation and awareness in the universe.

www.ingramcontent.com/pod-product-compliance
Lightning Source LLC
Chambersburg PA
CBHW070207260626
47160CB00002B/478